NINA

"ONE OF THE FANTASY
FIELD'S GREATEST TALENTS . . .
HER WORDS CREATE WORLDS
NO ONE HAS EVER SEEN BEFORE."
Kristine Kathryn Rusch, author of *White Mists of Power*

"THERE IS ABSOLUTELY NO OTHER VOICE IN
CONTEMPORARY FANTASY LIKE HOFFMAN'S.
HERE IS A WRITER TO FOLLOW, TO HEED,
AND, MOST OF ALL, TO READ WITH
WONDER AND ENORMOUS ENTHUSIASM."
Edward Bryant

"ONE OF THE FINEST WRITERS
WORKING THE BLURRY EDGE
OF FANTASY AND HORROR"
Locus

"ENORMOUSLY TALENTED . . .
A JOY TO READ . . .
WHAT A DELIGHTFUL ADDITION
TO THE FAMILY OF FANTASISTS SHE IS."
Kate Wilhelm, author of *Where Late the Sweet Birds Sang*

"SHE WEAVES WITH GOLD AND SILVER,
PLATINUM AND SPIDER SILK . . .
NINA KIRIKI HOFFMAN MAGIC.
THERE IS NO BETTER."
Algis Budrys

Other AvoNova Books
by Nina Kiriki Hoffman

THE THREAD THAT BINDS THE BONES

THE SILENT STRENGTH OF STONES

NINA KIRIKI HOFFMAN

AVON BOOKS • NEW YORK

THE SILENT STRENGTH OF STONES is an original publication of Avon Books. This work has never before appeared in book form. This work is a novel. Any similarity to actual persons or events is purely coincidental.

AVON BOOKS
A division of
The Hearst Corporation
1350 Avenue of the Americas
New York, New York 10019

Copyright © 1995 by Nina Kiriki Hoffman
Cover art by Matt Stawicki
Published by arrangement with the author
Library of Congress Catalog Card Number: 95-94152
ISBN: 0-380-77760-6

First AvoNova Printing: September 1995

AVONOVA TRADEMARK REG. U.S. PAT. OFF. AND IN OTHER COUNTRIES, MARCA REGISTRADA, HECHO EN U.S.A.

Printed in the U.S.A.

RA   10   9   8   7   6   5   4   3   2   1

This one is for Nancy Etchemendy, blood sister

Contents

1
Newcomers
1

2
Disappearances
20

3
Conjuring Acts
42

4
Questions of Ownership
68

5
Shocks to the System
100

6
Family Matters
135

7
Trouble Breathing
175

8
Business Affairs
195

9
Dirt
215

10
Stones
232

1

Newcomers

The first time I saw Willow disappear was a couple of days after I met her, and she didn't know I was watching her—not unless she was a lot more devious than I thought she was, and as a master of deviousness, I was pretty sure I would know.

It was almost by chance that I saw her disappear—but not quite. I was watching her on purpose. Willow's family had rented one of the Lacey cabins partway around the mountain lake from my father's dream come true, his crystal clear ice/piping hot coffee/firewood/nightcrawlers/fishing gear/all-round general store and six-room motel out back, the Venture Inn. I'd spent half my life on Sauterelle Lake in the Oregon Cascades, doing chores around the business or ducking work to spy on visitors. I usually knew where to find people to watch.

The community was mighty thin of interest in the winters, when most of the lowlanders went back to their valley towns, and I had to take an hour-and-fifteen-minute bus ride just to get to school, except when we were snowed in and I didn't go to school at all. But right now it was late spring, prime viewing time, with summer people moving in. I liked to check the long-termers out early on, get a feel for their habits and figure out which people I would spend the most time studying. There were lots of overnighters and two-weekers, too, so there were always new people to examine.

The Lacey cabins had the most interesting people in them. They were upscale fancy; the grounds held tennis courts, a four-star restaurant, a lounge, a swimming pool for those who couldn't stand lake slime, and a community room where people could gather for barbecues or videos. People with money used the Lacey's as a hideout, some of them people whose pictures I had seen in magazines. If they had a reason for hiding out, I figured I had a reason to be interested in them, even though I never told anybody any of the things I discovered.

Some of the more run-down lodgings around Sauterelle Lake were popular with people who thought they wanted to make love out in nature or under the moon or by a crackling fire, not figuring on bugs, poison oak, jumpy sparks, or splintery floors. I had watched enough of those people already and usually just checked to make sure they were that sort of people before dropping them from my spy route.

I met Willow at the store, same way I met most people. That was why I liked cash register duty. A grin and a "Hi, my name is Nick Verrou. Y'all enjoying our lake?" would usually get them talking.

Willow was a small dark person, probably about my age, seventeen, where you're not allowed to call them a girl anymore, but she didn't strike me as a woman yet. There was something soft about her face, like she didn't have any idea how pretty she was, with those amber eyes and that soft short black hair and not a touch of makeup.

"I'm Willow. The lake is wonderful," she said. Her voice was deeper than I had expected it would be, with an edge of honey in it. "The *skilliau* are so strong here."

Before I could say, "Huh?" she smiled, put out her hand for change from the bill she'd given me for a Mars Bar, accepted the money, and left.

I went to the window and peeked past all the taped-up notices of community affairs, decals about soft drinks, and neon about beer. She was climbing into the back of an old black Ford truck, late thirties vintage, where two dark-haired teenage boys and a thin, red-haired preteen girl already sat, all of them in sloganless white T-shirts and blue jeans. The girl had her arm around a very furry white dog, or maybe it was a wolf. None of the others reached out to help Willow in, though she ended up sitting awfully close—kissing close—to the older of the two boys.

A thin-faced man in the passenger seat up front leaned out the window and looked back, then said something to the driver. The dusty truck started up. It rattled away down the road past Mabel's Backwoods Café, taking the left turn toward the Lacey cabins and the Hidaway Motel. The driver was a heavier man with shoulder-length hair. I thought for sure they were Hidaway types. The truck didn't say anything like enough money for Lacey's.

But the next morning before opening time and after my first sets with the barbells, when I had dipped my fingers in the lake in my morning greeting and had walked part of my regular spy route, I saw the old black truck parked in front of the most remote Lacey cabin, the one closest to my secret forest path from the store, and farthest from the road.

Had to go sit on Father Boulder to think about that.

I had never told Pop or Granddad or anybody about Father Boulder—not even Mom when she was still living with us, though she had known more about me than anybody else. I tried not to make a track to the boulder, because I didn't want anybody else finding him. He was in a little clearing up among the Doug-firs and mountain hemlocks and ponderosa pines, the sword ferns and bracken, away from all roads. He huddled among a bunch of smaller rocks but stood taller than all of them with faint gray-green starbursts of lichen scattered over his pale, speckled gray sunside. I could climb up on top easily by stepping on the scatter of smaller stones around him, and I went there when I really needed quiet.

All you could hear from there was the ocean noise of wind in the treetops and waterfalls of bird notes and warbles. All you could smell was the spice of pine resin and the sand of stone and damp mossy earth. Most of the day, sun touched the top of Father Boulder, if there was any sun at all.

It wasn't like I thought Father Boulder talked to me or anything. It was just sometimes I lay on top and felt . . . naw, that's too stupid to say. I felt a way I never felt at home. When I fell asleep on Father Boulder I had weird dreams, too, not like any of my other ones (which were weird enough, in their way).

After I saw the deadbeat Ford parked in front of a Lacey cabin, I sneaked up the hill to Father Boulder and lay down. The stone was cold from the night; sun was still low enough so the trees shielded the clearing, but I was warm from hiking uphill.

Four kids, two grown-ups, one wolf dog, all living in Lacey number five, which had one master bedroom and two small singles. Crowded for six people and a dog. Big living room, though, with couches that could double as beds (I'd helped the Laceys with end-of-season cabin cleaning every year, and I knew all the layouts). What were these people doing in that cabin? What was *skilia,* or whatever Willow had said? Why did I care?

I didn't want to think about that particular question or the way my fingers had tingled after I had touched her hand, dropping change in her palm. Stupid. Should be thinking about Kristen, the blonde in Lacey number eight; she'd been coming up here three summers now, and she had flirted with me when she stopped in at the store, but she had ignored me majorly at the Friday night dances in Parsley's Hall. This winter I had been working out with weights and had some upper body development to show for it. I had only seen Kristen once so far this spring, but I thought maybe this year she'd take a second look at me. I was sure taking as many looks as I could at her, because her shape had improved over the winter, too, in front, and her hair was long and heavy and almost moon pale. I wanted to touch it and go on from there.

I lay on my stomach on Father Boulder, coolness soaking into me, and wondered if Paul and Jeremy were coming to the lake this summer. I had always had a hard time making friends, especially with guys, but by the end of last summer they had invited me to join them at the basketball hoop back of Parsley's Hall, at least—didn't need much conversation for that. I had even gone to the pool at Lacey's with them once or twice.

My watch alarm peeped at me. It sounded dumb, this little techno noise in the middle of nature, so I turned it off right away, then crept back down to the forest floor, slapping Father Boulder once to say thank you. I would have to skip the rest of the route and get right back to the store.

As I slipped past Lacey number five, I glanced between screening trees and saw something strange: Willow and the red-haired girl were standing between the cabin and the lake, their arms stretched to the sky. They were chanting something, their voices thin, blending perfectly. I stood and listened for a little while. They were singing to my lake, after all. My mother had taught me to touch water at sunrise, letting the lake taste me while I felt its touch, and there was something about these girls singing that reminded me of that; but

I couldn't catch the words, and the whole thing was making my back twitch.

At the store I spent at least half an hour arguing with some one-day visitors, yuppies who were upset because we didn't carry their favorite brand of sunscreen. I thought Pop should expand on sunscreen—people would spend almost ten dollars on a tube if it was the kind they wanted; I read up on it in *GQ*. But Pop never listened to advice from me.

For the longest time I couldn't convince these people that we didn't have a magic carpet that would fly down to the valley and pick up whatever they happened to want.

I finally talked them into buying the brand we carried by pitching it harder than it deserved. When at last they headed out, I breathed out a *whew* and turned to find Willow watching me.

She grinned.

"What?" I said, annoyed. I hated discovering that people were watching me without my knowing it. Go figure.

"You have a way with words," she said.

"Thanks. I think."

"They turn slippery when you use them," she said, "and they taste like fresh bread."

This was definitely the weirdest thing anybody had ever said to me directly. I raised my eyebrows at her, not knowing how to answer.

"Say something to me," she said, and there was a nudge in her voice stronger than the ones I used to get from my mom when she still lived with us.

"Uh—would you come to the dance Friday with me?"

Willow cocked her head and frowned. She ran her index finger over her lips. She shook her head.

"You don't dance?" I asked.

"You're not doing it," she said.

"I don't know what you're talking about."

She came and leaned her elbows on the counter, propping her chin in her hands, her dark yellow eyes staring into mine. "Nick," she said, her voice deep and velvety, "will you come to the dance with me on Friday?" Promises lay in her voice like baited fish hooks on a line.

I said yes before I even thought.

She grinned, dimples dancing in both cheeks. "See?" she said. "You could do that."

I locked the register and went out to straighten the magazines, not looking at Willow. Something about what had just happened made a hot lump lodge in my throat. I knew that when I really pushed, I was a hell of a salesman. A kind of energy filled me, a heat that brightened my brain until words slid from my mouth, smooth and elegant, convincing people of things they didn't want to believe. When I first figured it out I had a great time selling people things they didn't want. The problem with that was they came back later, upset, or they didn't come back at all because they didn't want me to do it again. Besides, it made me feel hollow and echoey and a little sick inside. So now I reserved the extra push for special occasions; but I didn't want anybody else to know about it.

"When should I pick you up?" Willow said from behind me. Her voice sounded subdued.

"Seven-thirty," I said. When I turned around, she was gone.

Mariah, a wild-haired forty-eight-year-old artist who spent the winters painting pictures and the summers selling them, came by at noon to spell me on the register, as she did every day. I went back past the storeroom to Pop's and Granddad's and my living room/dining room/kitchen and built myself a sandwich. A few minutes later Mariah ducked in to hand me the mail. There was another letter from Mom. I folded it in half and stuck it in my back pocket. When I finished eating and

washing up I put the other mail where Pop would find
it when he got back from his thrift-store raiding trip
to town.

With half an hour of lunch break left, I went upstairs
to my bedroom. It was narrow, just wide enough for a
bed, a dresser, and a small carpeted space where my
barbells sat. I used to have pictures of wild animals all
over the walls, ones Mom had bought for me or taken
out of nature magazines and helped me pin up. When
she left I took them all down and lived with blank
white walls pricked with tack holes.

I opened the bottom drawer of the dresser, got out
the stack of letters Mom had sent me, and stuck the
current one under the rubber band. When I had held
the first one in my hand, I could scarcely breathe, I
was so angry. I had had to put it down before I could
get any breath. It had reminded me of the panic attack
I'd had the day she left. Spooked, I had burned that
one, and for a while I burned them every month as soon
as they arrived, but they kept coming, and eventually I
started saving them. I hadn't read any of them. Didn't
know if I ever would. Each time one came, though,
about once a month, I felt faintly reassured. At least
she was still alive somewhere. I didn't any longer wish
she were dead.

I picked up the third volume in the Lord Calardane
series and read for a little while. My watch beeped just
when he discovered a nest of monsters in the sewers
and realized that they were actually nice and might help
him get the all-curing elixir from the Castle of Infinite
Illusion. I always liked that about Calardane, that he
didn't slice anybody's head off with his sword until he
was sure they were mean.

Mariah took off as soon as I got back. Something
was missing from the things hanging on the back wall
behind the register where Pop had mounted antique
fishing equipment. I had to study a bit until I figured

out it was the wicker creel Granddad used to use ages ago until he couldn't mend the leather strap any longer.

No wonder Mariah had run off. She knew she wasn't supposed to sell that stuff, but she couldn't say no to some people, especially light-haired men with sun crinkles next to their blue eyes and wide smiles full of teeth. She had been in love with somebody like that once, I figured, and she kept hoping he would come back. Or maybe she thought if she gave one of these guys what he really wanted she would get a reward.

I leaned against the counter for a while with my eyes closed. I could try to rearrange everything so there was no broad blank spot. Maybe Pop wouldn't notice the creel was gone. I had managed to fool him when Mariah had sold the bamboo rod, but that hadn't been anywhere near as important as the creel.

I sighed and ran out a register tape to see if she'd actually entered the sale. The first time I caught her at this, she had showed me that at least she hadn't kept the money. This time there was a sale labeled ''misc'' for twelve dollars, and I knew we didn't have anything in the store that cost twelve dollars. Everything cost something ninety-five, as if that fools anybody into thinking it costs a whole dollar less.

For a minute there I really wanted to hit Mariah. Twelve dollars couldn't buy a replacement for family history. It was a stupid amount. She'd sold me out to Pop for twelve dollars. I wanted to hit her—and kill the guy who had talked her into selling it. Instead, I just finished my shift and closed up the store at five, like always, leaving the big blank spot on the wall behind me, where Pop would see it right away. I ran out the end-of-day register tape and put it with the account book and sales graph paper on Pop's desk in the living room/dining room/kitchen in back, straightened stuff, restocked whatever I could from the storeroom, and then headed out for my evening prowl.

This time I decided to go the opposite direction. I

checked out the tumbledown cabins on Old Man Fortrey's property (nobody home), took a look at the law-
yer's weekender up the ridge (nobody home), and
cruised past some other places. Smelled steaks cooking
over an outdoor grill at Benningtons' and wished I was
invited. But I never had been.

There were a few other places up at the end of the
road, but I was too curious about Willow and her family
to finish out my route. None of the usual suspects who
took those cabins had been by the store yet, anyway.

So I turned around and headed toward Lacey's again,
stopping at the Venture to put three big baking potatoes
in the oven at 425 degrees. They'd keep for an hour.
Pop hated me to turn the oven on and leave, but with
no backup—Granddad had gone on the trip to the valley
with him—I didn't have much choice. I set my watch
alarm for forty-five minutes.

This time I went right by Willow's cabin and on to
Kristen's. She was sitting on the patio, looking out at
the lake, and some big muscular guy in tennis whites
and a crew cut was sitting next to her.

I watched them for a while. The guy talked to Kristen, but Kristen didn't even turn to look at him when
he spoke. So maybe there was hope. Eventually Kristen's mom came out with a tray of iced tea glasses and
a plate of cookies.

I decided they were boring and went to check the
other Lacey cabins. Four of them had families in them,
and one had a couple who obviously weren't married
to each other. Up at the tennis courts I saw Paul rallying
with some new guy. I decided to wait until he came
into the store before I said hello; that would give me
some idea of where we stood this year. I didn't want
to assume something stupid, like we were still friends,
if it wasn't true.

I should have gone on to check the Hidaway, but
somehow I couldn't stay away from Willow's cabin
any longer.

This time there were three grown-ups, the two men I'd already seen and a red-haired woman, and all four kids standing out on the back patio facing the lake. I didn't see the white wolf anywhere. A cooking smell drifted up from the cabin, but it didn't smell like meat, more like some sort of stew that included a few turnips and lots of onions.

The family wasn't talking. They just stood there, staring. Then the woman stretched her arms out in front of her, palms up, and said something. The rest of them murmured. Not a conversation. More like the statement/response part of the church services my mom used to take me to. The woman said something else, and the rest of them answered. I couldn't even move while this went on. There was something so intense about it. The phrase "true believers" drifted through my mind.

Suddenly all the others lifted their arms, too, holding their hands toward the sky. They sang something in harmony, and something shimmered around them all, maybe flickers of light reflected from the lake water. Maybe not.

I couldn't take it anymore, and I lit out running, which was a good thing, because my watch peeped about ten seconds later. I ran so fast that by the time I got home all I was thinking about was breathing, which was a relief.

Pop and Granddad hadn't made it home yet. I threw together some Dagwoods for them. The truck pulled up just as I poked the potatoes with a fork and discovered they were done. I turned the oven off and went outside.

It didn't take any time at all for Pop to figure the creel was gone. He waited until we'd unloaded the odds and ends of stuff he'd picked up at thrift stores for resale before he lit into me, though.

"You should have gotten the guy's name from her— I got a quarter says she wormed it out of him—and gone after him," he yelled when I told him Mariah had sold the creel.

I set a plate loaded with sandwich and steaming potato in front of him and got the butter dish out of the cupboard.

"What do you call this?"

"Dinner," I said. I never could control my mouth when it really counted.

Granddad was just as happy. He bit into his sandwich and chewed, then grinned at me.

"You go up to that woman's cabin and get that name from her! Ten cents says he's visiting her right now. You make him give you back that creel! She can't sell things like that, she just can't. Can't you make her understand a simple thing like that?"

I had only explained it to her twenty-six times, and no, I couldn't get her to understand it.

"If there was any single other person loose who would cover your danged lunch break I would fire Mariah in a minute!" But of course in the summer everybody else was working at a service job that paid at least minimum wage; Mariah was the only one who'd watch the store for three dollars an hour and a ten percent discount on her food bill. "Why don't you just eat your lunch behind the register?"

"Wouldn't look good," I said. It was the only way I had gotten him to give me a lunch break in the first place, by convincing him, really hard, with every slippery, bread-smelling word in me, that customers seeing me eat would not come up and try to buy something and we'd lose business.

"Tell you what," he said, his voice quieting just a touch from the full-scale yell, "from now on, you eat sitting right behind the curtain, and if you hear her bargaining with somebody for anything off the wall, you come out and fire that bitch right out on her ass! We can close up for half an hour while you eat!" Then he started chomping on his sandwich. I ate in silence.

After about ten minutes, he said, "Okay, you've

eaten enough. You get up to her cabin and get her to tell you what she's done, dammit!''

I slid my plate into a plastic bag and put it in the refrigerator, hoping the rest of my sandwich would be there when I got back. Pop didn't like me taking anything from the store unless he authorized it first, and I had thrown together supper from the last things he'd authorized. Sometimes when Pop was mad he got especially hungry, and tonight looked like one of those times. He'd eat anything he could find, including my leftover sandwich.

The way my stomach was clenching, I wasn't sure I'd be hungry later anyway.

Mariah lived in a shack up on the ridge, reachable only by footpath. She had a small parking area below where her rusty old VW bug stayed. She used the car so seldom she usually needed a jump to start it. I had crept up close to her house, but I'd never been inside it; she had never invited me. She liked her privacy, and she was generally pretty boring to watch, so I granted it to her.

I took a flashlight.

What if Pop was right, and she had some guy with her? He'd never told me I had to go accost Mariah before. Other than training her on the register at the beginning and telling her what she was doing wrong later, I hadn't exchanged many words with her, actually; what I knew about her, I knew from observing her interactions at the store.

I started for her place, flashing the light on fallen pine needles and gravel, dreading the confrontation. I reached her parking lot before it occurred to me that I could lie: just tell Pop I had gone to see Mariah, and she had sold the creel to a passing stranger whose name she didn't know, there was no chance of retrieval, we could kiss the creel good-bye, end of story. Mariah had no telephone. He wouldn't be able to check the story unless he stormed up the mountain himself, and I wasn't sure he even knew the way, for all we'd lived here half my life. I could catch her when she came to relieve me at lunch break, brief her before Pop could check with her.

Less psychic stress on all of us.

I switched off the flashlight and sat in Mariah's parking lot, studying the stars and listening to the silence of the night. A faint whiff of wood smoke in the air, a stronger scent of pine needles. Owls hooted somewhere nearby. Something more distant screeched, maybe its tiny death cry as a night hunter killed it. And even farther away, the quavering howl of—of what?

It came from the direction of the Lacey cabins.

The wolf dog, I thought.

Another howl rose and matched it.

Surely they had only had the one dog?

I had heard coyotes yipping, and dogs barking, but I'd never heard full-out howling before. It was less scary than just lonesome and sad, until I started thinking about wolves running loose around here. Bears were seldom things around Sauterelle Lake, but when one showed up the community response was slow-motion panic. I had heard that there had never been a documented case of a wolf attacking a human, but just the thought of some large creature with senses better than mine running through the night and maybe sizing me up as a meal was shuddery enough.

I could run home, or I could go up to Mariah's. What if Pop had an unlikely interest tomorrow and took a break from the motel desk to work the store before Mariah came in? Every once in a while he did that, especially after trips to the valley. He usually stopped at other stores along the way home, looking for ideas, and then he had to run our store for a little while to make sure it was up to the competition. Better if Mariah and I got our story straight tonight.

I switched my flashlight on and headed up the path.

Now I found the howls reassuring. At least if they howled I had some idea of where they were, whatever the hell they were, and they were pretty far away.

The bushes rustled on the left and I jumped a foot. When I shone the flashlight over there, I found nothing but leaves, some still moving.

Stop it! I thought.

By the time I reached Mariah's house, though, I had a pretty good head of steam. I knocked. She opened the door. I pushed in.

"Nick? Nick?" she said, her voice jumpy.

"I have to talk to you," I said. My voice had a trampoline quality, and I was having trouble catching my breath.

"Oh?" she said.

I looked around. Her house was log cabinlike, except that at one end where her studio was, the walls were windows, and I'd seen inside—just easel, canvases, paint, mess, table with paper cutter, mat boards. Stuff, not enough human attached to it to make it interesting.

This room I'd never seen; it was wide and windowless and had a big old bear skin, complete with growling, toothy head, on the floor in front of a riverstone fireplace. Above the fireplace loomed a glassy-eyed moose head. I could smell mildew and turpentine, moth balls, incense smoke, and boiled lentils. A small table stood across the room, with a kerosene lamp glowing on it. A doorway to the right had light coming through it, but I couldn't see anything except log walls. I wondered where she slept.

"What, Nick? You're interrupting me," Mariah said, having finally found her irritated voice.

I could see papers spread out on the table by the kerosene lantern, and a jar full of dark water with brushes sticking out.

"You sold the creel," I said.

Her outraged homeowner stance wilted a little.

"Pop told me I had to come up here and ask you

who you sold it to, find out where he is, so we can get it back.''

"But—"

"You really shouldn't sell that stuff, Mariah! It means a lot to us! Why did you do it?" I listened to my own wounded voice in horror. I had a plan, didn't I? I was supposed to stay cool and crush her with logic. Why was I losing it this way?

"I couldn't help it," she said.

"How can that be? Can't you just say something's not for sale?"

"I couldn't—it wasn't like that. It was a man with burning eyes—"

"And sandy hair and a nice smile," I said.

"No," she said, her face tightening, her mouth twisting into a frown. "No," she said, and this time it was a whisper. "A man with dark hair and burning eyes, and he spoke to me, so quietly, just telling me he had to have that creel and I had to give it to him and there really was no other way ... it reminded me ..." She broke off and looked toward the mantel. Following her gaze, I noticed a white ceramic unicorn with pink mane, tail, and hooves, and gold detailing. It looked weird below the moose head.

After a brainstorm, Pop had ordered a dozen of the unicorns, about two years ago, and nobody had wanted them. I had still been in supersalesman mode at the time. I really couldn't stand them, and I unloaded them quick. I think most of them got used for target practice.

"—of why I don't like to talk to you, Nick," Mariah said.

"I haven't done that to you since then, have I?"

"I don't give you that chance," she said.

"I don't do that anymore," I said. "If I did, I'd talk you out of selling the private stuff." Maybe I should wake up that part of myself just long enough to do it. It had never occurred to me to use it for anything but sales.

She looked at me, her eyes full of darkness, and I thought that was a stupid idea and I better forget it. She said, slowly, "Well, it was just like that. He stared into my eyes and talked to me, and I didn't really know what I was doing. I took the creel down and sold it to him. He even told me the price."

"Did he tell you his name?" I asked. Even if I knew, would I go after this guy, given what Mariah was telling me about him?

"No," she said, "but I saw him drive away. It was in an old black truck like the one in *Paper Moon.*"

I stumbled down the hill, my flashlight making a circle of light on the path, but my feet stepping into darkness. In Mariah's parking lot I paused again. The wolves weren't howling anymore. I wanted to go to Willow's cabin, found I didn't really care what anyone else on Earth might be doing except for Willow and her family, no matter how many times I told myself my interest in everything was all embracing.

Instead, I went home, and hungry to bed.

The next morning I started my route at Mabel's Backwoods Café, which was across the road from the Venture Inn and depended on out-of-towners for its existence. I bought myself coffee and a side of greasy hash browns. Mabel was so surprised she kept staring at me from her position by the grill. Pop had drummed into me that we didn't eat out when we could fix for ourselves much more cheaply. Somehow I didn't want to face our kitchen, and maybe Pop, that morning, though.

After breakfast I started my route in the direction away from Lacey's, but then I decided that was stupid; what could have changed since last night? If people were driving up from the city, it would take them two hours to get here, and it was only around seven-thirty.

I could check back for new people on my evening rounds.

Besides, I didn't fear the wolves in broad daylight. I eased the other direction around the lake to scope out the Lacey's.

I stopped first at the tiny indent of lake just below the Venture Inn and dipped fingers into the cool water.

On the way over to Lacey's I saw a bald eagle flying low above the other side of the lake and decided that on my half day off on Saturday I'd try tracking him to his nest, if nothing else was going on.

I was almost to Willow's cabin when I heard a splash from the little inlet a stone's throw from the cabin. I veered, walking quietly, and dropped down behind bracken and a fallen log, then peered between fronds and saw Willow naked and beautiful in the water. Where she stood, close to shore, the water only came up to her knees. She dipped both hands in, scooping up water, carrying it above her head, then tilting her hands. The water traveled from her hands to the lake in a way I had never seen before: in silver threads instead of droplets. Morning sun snagged in the water threads as if they were dew-pearled spiderweb. Willow murmured something. She lifted more handfuls of water and let it run down her body as she sang.

I watched and imagined I was the water, sliding down her body in the closest possible embrace. It got tangled up in a winter memory I had, of a time just after Mom left, me going out on the lake after it had frozen, lying down on it, taking off my mittens, jacket, shirts, and freezing my upper body to the ice, except I had felt heat from the ice, warmth and comfort like I was feeling now, only now I felt even warmer and not so comfortable. Icy heat against my skin, water against Willow, and the lake, talking to each of us, talking to both of us, tasting us.

I tried to stop thinking about it because there wasn't much I could do to ease myself, but it was the most amazing thing I had ever seen, how the sun touched the wet edges of Willow and glowed, how free and comfortable she was out there in the open air, no self-consciousness, confident in her aloneness, how she was talking to something or someone who wasn't there, but it didn't matter. How wrong it was for me to watch her when she couldn't know I was there.

What a weird thought. I thrived on invading people's privacy. If they wanted to do interesting things where other people could see them, was that my fault?

The hairs were prickling on the back of my neck. Maybe she really wasn't alone. Maybe somebody else was watching me. I glanced behind me. Nobody.

I should leave, I thought. I could always watch Willow some more when she had clothes on. I pushed up, ready to climb to my feet as quietly as possible and sneak off, but I couldn't resist one last look.

Willow still had her back to me, but now her arms were stretched straight out toward the rising sun. Light glowed around her hands, spun around her body like liquid tinsel. She turned, still singing, her wet hands weaving in the air about her, and she flickered and was gone.

2

Disappearances

I dropped down behind the log and shook my head, then slapped my cheek to see if I'd wake up at home in bed, wondering what the symbolism of this dream was. All that happened was my cheek hurt. I lay listening to birds and trees and the rev of somebody's motorboat from across the lake, a noise like a far-off lawnmower in need of a muffler. The air tasted fresh and cool and wide awake. Gradually I realized something: it was Friday, and Willow, the girl I had just seen naked, seen vanish, was going to come by the store and pick me up tonight at seven-thirty for the dance. Unless she was just fooling with me.

I closed my eyes a moment, then opened them and stared at the water, wondering if Willow had dropped under the surface without a splash and would come up any minute now, gasping for air.

Nothing.

Maybe I made the whole thing up? When time stretched or I was feeling especially trapped, I did make things up. I knew I was making them up, though. I didn't think I was inventing this one.

I watched the water unblinking until my eyes hurt

from staring at reflected sunlight. No splash. No Willow. No sense.

Finally I climbed to my feet. The back of my neck still felt like static was attacking it. I glanced around, but not a leaf or pine needle twitched. I shook my head and eased away without looking back.

I had stocked the till from the safe box, switched on the lights, and was just turning the OPEN sign in the door around when Pop came downstairs. "Well?" he said.

"We need more groceries," I said.

"Make up the list and stock the cupboards and the fridge while there's no one in the store," he said impatiently. We had a jingle of bells hanging above the door that sounded whenever someone came into the store, which helped when I had to do back room stuff. "Don't eat anything until I have a chance to approve the list. You know what I want to know, Nick."

"Mariah told me who she sold the creel to, but I haven't had time to track him down," I said.

He looked at his watch. "Okay. It's nine o'clock now. I'll watch the store. Put the MANAGER IN STORE sign up in the motel office window, then go out and find the man, get the creel. Be back here by ten."

I shoved my hands into my pockets so he wouldn't see the clenched fists. I could hardly tell him that the man who took the creel came from a family that practiced a weird religion, hypnotized you with a glance, and could disappear from sight. I was having a hard enough time believing my own eyes. Pop was never any good at taking no for an answer, no matter what the reason, and he had trouble believing me sometimes, maybe with reason. So I just said, "I need twelve dollars. That's what he paid for it."

He got twelve dollars from the register and tossed it at me. I picked it off the floor and left.

This time I approached the Lacey cabins from the

road, like other people, but on foot, unlike most. Pop had taught me to drive the truck, but he never let me take it out for frivolous reasons, only for pickups and deliveries. I went to the front office and talked to Adam Lacey, the son of Frieda Lacey, who had started the business back in the forties and brought her three children up in it.

"Old black Ford pickup?" Adam asked. "Sure, I rented the cabin to 'em before I saw their transportation. Might have had my doubts, otherwise, but it was real money they gave me, so I can't complain now. They don't socialize much, anyways, aren't bothering any of our other people."

"What's their name?"

"Come on, Nick, no reason for me to tell you that. Why you want to know?"

"They bought something I need to get back."

"Like bad tuna or something?" Adam got worry rowels across his forehead. "You had a recall on any canned goods?"

"What do you care—you buy from the city," I said, then wished I hadn't. The Laceys and their Culinary Institute chef had produce and meat trucked in from wholesalers in Portland. They never even bought so much as a toothpick at Pop's store; but they were our neighbors, and I wanted to get along with them. Sometimes the Laceys gave me work.

"I need to warn my lodgers, don't I?" he said. All the cabins had kitchenettes, and some people bought food from us. Others brought gourmet stuff with them. I remembered some of their garbage fondly, mostly for the wild ingredients and multi-ethnicity of the labels on the cans and boxes.

He had a point. "Nothing like that," I said. "They bought something that wasn't for sale."

"Well, that's your problem, then," he said. "I won't tell you their name, but I'll tell you their cabin number, since you could find it out yourself anyway. It's number five.''

"Thanks, Mr. Lacey."

"Don't tell 'em I told you."

"I won't."

Having spiked his curiosity about why I might be wandering his grounds openly (I hoped he didn't know anything about my peripheral paths, even though he was almost as much of a sneak as I was), I strolled over to cabin five and knocked on the door.

Nothing happened.

I waited.

I knocked again, louder and a little longer.

The door eased open as if the wind had blown it. Standing in the narrow gap was the redheaded woman, scowling. The air coming from the cabin smelled like burnt spices. The woman was wearing a thin white ankle-length dress I could see through, and nothing underneath, so after a first startled glance at her breasts I kept my gaze fixed on her face.

"Excuse me," I said.

She jumped, her eyes widening. "We left instructions not to be disturbed," she said.

"Where?"

"Up at the office!"

"I'm sorry," I said. "I'm not on staff here and I didn't know."

"Well, whatever you're selling, we don't want any."

"Actually it's about something you bought. Or maybe your husband bought it? At the store?"

She stared into my eyes. Her own were light green-gray, and I wondered if she could convince me of anything, the way the man had convinced Mariah she had to sell him the creel. I wanted to look away—but at what? I looked at her mouth. It didn't change from its narrow frown. She wasn't wearing lipstick. She had no brackets beside her mouth, which made me wonder how old she was; she sure didn't give off any kid vibes.

After a couple uncomfortable minutes she closed the door in my face. I heard her faint footsteps moving away.

What now? It would have helped if I knew whether she was coming back. I didn't feel like knocking again, but if I left without even news of the damn creel Pop would get on my case. I looked at my watch. I had half an hour.

I wondered if Willow had ever reappeared. I glanced toward the inlet, but trees screened it from sight.

Heavier footsteps approached the door. I watched the knob turn, then looked up into the face of the man who must have been driving the truck the other day, the one I hadn't gotten a very good look at. He wore jeans and a white T-shirt, but somehow they didn't look like regular clothes, more like counterfeits made by an alien. He was pretty bulky around the shoulders. He had long dark hair. I could see what Mariah had meant about burning eyes. I couldn't even tell what color they were, because there was this layer of silvery flickers around the irises. I stared at *his* mouth, until he lowered his face to look into my eyes.

"Yes?" he said, his voice surprisingly gentle.

I blinked and licked my lips. "Did you buy a fishing creel from the store yesterday?"

"Yes?" he said, but I couldn't tell if it was an answer or if he was just ignoring the fact that I had spoken.

"It was my grandfather's, and it wasn't for sale. I need to buy it back."

He didn't answer, just stared at me. It was unnerving having conversations with people who refused to talk.

"I mean," I said, "what would you want with it? It belonged to my grandfather. He used it for years. It has memories for him. We'd like to have it back. I brought you a refund of your twelve dollars." I held the money out to him.

The flickering in his eyes had changed from white

to a sort of blue-green, with tiny gold and silver dots mixed in. I could feel my attention heightening. I wanted to see where the next flicker of gold would show up, whether the next green would be forest or olive. At the same time I felt a gathering heat behind my eyes, like a headache, only intoxicating.

Then I was walking away.

I didn't wake up until I was already on the road away from Lacey's, heading toward the store. Somebody in a maroon Mercedes drove past, scattering gravel. The airwash off the car startled me awake.

I glanced back at the car. It was turning into the Lacey's driveway, five hundred feet behind me. I tried to catch up to myself. What had happened? Why couldn't I remember?

I looked at my watch, and that brought me back. I had five minutes to get to the store. I started running.

"He burned it," I said to Pop.

"He what?"

"He burned it. I can't buy it back. He burned it." I dug the twelve dollars out of my pocket and put it on the counter in front of him. "It's gone."

"Gaw *damn* it, Nick! This is some story you made up, isn't it? Always making things up, you sly little— gaw *damn* it!"

I said, "*You* go ask him."

"Why would anybody burn it? It was beautiful! Useless, but beautiful."

"I don't know. He wasn't very talky."

"I'll get it out of him," he said. "Where is he?"

I told him.

"You stay here. Get us our groceries. Granddad's like to start gnawing on the furniture—you better make him some toast. Make sure you keep a list. I'll be back."

The day was shaping up for hot. A lot of people wanted ice and soda for their coolers, and some strang-

ers came in wondering where to rent a boat. I directed
them to Archie's Dock and sold them sunblock, sinkers,
and fish hooks. The Coke vendor stopped by, and I
gave him an order. The chip guy came and restocked
chips and beef jerky. Between all this I assembled groceries—bread, cheese, lunch meat, mayonnaise, lettuce,
tomatoes, bananas (gave one to Granddad), cookies,
chips, rice, noodles, jars of spaghetti sauce, cans of beef
stew, chili, soup, milk, cereal (gave Granddad some
Sugar Pops, too)—and wrote a list of them. I tossed in
some Twinkies and a few licorice whips and some beef
jerky, just so Pop would have something to cross off.
I tried one week not adding unnecessary extras, and he
crossed off three cans of stew. I had to shop twice that
week, which he hated.

Having finished his breakfast, Granddad came out
and sat by the stove, watching people come and go. He
got one young woman to stop long enough to listen as
he talked about pets he'd had sixty years earlier. I
leaned on the counter and listened again to the tale of
Buster, the cat who ate peanuts, and Brownie, a dog
who could chew through any rope you tied him with,
and no matter how many times you whapped him with
a newspaper he just wouldn't mind. I found these stories eerie in the extreme. People's attitudes toward pets
used to be much different. I couldn't imagine beating
a dog—not that Pop had ever let me have one.

I thought about that wolf dog in the back of the black
truck. With a dog like that, I could go roving all over
the country and never have to look in a back window
again. He would be a friend. We would explore. We
could trap and hunt and live off the land and never have
to come back to civilization. We could be desperados in
the wilderness. . . .

I glanced toward the door, then noticed that the white
wolf dog was in the store, sitting there big as life in
the middle of the floor, staring at me with yellow eyes,
silent as something dead. Granddad's voice was dron-

ing, and the woman was still smiling at him, and there was this wolf sitting there.

I went around in front of the counter and hunkered down, holding out a hand to him. He sniffed it along the top and along the bottom, then gave me a grin, his tongue curling up between his teeth, and I reached to pet him. *"Ruh!"* he said. He let me scratch the base of his ear.

Then I thought, *This is crazy. Pop will shoot him.*

"I don't know how you got in, but you better go," I said.

"Ruh!"

I heard Pop's truck pulling up. "Right away," I said. I scrambled to my feet. The door bells rang fiercely. The wolf darted around back of the counter. Pop stood in the doorway, steaming.

I went behind the counter. The wolf was lying there, but I still had enough room to stand at the cash register. How *had* he gotten in? I hadn't heard the bells ring between the time the woman had entered and when Pop came in. Maybe the wolf had followed the woman in?

"Lies!" Pop said to me, then noticed we had a customer. The woman stared at him. He throttled down his temper. "Howdy," he said, smiling, his face crimson.

She patted Granddad's hand and darted out the door.

"Lies!" Pop yelled.

"Why, what did the man tell you?" I asked. My voice had a wobble in it.

"There wasn't even a family in cabin five!"

Breath left me suddenly. For a solid half minute, I wondered if I'd hallucinated everything that had happened. Worked for me. Willow, talking about words that tasted like fresh bread. A whole family standing in the sunlight summoning light. Willow, vanishing. A man with silver fire in his eyes. Sure, I made up stories, especially when I had run out of books to read.

Like I had made up the story about the wolf.

I glanced down. The wolf laid his muzzle on my

foot, and his yellow eyes stared up at me. I could feel
the warm weight of his nose, the tickle of his whiskers
against my bare ankles above my tennis shoes, even
smell his dogginess. If I was making this up, my powers
of imagination had increased about a thousand times.

"Did you ask Mr. Lacey about that?" I said to Pop.

"What? Lacey? No, I just went over to the cabin,
and there was no truck there, and nobody in residence.
I went around back and looked through the windows.
No sign of occupation."

"But Pop, they were there just"—I checked my
watch—"forty-five minutes ago."

"You're protecting that damned Mariah woman,
aren't you?" he said.

"No, Pop, honest! They were there!"

He stared at me, his gray eyes blank. Gradually his
face turned from bright red to its normal ruddy color.
Without a word, he stalked past and headed to our
living quarters.

Sweat eased down the gulley of my spine. I reached
to straighten the *TV Guide*s and saw that my hand was
shaking. I looked down at the wolf.

"*Ruf,*" he said, more a breath than a sound.

"You better go," I whispered. I glanced toward the
back door, listened for Pop. Nothing. I walked around
the counter and over to the front door, held it open just
wide enough so that it didn't set off the bells. The wolf
dog trotted out the door. Through the glass I saw him
cast one look over his shoulder before he melted into
the woods.

"Nicky."

I turned to Granddad.

"You're a good boy, Nicky."

"Thanks, Granddad," I said. I was never sure how
aware Granddad was of what went on between me and
Pop. He never talked about it, just sat and watched
everything, or sat and smiled. He could tell stories, but
it was hard to have a conversation with him. I figured

he was sort of like a tape recorder with a bunch of different tapes. Press the play button and out would come some anecdote, but not a whole lot of new stuff.

"Good boy," he said again. "A boy needs a dog."

I stared toward the woods where the wolf had disappeared, and sighed.

"Boy needs a dog," he said. He stood up and shuffled over to join me. "Good dog," he said, but his eyes didn't look focused; the pupils were pinpoints.

Then he turned to me and his pupils flared wide, opening dark tunnels straight to his mind. He patted my shoulder. "Good dog," he said. "Good dog."

My throat closed up. He was old and couldn't even keep track of his words any longer. He didn't know what he was saying. He couldn't mean what I thought he meant.

The hairs on the back of my neck were prickling, and my scalp shivered.

Pop came out from the back with my list in his hand. He had, as expected, crossed off the jerky, licorice, and Twinkies, and he had them in a bag. "Put this junk where it belongs! Straighten those magazines!" he yelled. "Stop standing around. There's work to be done!"

I went to work. Granddad got a red lollipop from the penny candy jar and went back to sit by the stove, even though it wasn't lit. He sat with his booted feet propped on the stove, sucking the candy, the loop of stem sticking out of his mouth. Pop stared at him a moment, made a sour mouth as if he had sucked on a green lemon, and made a note on the inventory sheet.

Three people came in wanting to talk about the merits of various fishing rods, which kept Pop busy for a while, and I finished straightening and rented an X-rated video to old Mr. Fortrey.

I moved stock up to the fronts of the shelves, closest expiration date nearest the front. Having finished with the fishing rod people, who hadn't bought anything,

Pop stood with his arms crossed, staring at the antique fishing equipment on the wall back of the register. He hit the counter with his fist. "Nick, take all this stuff off the wall and put it in the attic!" he said. "Put some of those movie posters up here." He disappeared toward our living quarters again.

I knew Pop was gnawing at it, looking for truth. He didn't believe me. I bet he was trying to figure out why I was lying or where the lies would serve me. I wondered myself about the wolf. If he could understand human speech, he knew I had tried to betray his family. Pop had mentioned cabin five, so, if the wolf knew English, he knew. . . .

I remembered how scared of the wolf I had felt last night, and thought, *Now he's smelled me, and my dream is that when I go out to the woods tonight he's waiting to join me. I can show him some of the places I know, maybe even Father Boulder.* Or maybe the wolf would lie in wait and attack me for telling Pop which cabin to go to. I felt this heat in my chest, a yearning for the life where a wolf waited to walk with me and be my friend.

I got pliers from the toolbox under the counter and pried out the staples that were holding a fishing net to the wall. Granddad's old fishing hat came down next, its band alight with feathered flies. I blew the dust off them and glanced at Granddad's gnarled hands. He didn't have much fine control anymore. I had never seen him tie a fly, but I knew he had done these, and they were like little jewels. Granddad had been a lot more present when I was small and when Mom was still around and we lived in the valley. Pop had worked construction then, and Granddad and Mom had been the most important adults in my world. I remembered Granddad teaching me how to tie knots in rope and how to play gin and casino and hearts. He had tried to teach me chess, but checkers was more my speed when I was seven, and by the time I was interested in chess

Granddad had gone away in his head, too far away to play cards or anything else.

I took the hat over and showed it to Granddad. He accepted it and stroked a finger along the feathers of one of the flies, avoiding the hook. He smiled, staring down at the hat in his lap.

I finished dismantling the fishing display and stapled up some of the movie posters we had rolled up under the counter, sent to us when we ordered the videos: *Terminator II*, *Roger Rabbit*, *Moonstruck*, *Raiders of the Lost Ark*. I was putting the last staple in when Mariah spoke behind me.

"I'm sorry, Nick," she said in a small voice.

I put the staple gun in the toolbox. "Why?"

"I liked having the fishing things up."

I shrugged. "Anyway, it was like you said. Those eyes . . ."

"You saw them too?"

I hesitated. "The next thing I knew I was walking away. I never got an answer from him at all."

She hunched her shoulders. "So now you know how it feels."

I considered that. Had she come into the store three years ago, her mind on what she was intending to pick up, and then woken up halfway to her house, the stupid ceramic unicorn gripped in her hand? "But that doesn't make sense. I just thought I could convince people they liked things. It didn't seem like—"

She didn't say anything, just stared into my eyes, her gray eyes wide, her eyebrows up.

I tried again. "I didn't know—"

She looked at me a moment longer, then shook her head. "You knew," she said.

Heat tingled in my cheeks. "I stopped," I said.

She sighed and came around the counter. "Go get lunch."

I didn't know if Pop had gone back to the motel office, which was where he spent most of his days, watching movies and the occasional sports event on satellite TV and waiting for customers or Candy, the high school girl who cleaned rooms for him and whom he took great delight in ordering around. If he was still back in the kitchen I didn't want to run into him.

For the second time that day, I headed over to Mabel's.

"You're going to give me a heart attack," she said as I sat down.

I grinned at her and checked my wallet. I had some money I'd made doing chores for various people around the lake. I hadn't decided what I was saving for this summer. Last summer I had bought a portable CD/radio/tape deck with headphones, and it had made the winter a lot more bearable, until the night Pop got mad because I had had the headphones on and hadn't heard him call me to fix supper. I still had all the pieces. I was hoping Jeremy would be able to help me fix it. He had an aptitude for that.

Might as well spend money on food, no matter what Pop would say; at least once I had eaten food he couldn't take it away from me and break it.

"Why don't you just give me a cheeseburger instead?" I said.

"Well, sure," said Mabel. "You okay, Nick?"

"I'm not sick, if that's what you mean."

"It's not," she said, and walked away before I could think that through.

Junie brought my cheeseburger to the table. She was two years older than I, and I had always thought she'd leave Sauterelle as soon as she turned eighteen, the way I planned to leave next year. But here she was, waitressing at Mabel's. "Want ketchup?" she asked as she set the plate down. Golden fries lay like a logjam around the burger.

"Sure," I said. I watched her legs as she walked away. Great calf muscles, even in flat shoes. A bruise the size of a quarter behind her left knee, her stockings almost concealing it but not quite.

I had been thinking about leaving Sauterelle since I turned eleven and Pop made me work more than two hours a day. After Mom took off, I thought about leaving all day, every day. Then the lake would freeze hard enough to skate on, or I would find a bird's nest and see the gape-mouthed near-bald babies peeping in unison, or catch sight of a dew-laden spiderweb at dawn, or listen to the frog chorus on spring nights. I would lean against a pine tree in the spring when all the branchlets ended in light green bunches of needles, and I would feel the life rising up through the tree like a slow explosion. Places in the forest drew me to them. Stones and earth and fallen logs asked me to touch them. I would dip fingers in the lake in the morning, or press my cheek against Father Boulder, and I would wonder how I could ever leave.

I remembered what life had been like in the valley for the first half of my life, before Pop packed me and Mom up and brought us here: we had lived in a horrible basement apartment while Pop worked construction and saved money to buy the store. Mom had been afraid to let me leave the apartment by myself, and whenever we walked somewhere together, she was always pointing out trash or broken glass or graffiti, or telling me to avoid people who looked like that or that or that, and tugging me closer to her. At least when we came to Sauterelle Lake she let me go outside by myself.

I loved everything about the lake, except living at home with Pop. And even that had its moments.

One really hot summer evening three years earlier, with the sun taking forever to go down, Junie and I had sat on the Salomans' roof, smoking filched cigarettes, coughing, and talking about where we would go and what we would do when we left. She figured she'd be a movie star, or at least on TV. I thought maybe I'd be a cop or an FBI guy. At that point I hadn't gotten my spy route set up yet, but I had already started sneaking around and spying on people. I could find things out. I could keep secrets. I figured I had the basic traits necessary to be a good detective.

We spun dreams and exchanged smoke-flavored kisses and watched as Venus brightened out of the ashes of sunset, the sound of crickets sheeting through the night around us, and I believed my dreams, and I think she believed hers. That was before George found her.

George worked Archie's Dock during the summer and pretty much hibernated during the winter, aside from hunting everything when it was in season and sometimes when it wasn't. He lived back in the woods, and Junie had married him and lived there too now.

She brought me a red plastic squeeze bottle of ketchup. When I looked up, her gaze slipped sideways, not meeting mine. I watched her walk away, the bruise winking as her knee bent.

When I looked around again, the small red-haired girl from the back of the black truck stood beside my table, staring at me. I studied her. She looked around eleven, or possibly a stunted thirteen. She had pale, pale skin. The dusty rose of her lips was like a color seen through clouded glass; her eyes were an intense amber. Her off-white T-shirt was smudged with dirt and grass stains, and her pale arms bore the healing scabs of scrapes.

I tried half a smile on her. "Want a French fry?" I asked, holding one up.

"Can you see me?" she said.

I looked behind myself, then back at her. "Huh?"

"Can you see me? Can you hear me?"

"Sure. Why not?"

She slid into the chair opposite mine. She reached out tentatively, then plucked a French fry from my plate and nibbled it. Her brow furrowed. "What is it?" she whispered.

I blinked. "It's made from a potato."

She licked her upper lip. She nibbled the fry. "Salt," she said.

"Yeah. You deep fat fry a chunk of potato, and salt it afterward."

"Salt between us." She looked at me with narrowed eyes.

I glanced at the salt shaker on the table between us, then up into her face.

"What's your name?" she asked.

"Nick Verrou. What's yours?"

She stared at the tabletop. She bit her fry in half, chewed, and swallowed. After a moment, she said, "Lauren Keye."

"Pleased to meet you," I said, holding out a hand.

She had a tiny smile, just a slight stretching of the corners of her mouth. She gripped my hand but didn't shake it. Her hand was small and tough and warm. She held on for what seemed like a long time.

"Nick?" Mabel came over to the table. "Who are you talking to? What are you doing?"

I cocked my head at Lauren. I wondered if just holding hands with her in public could be misconstrued. It wasn't like I was doing anything to her. She gave me a wide grin and released my hand, her eyes dancing.

I flexed my hand and grabbed a French fry. "What does it look like I'm doing?"

"Well, it was hard to tell," said Mabel. "You were sitting there with your hand out, like you forgot how to move your arm. You *sure* you're all right?"

I stared at Lauren. She leaned her head back and laughed. Mabel didn't respond to her at all.

A paralyzing cold gripped me for a moment, then thawed, leaving me strangely relaxed. I wiped cold sweat off my forehead and upper lip with my napkin. I must be imagining this little redheaded kid. If I could conjure up Willow and a wolf, why not this? I said, "I was trying to think through a yoga exercise I saw in a book." My voice wobbled.

"You haven't touched your burger."

I looked at my plate. I looked at my watch. I grabbed my cheeseburger and bit it. "It's great. Sorry, Mabel, I'm kind of distracted right now."

She patted me on the head and went back behind the counter, casting an anxious glance at me before disappearing into the kitchen.

I stared at my plate for a little while, then, feeling shivery, looked at Lauren. Maybe I was really in bed and almost asleep, and everything that had happened so far today was stories I had made up. But I sure *felt* awake.

"Ha!" she said.

I picked up my cheeseburger and munched. I couldn't taste it, and it was hard to swallow. I washed it down with water.

"Oh, come on," said Lauren.

I chewed. I looked at her and away. I drank water.

She took one of my fries and ate it.

"How does that work?" I whispered. "How come they don't see a fry floating in the air?"

"When I touch it, it disappears," she said, and giggled.

"But you touched me, and I didn't—"

"You're alive, silly!"

I wasn't sure that made the perfect sense she seemed to think it made. I swallowed the last of my hamburger and wrapped the rest of the fries in a paper napkin; Pop was scornful of waste. I checked my watch. Pop had said I could have just a half hour lunch, but I had always taken an hour. Mariah would want to leave as soon as she could, I thought; she hated facing Pop even more than she hated facing me. But I wasn't ready to go home yet. "Come on," I whispered to Lauren. I put a tip on the table for Junie, paid for my meal, and left without looking back.

I walked around back of Mabel's to the path up the hill, then perched on a rock in the first clearing. Sun struck down through the pines. Lauren jumped up and sat beside me, her hard muscular little shoulder pressed against my arm. "Can I have another?" she said.

I opened the grease-soaked napkin. We ate silently for a while. For an invisible and possibly imaginary kid she could really eat. Her shoulder felt intensely real, as real as the rock under me. She even smelled like a kid who hadn't bathed in a little too long. I kept trying to think this through and stubbing my mind on it. The edges refused to match up.

What would Lord Calardane do?

Cancel that. What would my science teacher say? Collect data, observe phenomena, come up with hypotheses. Data: something had helped me eat my French fries. I could see this kid, and apparently Mabel couldn't. That wasn't very scientific, but just for a little while, maybe I should entertain the hypothesis that this kid was real and other people couldn't see her. If I thought it through, I could probably devise a test to prove she was real. I would need some other observers for that, though, and I didn't have time to work on it now.

I could taste again, even though I still felt terminally confused.

"Salt between us," she said when we had finished.

"What does that mean?"

She cocked her head. "It means we mustn't hurt each other in a lasting way. You can't eat with your enemy."

"That's weird," I said. I'd heard about food taboos, but I'd never heard about this one before. I shook out the empty napkin, wadded it up, keeping the least greasy parts on the outside, and put it in my pocket. "Lauren?"

"What?"

"What are you—who—why'd you come up to me in the restaurant? What do you want with me?"

"Mama said you could see us even when we were warded, and I just wanted to check it out."

"Warded," I said.

"Mmm." She launched herself from the rock, floated through air and landed without a sound on the path below. "Fixed so people can't see us. You saw Mama and Dad at the house."

"And Pop didn't," I whispered. I remembered Willow's morning comfort in the water and her nakedness, the sense flowing from her that she was free of any watchers, even though I watched.

I looked at the girl on the path below me, and thought, this isn't happening. N-O, no. No way.

Or maybe it was. Wine and dine that hypothesis. Take it out to dinner. See if it wants a second date.

"So I just thought I'd check," she said. She grinned wide. "Then I had to try that food. Now we have salt between us, Nick."

"How come I can see you?"

"I don't know."

"But other people can't. Other people really can't?"

She shook her head. "There are some *Domishti* people with whatchamacallit, second sight. They've been a problem for us in the past. Mama says they're rare. She's irritated that you happen to be one, 'cause it can really mess things up for us. Other than that, only people warded the same way I am can see us. And I am warded. I'm not strong in my other disciplines yet, but I know my warding. Light is my friend, and it hides me."

I squinted at her. "But you're right there." I reached out and touched her shoulder. Solid and warm.

"Well, yes." She touched her index finger to her mouth. "For you. Not for anybody else in the restaurant, though, unless I bump into them. Maybe light likes you too. Maybe you see more than light. I don't know."

I thought of my mother, how she had curled my

fingers around a green rock. Her hand was so much bigger than mine in this memory, I must have been just a little kid. "Hold it tight. Hold it tight," she had said, stroking the tips of her fingers along the backs of mine. She had whispered words. Light leaked out between my fingers.

I blinked and the memory vanished. "Light likes me?"

"Maybe," said Lauren.

Well, it was almost a hypothesis. Coming up with a test for this one would be harder than for the other one, but it would be fun to think about. I said, "This salt-between-us thing. Does that work just between you and me, or does it count for your whole family?"

"If you make a promise, does it bind your whole family?" she asked.

I imagined trying to get Pop to honor a promise I might make, like, say, being nice to Lauren, and knew it was stupid to even think of it. "Nope," I said.

"Well, it does for my family, unless I forget to tell them. 'Bye." She turned and ran up the hill, so quickly and silently she vanished like smoke.

"Ruf."

I paused just before stepping from the woods into the parking lot behind Mabel's, and glanced to the right.

"Ruh," said the wolf, poking his muzzle out between bracken and thimbleberries.

I was late to relieve Mariah. Pop was probably pitching a fit, and it wasn't fair to Mariah to leave her there like a horseshoe stake. I thought that, and then I was squatting, holding out my hand to the wolf, who edged out of the brush and nosed my hand and wrist. When we had finished this greeting, I stroked his head. He pushed up and licked me on the face, and I hugged him, feeling very strange, pressing my face against his warm furry neck and smelling dog and a wilderness of crushed herbs and, faintly, manure. He stood still and tense in my embrace for a long moment, then said, *"Uff."*

"I'm sorry," I said, releasing him. The dream was alive in my mind. The wolf and I belonged to each other, and our whole purpose was to explore. We went places without fear, night or day. Even home. Pop might think twice if I had a wolf beside me.

Pop might think once and go grab his double-barreled shotgun.

"Ruh," said the wolf, and licked my face again.

"If I hear you at night, if you hear me, you're not going to come eat me, are you?"

He grinned wide, his tongue lolling between his icicle teeth. A chuckle of air huffed from his mouth.

"Easy for you to say," I said. "I bet you're not scared when you're running around at night. Was that you howling last night? Who was with you?"

He closed his mouth and stared at me, then turned and vanished into the underbrush.

I felt strange. Abandoned and bereft, for the second time in ten minutes. Was it just ten minutes? I checked my watch. Mariah was going to kill me.

These summer people had turned things around. *I* was supposed to be the one watching everybody else in secrecy, and here they were, sneaking up on me, watching me when I didn't even know they were there.

I hit the parking lot running, touched a finger to my face where the wolf had licked it. A wolf, an ultimate wild thing, had let me touch him. Had touched me back. I could put up with a lot for that moment.

"For that, you're going to spend the evening doing inventory," Pop said.

"We did inventory two weeks ago," I said. We did it every quarter, and I hated it.

"Doesn't matter," said Pop. "You're doing it not because it's useful but because you need discipline, understand?"

"But—" But tonight was the dance. Friday night. My night off. I wasn't sure if Willow would ever return from the place she had vanished to, but maybe, just maybe, she was real, and she was planning to stop by and pick me up. Paul might be at the dance—he usually went—and maybe I could find out if we were still friends. Maybe somebody else from Willow's family would be there, too, and I could try to detect more about them. Maybe I could talk to Kristen . . .

Maybe I was going to spend the night in the store, counting tubes of sunscreen and bottles of bug repellent.

"And while you're doing it, you be thinking about common courtesy, good business, and keeping your word. I bought you that damned fancy watch for a reason."

I stared into his eyes, then lowered my gaze to the floor. It was never a good idea to look Pop in the eye for very long.

"Now I have to get back to the motel. I heard a car pull up." He stalked past me and out the door, leaving the sound of bells behind.

I closed up the store at five, as usual, and made dinner for me and granddad and Pop. We ate in silence.

After dinner cleanup I went back to the store and started counting things, making hash marks on a yellow legal pad. I had just finished totaling the candy bar rack when Willow tapped on the door's window glass.

3

Conjuring Acts

I felt a clenching in my throat, and realized I had stopped breathing. I pulled in breath and looked at Willow through the smeared glass. She was completely visible. She had on a close-fitting red dress scooped low in front, with a full, frilly skirt that only came down to mid-thigh. Yellow Klamath weed sat like a twined halo on her dark head. It was a small flower I had never considered pretty before, but on her it glowed. Her eyes were only slightly more orange.

She looked like a wicked angel.

She smiled at me and rattled the doorknob. The door was locked. For a moment I just stood there, jaw dropped, and then I unlatched the door and let her in.

"You ready?" she said.

"I can't," I said, swallowed, and said, "go."

"What?"

"I'm being punished. Gotta stay home and count stuff."

"Punished? What for?" She walked to the counter, jumped or floated up, and sat there, her hands quiet in her lap.

"For taking a long lunch." I turned away and counted decks of cards, foil bags of pipe tobacco, jars of pink salmon eggs. I glanced at her. She was still there.

She cocked her head, staring at the wooden floor. Her brow furrowed. "Do you work here every day?"

"I get half of Saturday off." That had taken some real strong convincing. Weekends were our busiest times. Pop was still suspicious about why Saturday was my half day, and I thought maybe I should relax and let him pick some other day, like Wednesday. But there wasn't as much going on around the lake most Wednesdays. Saturdays, people were always up to something interesting.

"Six other days of the week you're in this store?" Willow asked.

"During the season. We open an hour later on Sunday, too. Oh, and at the moment, I get to take lunch, but that might change."

"But—" She frowned.

"Sorry about our date," I said.

She drifted down from the counter and wandered around the store as I counted lighters and packs of cigarettes and sticks of beef jerky. After a while, she said, "You're counting. You're counting what's here? And you're in here every single day?"

"Yep."

"Then you already know what's in the store." She came toward me, reached up, and touched my forehead. The tips of her fingers were cool. "Write," she said in her velvet voice.

I blinked and wrote, feeling four cold spots on my forehead and thinking about nothing at all. I flipped pages on the yellow legal pad and wrote more. My hand cramped, but I didn't stop to shake it. Seven pages later I dropped the pad and pen and tried to flex my fingers. Man, they hurt.

Willow stopped touching me.

"Don't do that," I said. My voice shook. My fingers were twitching. Don't do it? How had she done it? I had heard of hypnosis, but this was something else. The pain in my hand was real, and so were all the pages of scribbling. I looked at them because I didn't want to look at her.

Maybe I did know everything that was in the store. I might have listed things we had lost to pilfering. Or maybe I knew about those too, and didn't know I knew.

I could see me knowing everything. I couldn't see her just kind of ordering me to make a list and me doing it. N-O. No.

"No" hadn't gotten me anywhere with disappearing Lauren, either.

Something about this whole situation reminded me of my mother. Had she touched my forehead the way Willow had?

Willow took the pad from me and dropped it on the floor, then gripped my hands in hers, and smoothed her cool, callused thumbs down over my fingers and palms. My left hand was curled with cramp from holding the pen. She took it in both her hands and worked it with her fingers, stroking along the tensed muscles, pressing her thumb against my palm. Gradually her fingers warmed against mine. I felt very strange, standing there while she massaged my hand. I could smell her—a wild animal scent, crushed herbs, musky warmth, the tantalizing smell of clean, glossy hair. "I'm sorry, Nick," she said, staring down at our hands. Her eyes drifted shut.

I closed my hand around one of hers. My fingers worked okay again. Willow sighed faintly and moved a little closer to me, and my arm slid around her shoulders without thought. Her warmth felt good against me. I remembered her standing in the water in the morning sun. I wanted to get really close to her and at the same time I wanted to stand there and not move because so far it hadn't been a mistake, but once it turned into a mistake we'd never get back to here, where I could stand with her hand in mine, my arm around her, my cheek against her hair and her flowers, her breast nudging my chest, and all my ideas for what came next bright and untarnished.

She tilted her head back. Her eyes were still closed, but her mouth was coming closer to mine. Her lips looked soft, dark pink like the inside of a cherry, and her breath smelled of honey. I felt like I was standing on the edge of a cliff, about to dive off, without knowing what was waiting for me when I landed. Fear heightened my awareness; all I could see was her face. Each dark eyelash, each smooth curved dark hair in her eyebrows; a gentle lace of golden freckles across her nose and cheeks, almost too faint to notice. I heard the breath moving in and out of her, and the thought of that intimacy of air was almost unbearably exciting.

I closed my eyes and touched her lips with mine, and her lips touched back. Not like kissing Junie, who had been convinced sucking was important. A pressure, a softening, a moving pressure again, and the sweet taste of summer afternoon flowers. Heat and fear tremored through me. My pants were way too tight.

Her free hand came up and gripped my head. I couldn't think. All there was was pressure and heat and taste, discomfort and excitement, and something building.

"Nick!" Pop's voice.

One word, and I jerked, feeling as though I'd been dipped in liquid nitrogen. Everything inside switched from desire to panic. My eyes were open. I was staring down into Willow's left eye, looking into an eternity of gold around a deep well of darkness, fuzzy because it was too close to focus on. For a moment Willow's hand kept my head down, my lips against hers. Her strength scared me. Then she let go, and my head snapped up.

"Nick!" cried Pop again. "What are you doing?"

My face heated. I felt wobbly. What did he think I

was doing? "Inventory," I said. It came out hoarse
and scratchy.

"You lie! You lie and lie! You lie to my face."

Heat flushed my back. He was tearing me down in
front of My Girl. I stooped and retrieved the legal pad,
slapped it on the counter in front of him. "Inventory,"
I said. My voice was so cool and distant it tasted like
it didn't belong to me. "I've finished." I crossed my
arms, tucking my hands into my armpits. Willow stood
silent beside me.

He picked the pad up, his eyes wide, and flipped
back through all the pages. After a moment's study, he
said, "But this takes both of us eight hours." He turned
a page, went over and opened the drawer where we
kept spare sewing supplies. He counted needle packets,
checked my list. His eyes narrowed as he glared at me.

"What?" I said. "Is it wrong?"

After a moment, he said, waving a five-pack of needles, "These are dusty."

"You didn't say to dust. You said to count."

He counted spools of thread and checked my list.
Willow leaned against me. She covered a small yawn
with the back of her hand.

Pop glared at me again.

"I'm done," I said, "and I'm taking Willow to the
dance now."

"You're grounded!"

"Think twice," I said. The words came from deep
in my chest, in the voice of a stranger, dangerous and
persuasive.

Pop blinked three times, then said, "See you later."

The warm night smelled of lake bottom, dust, and
trees. Somewhere in the distance a skunk had sprayed.
Wind sent pine needles whispering against one another.
Frogs chorused from the lake, and cricket calls punctu-
ated the air from the roadside. Music left faint foot-

prints on the air. From the motel building behind the store blue and pink neon flickered: VENTURE INN VACAN Y.

Willow laughed. It was like hearing a lark at midnight. She hooked her arm through mine and set off toward Parsley's Hall, tracking music to its lair.

We had passed Mabel's, Fortrey's, the Lakeside Tavern, and Archie's Boat Dock. I pulled Willow to a sudden stop in the darkness between two yard lights and listened. The music was louder now, almost masking the faintest of brushing and clicking sounds from behind us. I turned back.

The wolf was there, a dark shadow shape, his furred edges tipped with left-behind light. He lowered his head and hunched his shoulders. He looked completely wild and unapproachable. A growl spun in his throat.

"Evan!" Willow said.

Wind touched the damp on my forehead, chilling me. I squatted in the road and held my hand out to the wolf, wondering if night transformed him into some other kind of creature from the one I had touched and even hugged by sunlight.

After a moment he straightened and edged close enough to sniff my hand. *"Ruh,"* he said.

I leaned forward onto my knees and put my arms around him. "Thanks," I whispered. "You scared me."

"Ruf!" He broke free of my embrace. *"Uff,"* he said on a breath, hanging his head and peering sideways at Willow.

"Nick!" said Willow, her voice light with stifled laughter. "What are you doing?"

"Nothing." I jumped up and dusted off my knees. I suddenly realized I was wearing dirty jeans and a dust-streaked black T-shirt with the logo of a valley country music station in white on the front. I had expected to spend the whole evening in the store counting things.

There was no actual dress code at the Friday night dances, but I had planned a better outfit when I still thought I was going—wanted to look good at my first dance of the summer. Who knew who might be there?

Though Willow didn't seem to care how I was dressed, and it didn't feel so important to impress Kristen anymore.

Willow said, "You were hugging Evan."

"It wasn't his idea. I just . . ."

"Just what?" she said after a moment, her voice soft as warm chocolate.

"Just always wanted a dog," I said before I could stop the words. I remembered looking out the door as the wolf vanished into the woods, and Granddad telling me a boy needed a dog.

"Evan's not exactly a dog," Willow said. Some of the dance had seeped out of her voice.

"I know that," I said. "He's wild, and he owns himself. Anyway, Pop would never let me have a pet."

She slid her arm through mine again. We walked without words toward the hall. The wolf wisped along beside us. He licked my hand once, a brief damp contact, then darted a few feet away as if to pretend he hadn't done it.

Cars were parked haphazardly all around Parsley's Hall, staggering across grass and gravel parking space, huddled in under the skirts of trees. The night smelled of stale cigarette smoke and crushed grass. Orange lights on poles copper-edged the big summer leaves of maples, copper-sheathed the pine needles. Moths surfed the air currents near the lights. The hall's open double doors spilled yellow light and bright music out into the road. Fiddles wailed, an amplified voice sang garbled words, and shoes shuffled on the rosin-dusted wooden dance floor. Beyond the small high curtained windows, shadows moved.

I took Willow's hand. We both looked at Evan.

"RooOoOOoo," he said softly, and faded off into the forest.

"Did you put a spell on him?" Willow said.

"What do you mean?"

"Evan hates everybody. He was so angry when the family sent us to live with these cousins, he's been resisting everything ever since. How come he likes you?"

"Cousins," I said, letting the word curl upward at the end into a question. I wanted to ask her about spells, Evan, everything she had just said, but decided to start small. I had thought maybe Lauren was Willow's sister.

"Oh, I guess I haven't explained any of that. I'm pretty sure I'm supposed to marry one of them."

"What?"

"Probably Joshua. He's only a year younger than I am. But there haven't been any definite signs about it, not since the night Aunt Agatha threw the bones. And all that told us was that I belonged with this family for now. Joshua doesn't even like me yet."

"What?"

She looked up into my face and laughed, then pulled me along into the light coming from the open doors.

Friday night dances at Parsley's Hall brought people out of the woodwork. The dances were the equivalent of a weekly newspaper; for locals, it was the best way to get news and to make news. Parsley scheduled a break in the middle of the evening for public service announcements, birthday and anniversary best wishes, and a raffle. Even though there was a private rec hall at Lacey's, a lot of the Lacey's guests came to the dances, and people from all the other rent-a-cabins or lodgings who were starved for entertainment came too. Musicians drove up from the valley and down from the hills to jam just for fun, but they always played danceable stuff with a strong beat, whether they played well or not. Kids came with their families, and old folks came with their spouses or alone. A coffee can with a slot cut in its lid stood by the door for donations for hall upkeep. Other than that, there was no charge.

The front hall was mostly dance floor, with benches along the side walls and a sound system set up at the far end in front of a stage nobody used except as a place to park instrument cases. The back room had long tables lined up and surrounded by unfolded metal chairs, and a kitchen complete with a counter where Parsley's wife and sister sold fair to middling slices of pie for a dollar each and coffee from a twenty-five-gallon pot for fifty cents a Styrofoam cup. They also sold weak punch to younger people.

A lot of the musicians were old-timers from other states who had ended up here. Many of them were men. While they played music their wives sat in the back room playing cards and telling tales.

I'd been hearing the music here half my life. It had all been brand new to me when I was eight, just up from the valley, where Mom had listened to classical music and I had listened to rock like the kids I knew in school. At first I had thought this new music was strange, weird, and stupid. I had never heard any of the songs on radio or TV. Now they were more familiar to me than any other music, and there were enough different songs that they didn't get old and irritating, just familiar and comfortable.

Jake was singing "Storms Never Last" when we stepped into the hall, and lots of couples were two-stepping around to it. Kristen, Paul, a dark-haired girl I'd never seen before, Jeremy, and the tennis-whites guy sat on the bench to the left, holding cups of something and talking with their heads together. Kristen's parents were dancing with each other, and didn't look as though they had even a bit of a buzz on. There was the usual assortment of women in blouses and frothy skirts and men in cowboy boots, jeans, belts with big buckles, cowboy shirts with embroidery on the yokes, and cowboy hats. Mabel had on her dancing sandals, which were studded with sparkly fake jewels. Then there were other people wearing jeans and tennis shoes, shorts and halter tops and sandals, relaxed and not out of place.

I wished I had washed before I'd left the store, but all in all Willow and I looked like we could belong if we wanted to. Jeremy glanced up, smiled, and beckoned us to join them. Clutching Willow's hand, I edged around dancing couples and went over to him.

He, too, had done some growing during the winter. He was now tall enough to play basketball without embarrassment, and on him it looked good. "Hi, Nick," he said. His voice had dropped and stabilized into a warm bass.

"Hi, Jeremy. This is Willow. Willow, Jeremy."

His smile stretched wider as he took her hand. He wasn't in any hurry to let go.

"Willow," I said, after a minute during which her smile tightened, "this is Kristen, Paul—hi, Paul!— and who?"

Willow slipped her hand out of Jeremy's. It looked like an effort.

"Ian," said Kristen, waving at the big blond tennis-whites guy (actually in dark slacks and an alligator-emblem shirt at the moment), "and Megan," gesturing toward the brunette, who looked relaxed and wore jeans and a green shirt. Kristen's smile looked real. We shook hands all around. "Nice to meet you, Willow. Good to see you, Nick," Kristen said.

"Thanks," I said, feeling very conscious of how messy my clothes were and how pristine she looked, all in white. "Good to see you, too." Then suddenly it was awkward. I had no more words for them, and they didn't speak either.

"Let's dance," Willow said.

I straightened and looked toward the musicians. Holly Waggoner stepped up to the microphone, fiddle tucked into the crook between her chin and shoulder. I grinned. She had taken some second and third places in the state fiddling contests. " 'Scuse us," I said, and led Willow away from the others. I slid my arm around her waist and took her right hand in mine. Holly played "Chinese Breakdown" with verve and style.

Willow, it developed, did not know how to dance at all. I could feel from the way she swayed in my embrace that she understood rhythm, but she didn't seem to know what to do with her feet, and she put her left hand first over my arm, then gripped my arm, as if afraid I would let go of her. "Rest your hand on my shoulder," I whispered. She did. Her fingers were kind of tight. She kept glancing around, looking at what other people were doing and trying to imitate them. Since the tune was a fast one, I wondered if we wouldn't be better off sitting this one out, or at least heading outside to practice where we could still hear music but not be seen.

Willow muttered something in her velvet voice, and suddenly we were dancing just fine, her steps matching mine with a prescience that was eerie. I felt peculiar, as if I had four legs, four arms, two hearts, and an imperative: music was the brain that governed my actions. So I didn't really need to think; but I felt sweat on my forehead, upper lip, back, and the back of my neck, and as we danced heat generated in my chest until I was sucking in breaths to try to blow the fire out.

When the tune ended I rubbed my forehead on the arm of my T-shirt, even though Willow's and my fingers were still intertwined. "Don't do that," I said, my voice ragged.

"What?" She stared at me, wide-eyed. All around us couples were breaking up, walking to the side, matching with others, wandering off for punch, and we still stood in dance pose, attached to each other, encircling each other. I felt fear flare through her, a cold creeping fire where the one in me had been hot.

"Don't," I said. Now that we were standing still,

the fire in me was settling to embers. "Don't ... let go. Let go."

She stared up into my face, unblinking, the fear in her flashing to panic.

"Willow." Our hearts were beating fast, matching rhythms, mine speeding as hers raced. "Stop it," I said, putting an edge into my voice. Her head jerked, and then the connection broke and I could breathe again. I drew in heavy drafts of air as I felt my muscles relaxing. Willow closed her eyes tight and turned her head away as if waiting for a slap.

I tightened my arm around her, dropped our hands, and led her out of the hall, across the road, beyond the lamplight into the darkness of the trees, closer to the lake. "You've got to stop doing that," I said, sitting us down on a low maple branch. Her face and arms were paler than the leaf-shadowed darkness. She was warm beside me.

"Doing what," she said in a toneless voice.

"Making me do stuff without asking." I had said it out loud. I couldn't think of any other explanation for what had happened. I'd go with this one until something knocked it out of the running. It might not make logical sense, but it made internal sense.

Besides, I could sort of almost remember a few times Mom had stared into my eyes and then shared her heartbeat with me. I couldn't remember why.

"What are you talking about." Willow sounded like a robot.

"Willow!" I gave her a little shake. "I'll teach you to dance. I'll write down a list. Just ask."

"What," she said. She stared straight ahead, though I was beside her.

I pressed fingers against the pulse at her wrist, trying to feel her heartbeat again, trying to feel mine, relieved that the heat had died, wanting the connection. Had it hurt her to break it? "Look, I liked being hooked to you, but it was making me breathe funny," I said.

"What?" She sounded a little more awake.

"And I don't really understand it," I said. "Maybe if I knew more about it, it wouldn't scare me."

"Nick?" she said after a moment.

"What?"

"I'm not supposed to do things like that. That's why my parents sent me away. I'm not supposed to *kilianish*, to *fetchkva*—to hook to—I'm not—especially not with—they're going to lock me up. I'm sorry, Nick. I'm really sorry."

She was going to get grounded? For reasons that didn't make much sense to me—what had happened was between us, wasn't it? "Look, it's not like I'm going to tell anybody. What would I say?" I focused on the pulse at her wrist. Her heart was still beating too fast.

"I'm not supposed to do it. I'm not supposed to own boys, even though I have a special, secret reason for it. Mom and Dad explained to me that it's wrong, even though my cousins at home kept doing it, even though our teacher told us to do it. Uncle Bennet and Aunt Elissa explained it to me. That's why Mom and Dad sent me to them. Uncle Bennet and Aunt Elissa think it's awful to own other people. I even understand that it is. I'm not supposed to do it, and I don't want to do it anymore, and I start to do it anyway."

I swallowed. "Own boys?"

"Own people. It's the best—it's the most—it—" She shook her head. "That's wrong. That's wrong. Oh, Nick."

"Own people . . ." I said, thinking about my mother and my father. My mother had made me feel like I was a part of her. My father seemed to think I belonged to him. I wasn't sure either of them was wrong.

"I . . ." she said, "I need to learn not to want to." Her pulse was slowing under my fingers. "Or unlearn how to do it. Some lessons I was just too good at." She took my hand and stroked the rough callus on her thumb's outer edge along my palm and down my fingers, one at a time. "Some urges are hard to fight. I am so totally tempted to own you, Nick."

A sliver of ice zipped down my spine. Some part of me wondered: what would that be like? If I did what she wanted—danced when she wished, wrote when and what she wished, followed her and served her in ways pleasant and uncomfortable? "No," I said, my shoulders twitching. Though really, wouldn't it be more interesting to do what Willow wanted than what my father wanted? The demands were sure to be different.

"Well, I won't," she said. She raised my hand to her mouth and pressed a kiss into my palm. "I won't own you. If I even started the procedure that makes you mine, my aunt and uncle would release you and punish me. I'm trying not to do anything to you. But then I get scared, and I'm not sure how to *not* start the *kilianishkya*. I've never just tried to ... to know somebody without putting the pulling-threads into the *veshka*. . . . You seem so calm about all this. As if you understand it."

"No," I whispered. If I waited until I understood everything, I might go crazy before I got there. Too many weird things had happened already today. What else could possibly happen?

I thought of the longing I had for the wolf dog, my wish that we could be traveling companions. But that wasn't the same. I didn't want to own him. I just wanted us to be very good friends. He would care about me and I would care about him and we would take care of each other.

"I want you," Willow murmured. "I want you."

I couldn't remember anybody ever saying that to me—not Pop, not Junie, certainly not Mom. The heat rose in me again: not the heat of our dancing connection, as if I were struggling to either get away from or live with something new and foreign, but the heat of blood. It felt exciting and sexy and scary. I put my arm around her and kissed her. She tasted like warm golden flowers and the juicy ends of grass stems. She gripped my head again. Her kisses were still tentative, but her hands were certain.

Heat was building in me again, but it wasn't a mirror of her heat, or if it was, I didn't know. Her hair felt soft as cat fur when I worked my fingers through it and dislodged the flowers there. Her skin was almost as soft as the surface of warm water, and she smelled faintly of cinnamon. My fear seeped away. I knew there was something I wanted, but I was thinking with something other than my brain, just feeling and waiting and wanting and knowing, gathering her to me, wanting her against me, sensing her heat and her longing, wanting to be inside of her.

"Ruf!" A weight hit me, knocking me and Willow right off the branch to the ground beyond. I cracked my elbow against a buried root, and it hurt; Willow spilled loose of my embrace, and the cold where her warmth had been hurt, too. Then the wolf was standing on me, his forepaws pinning my shoulders, his hind-paws planted on my thighs, a growl simmering from him—and his nose pointed at Willow.

"I wasn't," she said, elbowing herself up and straightening her hem.

"Wuf. Raroor," he muttered.

She sighed. "All right. I started to, but I stopped myself. I wasn't doing it right then."

The wolf lay down on me, heavy and warm, and snuffed at my face. His bristly whiskers tickled. I still felt shocky from the suddenness of his attack, but I also felt strangely relaxed, as if huge wild animals lay on me all the time. He raised his head and stared down into my eyes. I felt his regard more than saw it in the darkness. Then he muttered little barks and growls.

"Evan . . ." Willow said, her voice rising but soft.

I felt sleepy and strange. The wolf's noises seemed more and more like words. I wanted to close my eyes, but I couldn't even blink. My breathing shifted. I was panting. The inrush of air woke me up.

"*—nishti fetchayim shtoi veshkuti minish minish minish,*" said the wolf, and I felt cold all over. Every voluntary muscle in my body tensed and froze, as if I were straining to lift a rock that was really part of the Earth and wouldn't come loose. The wolf licked my nose.

"Evan," Willow said. Her voice was bereft of hope.

"Can't have him now," said the wolf, his voice low and gruff. "I got him." I could feel his heart beating and knew mine matched its rhythm. My own pulses ran loud in my ears, the sound of a fingertip rubbing back and forth on fabric.

"No," she whispered. "They'll punish you."

"They won't know," he said. "I'm never going back to the cabin. I'll stay here. With Nick." He licked my cheek. His breath smelled doggy. His tongue was warm, but the wet it left behind cooled instantly. I couldn't summon the energy to be scared, even though I was still totally tense and I had the feeling something monumental had just happened. It occurred to me that it was odd I could understand a wolf.

"Evan, you can't—you can't—what are you going to—" She was crying.

"Point is," he said, "now *you* can't." He snuffed, then said, "Relax, Nick. Relax."

My muscles melted like wax, and my eyelids fell shut.

"Not that much," said the wolf. "Be comfortable."

I felt totally disabled, but comfortable. Evan slipped off me, stood over me, sniffing. "Are you all right?" he asked after a moment.

"I don't know." My voice came out high and drifty.

"What's wrong?"

"I don't know," I said.

"Be well," he said.

I took some deep breaths and felt health running through me like alcohol. I sat up. "What—" I said.

"You wanted a dog," said the wolf. "Now you're my boy."

"But—"

"I'll give you a long leash. Be well. Be independent. Do whatever you need to. Take good care of yourself."

"What?" I said. "What?"

He huffed a laugh. "See you later," he said, and trotted off into the darkness.

I rubbed my elbow where I had hit it. It didn't hurt anymore. "What—" I said.

Willow rubbed her eyes, climbed to her feet, and brushed off her skirt. "Come on, Nick." Her voice sounded shaky. She held a hand out to me.

"What just happened?"

She gripped my hand and didn't say anything. Her hand was cold again. She pulled me to my feet even though I wasn't sure I was ready to stand up.

"Willow . . ."

"He fetched you," she said, her voice low and flat. "He owns you. You belong to him now."

I shivered. "But that's not—"

"He did it so I wouldn't. You're fetched, Nick. Let's go back to the dance."

"But—wait a second—how can a—how can I—?"

"You'll have to ask him."

I took a few more deep breaths, feeling better with each one, even though I was scared. "That's not fair," I said. "He's gone. How can a wolf own a human being, anyway?" *What would a wolf want with a human being? What did Evan want with me?* "Don't I get to say anything about this?"

She threaded her fingers through mine. "Teach me to dance," she said, tugging me back toward Parsley's Hall and light and music. My fear stayed with me, but I knew I wasn't going to get any more answers from Willow, so I dropped the subject.

We danced in the road to music coming out the door until her black slippers turned dust-gray and her steps came without effort. There was never another moment when I felt our hearts beating like two halves of one heart, but presently our steps matched and meshed and it was like she could read my mind, anticipating our next move. Holding her felt comfortable and right.

"You're ready to go inside," I said, when she knew the basics of the waltz, the two-step, and the schottische.

"Mm." She stepped back and looked down at herself. "Not quite." She held up her hands and caught orange light from the streetlights, then poured it down on her dress and legs and shoes. The light washed the dust away. "You want?" she asked.

My throat felt tight. Every time she touched something I thought I knew, she turned it into something unexpected. How was I supposed to think about this? Light liked Lauren. Light liked me. Maybe it liked Willow too. I managed to say yes. She walked around me, aiming a wash of light at me. It tickled like a soft breeze. When she was done, my clothes were cleaner than they had been when I left the store. I sniffed my shoulder. No sweat smell at all, just something like the edge of lightning, ozone and electric. Well, after everything else that had happened, why not?

"Thanks," I said. "You lost your flowers."

"Those were for you, anyway," she said, combing her fingers through her hair, then shaking her head till her hair settled in soft curls.

"What?"

"People usually dress for a date, don't they?"

"Unless they're idiots," I said, burying my hands in my jean pockets.

"Come on, idiot." She took my arm and we went back inside, where Jeremy immediately came over and asked Willow to dance.

She glanced at me. "But I came with you."

"People switch," I said.

Her forehead furrowed. Then she gave Jeremy a small tight smile and her hand, and he led her to the floor. I wandered over and asked Megan for a dance.

"Haven't seen you at Lacey's," she said when we had gotten the first adjustments to each other's styles out of the way. Her breath smelled of spearmint. Sanders was playing "Earl's Waltz" really slowly, and for once I didn't mind; it would make it easy for Willow in her first dance with somebody else, I figured.

"I work at the Venture Inn store," I said.

"You do? You sell bathing suits there? Mine's old. It tore when I put it on."

The inventory came into my mind. "Sure. We have one that would fit you. Black with a rainbow stripe from the shoulder to the opposite hip."

She stared at me, eyes wide. "What size?" she said after a moment.

I knew I had written everything on the legal pad, but I couldn't see the writing anymore. "Four, six, something like that," I said.

"How would you know my size?" she said.

"I've got my arm around you," I said. Still, it was a good question. I had never paid attention to women's clothes, beyond knowing we had a few in stock. "Could be wrong," I said.

"Is this a line?" she asked.

"Huh?"

"It seems like a really weird way to pick up girls."

I tried to think of a way of answering that without being insulting. I wasn't interested in her except as someone to dance with while Willow was off with someone else. "I don't have much experience," I said. "What works?" I would never have said anything like that before tonight, but tonight I already had a date. A really, really weird date.

Megan laughed. " 'Has anyone ever told you you have very beautiful eyes?' " she said.

"That works?"

She fluttered her eyelashes at me, grinning.

"Well, you do have beautiful eyes," I said, noticing them. They were an intense turquoise blue.

"Thanks. It's the contacts."

"Wow, I always wanted those! Brown ones and green ones. Turquoise seemed like it would be too easy to tell."

"Fooled you for a minute though, didn't I?"

"Yeah."

She looked at me. "I don't know. I don't think brown eyes would look natural on you. Green, I could see."

"What if I changed my hair color?" My eyes were gray-blue, and my hair was dark. I had thought a lot about disguises, which would come in handy whether I was being a detective or just running away from home.

"Somehow I can't picture you with some other color hair. You should get that spray-on, wash-out color and experiment."

"We don't carry it at the store," I said.

The tune was coming to an end. "I've got some at cabin nine," she said slowly. "Red and blond, silver even."

"I've got a girlfriend. I think," I said. I was watching Willow. Jeremy was holding her a lot closer than I was holding Megan, and Willow didn't look happy.

"I know," Megan said slowly. "Bring her if you want."

"Is that a line?" I said.

She grinned.

Sanders played a final flourish. I released Megan and clapped, and she clapped too. Willow pushed at Jeremy's chest. He laughed. Finally he let her go, and she came straight to me and pressed herself against my chest, hiding her face. I put my arms around her. "Thanks for the dance," I said to Megan, who was looking at Willow and frowning.

"Any time," she said. She gave me a little wave and wandered back toward their stretch of bench.

"What's the matter?" I murmured to Willow.

After a pause, she looked up and said, "He was trying to *kilianish* me. Without waiting for a yes."

She had talked of *kilianish* and owning a person when I had talked about being hooked. Jeremy was trying to connect with her, own her? But I knew that, didn't I, the way he had held her too close? Maybe he thought he was just goofing around. Maybe not. I said, "Bad. But you're okay now?"

She closed her eyes and, after a moment, nodded.

I let a moment slip by. "You have to say yes?"

"Mm-hmm," she said, "for it to work right."

I remembered saying no and yes to Willow. She had stopped pushing when I told her no. "Did I say yes to Evan?"

She stirred. She looked up at me. "Yes," she said, "and he didn't even ask you. You put your arms around him. You said you had always wanted him. He wasn't even trying to fetch you, but you came."

"Oh." I had dreamed of him and longed for him. I wondered if I would be able to live my dreams, or if this would turn out like all those stories about people who get their wishes and find out just how sorry they can be. "If Jeremy is doing something you don't like, you have to tell him so he believes you that you want him to stop. You can do that," I said, thinking of how her voice had made me do things.

She stared into my eyes for a moment, then smiled. "Yes," she said. "Of course." She pulled my head down and gave me a little kiss.

Alison and Murray began a twin-fiddle version of "Ozark Moon." Willow and I waltzed. I remembered how afraid I had been in the store when we first touched, and thought it was weird how comfortable I felt with her now, as if we had exchanged some sort of vows, even though I knew more scary things about

her than I had before. "Are you my girlfriend?" I
asked her after the music stopped.

"What?" she said, startled.

"I feel like you are."

"But I can't marry you. I can't marry anyone unless
the Presences sanction it."

"I'm not talking about marriage," I said, alarmed. I
knew even less about her than I had thought.

"What *are* you talking about?"

"I like you, you like me. We date. We don't go out
with other people as long as you're my girlfriend and
I'm your boyfriend."

"How long does it last?"

"Until we break up. You can do that whenever you
want. How much longer will your family be staying?"
Suddenly I wondered: if Evan owned me, and he left
with Willow and her folks, would I have to go too?
Could he make me? Or was it all just a joke? Ridiculous. Absurd! It had to be a joke. People didn't own
each other, not anymore, and how could a wolf prove
ownership of a person? It would never hold up in any
court I'd seen on television.

Then again, it wasn't a legal matter. Something had
happened to me. I had heard and understood a wolf
speaking, and the words he had said had done involuntary things to me.

What if it wasn't a joke? Pop would stop it. I didn't
know how I was going to get away even when I was
eighteen, a moment I'd been planning for years (pack
what I needed, what little money I had saved, slip away
and catch a ride with Hank, the Laceys' produce driver,
whose acquaintance I'd been cultivating. Pop might
check with all our regular vendors to see if one of them
had given me a ride, but he probably wouldn't think of
Hank. At least not right away . . . Get down to the valley and disappear). Pop's expectation that I would stay
and work at the store was so strong it was smothery.

Pop would just expect me to stay; how could Evan fight that?

What if he could fight it, though?

"As long as we must," said Willow. "The *skilliau* are strong here and listen to us, but they are stubborn and want courting. You can't just take one by force."

"Skilly-what?"

She laughed and said, "We'll be here a while."

"So while you're here . . ."

"All right."

I gave her a kiss. "And then if Jeremy still bothers you, you tell him you're my girlfriend, and I can rescue you."

She glanced toward the bench, studying Jeremy, who was talking to Megan now. "Voice will work on him, Nick. It's very strange. I do things to you that Aunt Elissa and Uncle Bennet told me over and over never to do to anyone in public, but I haven't been thinking of doing them to other *Domishti*, not since Mama and Papa sent me south; just to you. Maybe because you're not *Domishti*." She put her hand over her mouth. "Not *Domishti*," she whispered behind her fingers.

The music had started again, and people were dancing around us. Willow gripped my hand. "Come outside," she said, and led me toward the door again.

We walked past Junie, dancing with George. Junie winked at me. It suddenly occurred to me that Willow and I had kissed right there in public, more than once, and I hadn't been paying attention to the fact that everyone in the hall except a few summer transients knew me. Pretty flagrant stuff for Parsley's. Just part of the newspaper report now.

Willow led me under the trees, then gripped my fingers, pushing my hand down until my palm faced up. With her free hand she made a series of gestures above my hand. A little ring of gas-blue flame glowed above my hand, giving off no heat at all.

"*Sirella*," she muttered.

With my free hand, I passed my index finger through the flames. Couldn't feel a thing. Not bright enough to read by, but still pretty as a firework. "Can you make lights like this anywhere?" I said.

"No," she said. The blue ring faded. "Just special places." She released my hand, then held her left hand flat and gestured above it with her right. A spire of clear lemon-yellow flame rose above her hand, almost too bright to look at. Heat came from it. She snapped her fingers and it disappeared.

"I knew you were safe," she said. My eyes, burned from staring at the flame, showed me a tall dark streak everywhere I looked. "Somehow I knew it."

"Define 'safe,' " I said.

"Kin," she said.

I lost breath and for a moment couldn't find it again.

"Maybe not close kin," she said. "I haven't seen a sign like yours before, though the color is air. But somehow kin."

"But what does—" For about the fifteenth time since I'd met Willow, I didn't know what questions to ask. How could she gesture and make light? Was she a magician? She was probably a witch. Well, she pretty much had to be, didn't she? And all her family with her? What she had just done, was it some kind of blood test? Was Pop related to Willow's family? Was Mom? Mom seemed like a likelier candidate, now that I thought about it. . . .

Oh, boy, who needed any more relatives?

Except, of course, my new brother, the wolf; or maybe he was my new pop.

Suddenly the air carried people noise, a chorus of good nights and good wishes, promises to get together for lunch or swimming or barbecue, and the rev of car and pickup engines. Exhaust flavored the air. Red lights shone as cars backed and reversed, then arrowed off down the road. The dance was over.

"What time is it?" Willow asked.

I pressed a button on my watch and the face lit up. "Almost eleven."

"Oh, no! I have to go home," said Willow. "They told me to be back by ten at the latest. Nick . . ."

"I'll walk you back. I know a few short cuts."

I didn't stick around once we got back to Lacey number five. I asked her if she wanted support and she said it would be much better if her aunt and uncle didn't even see me.

"Where did you tell them you were going?"

She smiled. "Out to commune with nature," she said.

"Boy, if I said something like that to Pop, he'd tell me to stop smart-mouthing him."

"I used different words, but that's one of my jobs, *klishka y varyan*. Speaking to wood spirits."

"Tell 'em some of the spirits were long-winded."

She gave me a brief kiss, then ran across the clearing to the cabin's front door. I stood in the forest's fringe and watched the door open, with golden light beyond it turning Willow into a silhouette. A murmur of voices, and then she was inside, shutting the night out again.

So the magic was over, and now I had to go home and face Pop, who would be waiting up, I was sure, and would have a lot to say. Might as well get it over with, and then maybe I could go to bed and think about everything that had happened. Write down a list of questions so the next time I saw Willow I could get some real information. Like: how did she make that fire ring show up? Did it mean I was a witch too? Was it something I could learn? Lights could come in handy on a night like this, when there was no moon and the forest path was dark and I was hearing things rustling around me.

I knew this path. I had made this path, and walked it at least once and usually twice every summer day for almost nine years. I could run it. But if I ran, wouldn't that tell what was following me that I was scared?

The rustle was loudest to my left. I walked faster, trying not to think about bears. No reason on Earth why a bear should be pacing me. I was pretty sure I didn't smell like any food I had eaten, and humans weren't bears' preferred dinners. Still . . . I picked up the pace some more. No. I wasn't running. Just walking very, very fast.

"Nick."

I tripped over nothing and sprawled on the path. The heels of my hands skidded on the ground as I fell, and they started hurting. I groaned. "Evan! Cripes, you scared me!"

He laughed, more breath than sound, then said, "Sorry." Then he laughed some more while I was catching my breath, calming my heart, and pushing myself up until I was sitting instead of sprawling. "Sorry!" he said. He laughed. He apologized again.

"Yeah, sure," I said. "If this is your idea of fun, I'll be good for lots of laughs, I'm sure." My hands were throbbing. I tried to think of all the questions I wanted to ask him. Like, how could he own me, and what did it mean? How could he talk? How could I understand him? What did he want from me?

"Blood?" he said.

"What?"

"I smell blood. What happened?"

"Oh. Skinned my palms."

"I'm sorry," he said, and this time he sounded like he meant it. "Heal."

My hands tingled, then itched; it felt like bees were swarming across my palms, prickles and wing brushes. Under the skin, heat grew, peaked, faded, leaving a shadowed-stone cool behind.

The hairs on my neck and forearms prickled. I touched one hand with another and felt only smooth skin.

4

Questions of Ownership

I pressed my hands together, feeling a bone-deep chill because the skin of my palms was smooth and the pain had gone. I had a strong sense that I had done this to myself, the prickling and the heat and the strangeness, that it had come from inside me. How could a wolf order me to do something impossible and have me accomplish it?

I could persuade people to do things they didn't want to do, but he hadn't bothered with persuasion. He had told me, and I had done it.

I lay face up on the path, folded my hands on my stomach, and closed my eyes. I had crossed my believing-unbelievable-things threshold. I wasn't sure when I was going to move again.

"Nick?" Evan said. His cold nose touched my hand. "What's the matter now?"

I lay quiet for a while, trying to sort facts out in my head. They lay like beached fish, a flopping fact here, a shivering fact there, a gasping fact over there, no cohesive net of sense pulling them together. Unconsciousness beckoned. The cradle of drifty sleep thoughts and slowed breathing rocked me a few inches away from myself.

"Nick?"

Be comfortable, he had told me some hours earlier. It was odd how comfortable hard ground and twisted roots and pine needles could be. Pine needles, the best smell in the world. Be well, he had said. I wondered how long that would last. The rest of my life? Maybe this was a good thing. What if he decided he didn't like me, though? What if he said, *Be sick?* My thoughts warped and stretched taffy thin. What sort of sick? Maybe he'd be specific. He could say *spots* and I would be leopard-spotted, or *hairy,* and I would grow my own fur. I saw a courtroom with a wolf in the witness stand, and all the jurors wild animals. The judge was Pop, of course. Pop was always the judge, and I was always on trial.

"Nick. Wake up."

I blinked, wide awake.

He said, "Talk to me."

"About what?"

"Tell me what's the matter with you."

His voice was nothing like Willow's when she was persuading me to say something I would rather keep to myself. I could still hear the edge of a growl in it, and thought that if somebody else was around, Evan would sound like a wolf to them. His voice wasn't beautiful or soothing, but still, words came from my mouth whether I wanted them to or not. "Did anybody ever own you?"

After a moment, he said, "Yes."

"Did you like it?"

"No."

I hesitated, then said, "How can you tell me to do something and I do it, even though I don't know how?"

"When did I?"

"You said, 'Heal.' "

"But you know how to do that."

"What?"

"You don't strike me as particularly cautious. You

must have scraped yourself before. Of course your body knows how to heal. Otherwise you'd be all sores."

"But it doesn't happen in a moment."

"It could, though." I felt him sniffing my hands, tiny puffs of warm breath against my skin. "You have the energy for it." He sounded puzzled. "How odd."

It occurred to me that I hadn't answered his question, anyway, and I said, "What's the matter with me is there are too many things I don't understand, things I don't know how to believe in. All day, one thing after another."

He sat. "It's all right," he said. "You're fine. Believe what's true, what's actually happening. It won't hurt you."

Something hot and hard caught in my throat. For a little while I couldn't breathe. I saw darkness inside my eyelids, and then an explosion of fireworks, and then I moved my throat and swallowed the hot hard thing and my body relaxed. I felt much better. It was inside me now, out of my head and into my stomach, all the doubts and resistance, dissolving, changing into different things I could absorb. I took deep night-flavored breaths, tasting starlight and possibilities.

Evan said, "See? Feel better?"

"Yeah."

"Good."

"Evan, Willow says you own me, and I'm scared. She says I asked for it, and that scares me too."

"You didn't ask for it. I took you. You consented, but you didn't ask for it. I took you so Willow wouldn't. I never meant to do anything with you, Nick, except protect you." He lay down beside me and rested his muzzle on my chest.

After a moment, he said, "Willow was getting trained to take people and own them, and our parents didn't like that, but they couldn't figure out how to stop it. They couldn't see where it was coming from. Even now I'm not sure. I didn't get that training; I mean, I knew how to fetch you, but I don't crave owning people the way she does. Anyway, they sent us to live with our cousins, hoping that would change Willow's mind. With the help of our aunt and uncles, she's fighting the training, but she still has this hunger."

There was something very odd about what he was saying, but it took me a moment to figure out what. "Your parents are Willow's parents?"

"She's my sister; what did you think?"

"I thought you were a wolf," I whispered.

"Oh." He lifted his head and looked down at me. In the darkness all I saw was a moving shadow. After a moment, he lowered his head to my chest again and muttered, "I forgot."

"You're *not* a wolf?"

"I am now."

I thought about that for a while, about all the assumptions I had made because I had thought he was an animal; that I had held out my hand for him to smell, touched him, scratched his ears, hugged him, that even now I was lying here with his head on my chest, which was a magical connection to an animal one had made friends with, but very strange if I considered Evan a human male.

I tried to imagine him as a man or a boy, but I could only picture him as a wolf. I lifted the arm he wasn't lying against and stroked his head. It felt natural and right. And he had licked my nose, and that had felt okay, too. I decided not to think about it too hard.

After a little while, I said, "How long have you been a wolf?"

"Six months." He moaned the way a dog would. "Ever since they sent us to live with Aunt Elissa and Uncle Bennet. I hate the way they live."

"That's what Willow said," I murmured.

"I didn't want to leave our home. I mean, I didn't have Willow's problem. But Ma and Pa were worried that something else was happening to me. Maybe because I . . . well, anyway, Pa put a pusher on me to go, even though he and Ma cried when Willow and I left. So as I left, I turned myself into a wolf, and I'm sticking with it.''

"Mmm," I said. "Would you really stay here with me, like you said?"

"Sure," he said. He laughed, this time a deep chuckle that sounded almost like a growl. "I'll be your dog. And then sometimes . . ."

"What?"

"You'll be my wolf." He urfed.

I tensed. Images of late night horror movies flashed through my mind, men turning into beasts and committing horrible crimes, then living to rue the night.

"What's the matter now?"

"I—" How could I explain that to him? "You ever watch TV?"

"No," he said.

"Never mind, then." He was probably joking, anyway. He certainly laughed a lot. I felt sleepy again. Suddenly I remembered that Pop was probably sitting up, waiting for me, and the longer I stayed out, the madder he would get. I was pretty sure I could already kiss my half-day Saturday good-bye just for insolence, let alone staying out too late, and the regret I felt—I had an eagle to track down and finally a wolf who would go out with me and look—struck so deep it felt like a wound. "Evan? I have to go home."

He lifted his head and I sat up, then got to my feet. The path was familiar to me again, even in the dark, and my fear had gone. Evan followed at my heels. Was this what it was like? To have a dog and not be scared of anything in the night. Even better, to have a wolf. A fierce joy flowed through me, in spite of everything. For a little while I imagined we were leaving, me with a pack full of supplies and a sleeping bag, heading into the wild together. We would find the perfect campsite, and in the morning I would catch rainbow trout—add

fishing gear and a frying pan to what I was carrying—
and fry them over a tiny fire, and . . .

Light from the store woke me out of this dream. "I
don't think you should come in," I said to Evan. I
could see Pop sitting behind the cash register in the old
swivel chair he had found at a yard sale, his boots
propped on the counter. He was reading *Alfred Hitchcock's Mystery Magazine*.

"He's got to know sometime, doesn't he?" Evan
said.

"I'm just about to get in a lot of trouble. This
wouldn't be the best time for me to tell him I have a,
a, well, a pet."

Evan laughed. "See you tomorrow," he said, and
trotted off into the woods.

I opened the door, and the bells rang. Pop looked
up, his face still ruddy as normal, not bright red like
when he was about to shout. "Nick," he said, putting
down his magazine, lowering his boots to the floor.

"Hi, Pop."

"I ever tell you how much I need you here?"

I felt staggered. He'd never said anything like that
to me before.

"Place couldn't run without you."

I stuffed my hands in my pockets, feeling a weird
combination of hope and fear. Was this actual, honest-
to-god appreciation? Or was he setting me up for
something?

"I know you don't get to have all the fun the other
kids do, but then, their dads are different. Their dads
make plenty of money. Their dads don't depend on 'em
the way I depend on you."

I stared at the worn hardwood floor, at the grime that
had worked its way down into the cracks despite once-
a-week sweeping and mopping Sunday evenings. My
feelings crystallized into one solid sensation: dread.
How could I leave him if he was going to be nice
to me?

"I know I kept the leash pretty tight on you all these years," he said, and I heard a faint echo of Evan's voice murmuring, "I'll give you a long leash." Pop continued, "You seen what happens when the parents get too loose on the reins with the kids. Remember those Clark kids from last summer?"

I remembered them, Alicia and John Clark. A nastier pair I had never met. They had been convinced that everybody who worked where they could see it was some sort of subspecies, to be ignored if the work got done properly, abused if anything displeased John and Alicia. Kristen had been in the store one time when John came in and cussed me out because a fish hook got caught in his thumb (real fish hooks only worked on fish, not people!). She had gone red listening to him, and drifted farther from the cash register, I guess to spare me embarrassment; it worked out for me, because with Kristen out of earshot I could lean forward, stare into John's eyes, and say, "Leave. Now." Kristen came over with a *People* magazine after John had gone, and said she was sorry. I had shrugged, wishing that she hadn't been there to hear it and to see me stand there and take it as if I deserved it.

"Yeah," I told Pop. "I remember."

"That's what happens when there's no leash. You wouldn't want to be like them, would you?"

"No," I said. I had the feeling there were other factors contributing to the way the Clarks behaved—I had seen the way their parents were with them—but decided not to mention it.

"And you aren't," Pop said. "Anyway, I guess you're growing up now, and I need to ... I need to ..." He blew breath up, riffling his bangs a little. "I need to let you go," he said, then glared at me. "To dances, anyway."

I just looked at him, not knowing how to respond.

"And dates, I guess. Look, I don't want to reward you for insubordination. I hate it when you tell me made-up stories, and what you did tonight was wrong, defying me. I don't want you to do that again. But I got to thinking about it.'' His eyes shifted, till he was looking over my shoulder, but not at anything in sight. ''Got to remembering what it was like when I was your age. Gaw dang.'' He shook his head slowly. ''Your granddad and I sure didn't see eye to eye in those days, no sir.''

I straightened. I had never heard him talk about his childhood.

''I was the second boy,'' he said. ''Your uncle, Luke, was the important boy, Dad's favorite. He was as fine and golden as they come, not smart, but such an athlete. Granddad never paid any mind to me. I never knew he cared about me at all, not till much later.''

''Uncle Luke?'' I'd never heard of an Uncle Luke.

''He went off to Vietnam and died.'' Pop frowned. ''You know I care about you, don't you, Nick?''

''I guess,'' I said. I had never thought about it much. I knew he valued my work even though he had never said so. I knew he trusted me to run the store, and that had been hard for him—to let go control enough not to supervise my every move.

I knew he couldn't get along without me, even though this was the first time I'd heard him say it aloud. When he first started me on a full-day shift I had been proud of that, that I was helping us survive. When Mom left and I took over the cooking, I had felt the same. I liked knowing what I knew. I liked being able to take care of Pop and Granddad the way Mom had taken care of all of us. At first, I swore to myself that I would never leave the way she did, ripping the hearts out of us. Lately I had started feeling differently. I was glad I hadn't made my vow aloud. I figured I could take my skills other places and use them to survive.

Resentment and frustration had started building. How come Pop paid Mariah a token wage and me nothing at all, except a monthly allowance any kid might have gotten without any work? How come he never let me learn how to do the books?

Pop said, "I do care about you. I'm glad you're here. I need you bad. I know I've been tough on you. I think it's time for me to ease up. Go to dances. Go on dates. But you got to be careful. Don't get too moony about anybody staying at Lacey's. That would never work. I mean, you can have a good time with those girls, but don't be getting any ideas. They'd never plan to settle out here away from everything and run a store and a motel."

The dread took root in my stomach and spread through my body, made my legs and arms feel very heavy, as if I couldn't walk, let alone run. *I am going to get away from here. I'm going somewhere else.* I heard Junie saying those words in my mind. How far away had she gotten? Halfway around the lake.

"Anyway," said Pop, "I guess what I'm trying to say, your time off the job, it's yours. I know you been running around, morning and evening, but you get stuff done. You get our meals on the table. You do the chores. You run the store. I appreciate that. I really do. So no more grounding or anything like that. Listen, maybe you could even drive down to the valley sometime if you want. You do something really screwy, though, and—well, just don't, all right?"

I felt the cement setting around my feet. I was going to be stuck here running the store forever. "Pop?"

"What?"

"Can I have a dog?"

"Wha-a-a-a-at?"

"He won't get in the way, I promise, and I don't think we'll have to pay much for food. He hunts for himself."

"Well, this is very strange," said Pop. "Not exactly what I expected you to say."

I half wanted to ask him what he had expected me to say. Thanks very much, Pop? Gee, I'm glad you noticed, Pop? I'll stay here forever, Pop? You're the best?

"But okay," he said. "Whose bitch has puppies?"

"Uh," I said. I went to the door and opened it. "Evan?" I called softly.

A moment later the wolf stood in front of me. He looked bigger than I remembered, and much more ominous. *He had had his head on my chest,* I remembered. Now that I could actually see him by security light, I felt a small thrill of fear.

I held the door open. "Come on in."

He walked past me.

Pop scrambled to his feet, grabbing for the broom in the corner.

"It's all right," I said, telling Pop and myself. "This is Evan, Pop. He's—he's my dog."

"Since when?" whispered Pop.

"Tonight, I guess."

"Son, that is a wild animal."

"He does look pretty scary, doesn't he?"

"That is a wild animal, Nick. It'll tear out your throat the instant you go to sleep."

"No, he won't," I said. I put my hand on Evan's head, and he glanced up at me, jaw dropping into a grin, tongue lolling between his teeth. "You're not interested in tearing my throat out, are ya?"

"Naw," he said.

"And you can do tricks."

"What!"

"Show Pop."

"Nick," Evan said. It came out in a growl.

"If you want to stay in the house, you gotta act like a dog." I stroked his head. "Speak," I said.

"This is ridiculous," he said.

"If I had one of those doggie treats, I'd give it to you, but I don't have one. Sorry. I could give you a piece of jerky."

"No thanks."

He didn't like jerky? I'd never met anybody who didn't like jerky. I shrugged and said, "Sit."

He glared at me, then sat, his tail curling around his front paws.

"Thanks," I said. "How about shaking hands?"

He huffed, then held out a drooping paw, his eyes narrowed with disdain. I gripped his paw and released it. "We gotta work on that one," I said.

"*Ffff,*" he said.

"Would he attack people for you?" Pop asked.

"I don't know," I said. "I only got him tonight."

"Where'd you get him?"

"Somebody at the dance gave him to me."

"So you planned to have him even before you asked me."

"I hoped you'd say yes," I said.

"And if I said no?"

"I'd just have to let him go."

Evan said, "I would then turn you into a chihuahua and take you into the woods with me. Tell him that." He laughed.

"A chihuahua?" I cried. It was too horrible to contemplate.

Pop said, "Well, thank God you didn't get one of those toy dogs, Nick. Guess I should just be glad you got a respectable critter, huh?"

"Please," I said.

"A chihuahua," Evan muttered, "or a poodle. A little white toy one. With pink bows."

"Can you do that?" I asked him, feeling worms crawling among my guts.

"Guess I can," said Pop.

"Of course," said Evan. "I know lots of tricks." He padded over to the sewing supplies and stared at a spool of pink ribbon.

"Thanks, Pop," I said, looking away from Evan with effort.

"Just don't let him scare the customers away, that's all I ask."

"Okay," I said. "Thanks, Pop. Thanks."

"You're welcome. Never even knew you wanted a dog. Should have told me."

Something hot and sweet and hurting twisted in my chest at that. All these years alone. I went to Evan and knelt beside him and put my arms around him, pressing my cheek to his fur and thinking about nothing at all. He smelled like wilderness.

"He's sure patient," Pop said after a while.

I took a deep breath and let go of Evan. He swiped my face with his tongue. I rubbed my cheek on the sleeve of my T-shirt and said, "He's the best." I glanced at my watch. I blinked. It was after one.

"Yeah," said Pop. "It's late. Hope you were having fun tonight."

"You could put it that way."

"Two guests up at the motel. They'll be needing coffee and rolls around eight tomorrow morning."

"Okay," I said, climbing to my feet. I set my watch alarm for six. "Good night, Pop."

"Night, Nick."

Evan watched with interest as I did a short set with my weights, then washed up, brushed teeth, and got ready for bed. "Are you hungry? Thirsty?" I asked him.

"No," he said.

"Need to go out?"

"I'll let you know," he said, grinning.

"Are you really going to turn me into a poodle?"

He laughed and rolled the barbells off the rug with his nose. "Wonder if I'll like being domesticated," he said, turning around three times and then curling nose to tail.

I switched off the light. "Good night," I said. "This has been the weirdest day of my life."

"Good night, Nick. Go to sleep."

           *   *   *

"What's that noise?" someone asked loudly in my ear.

"What!" I struggled up, fighting covers, to discover my watch alarm peeping and a wolf beside the bed. "Ow!" My head felt thick.

"Wake up," said the wolf, and my head cleared instantly. I switched off the alarm.

"Thanks," I said. I got out of bed and did an extended workout with the weights. Evan lay down, muzzle on front paws, eyes watching me.

"Got to shower," I said. "God, I'm tired."

"No you're not," said Evan. "You feel rested and energized."

And I did. "That's spooky," I said.

He laughed.

I took my shower, did my Saturday morning shave, then asked Evan as I got dressed, "Do I need to sleep at all?" Not that I would know what to do with that many more hours. If everybody else was sleeping, there wouldn't be anything to watch. On the other hand, I could still explore the lake and the forest, though my night vision wasn't any better than anybody else's, as far as I could tell. On the third hand, maybe not everybody else was sleeping. Willow's family, for instance, might have odd night habits worth investigating. Everything else about them certainly bore further study, and now I had a double agent right in the room with me.

"You do," he said. "At least . . . I think you do. We could experiment. I *like* to sleep."

"Sometimes I really like to sleep." Especially if everything was rotten in the waking world. "You hungry yet?"

"I'll catch something when we go out."

I tied my shoelaces and led him downstairs, where I set out a bowl of dry cereal for Granddad and checked the expiration date on the milk carton. Still good. I got a salad bowl we hadn't used in ages out of a cupboard and filled it with water. I put it on the floor. Evan looked at me, then drank long and deep. Ate a quick bowl of cereal myself. I loaded the coffeemaker's filter with fresh grounds, poured water in and flipped the switch, set up and switched on the coffee maker in the store, and led the way up to the motel office, where I started that coffeemaker and microwaved some frozen pastries and rolls, then stocked the buffet with napkins, cups, plates, plastic spoons and knives, a dish of margarine, and things to put in coffee. The pastries and the coffee smelled good. I offered Evan a croissant, but he wasn't interested. By that time it was almost seven-thirty.

Evan watched everything I did without comment.

At last we stepped outside and headed for my trail.

I stopped first and dipped fingers in the lake. Evan watched me, his head to the side.

For the first time in an age, I thought about what I was doing. Mom had taught me this lake greeting. After she left, I had ditched a lot of what she had given me, but this one was important, still. Ever since that winter day when I lay on the ice and tried to let it freeze me, I had felt an intense connection to the lake. Ice had crept up over my bare hands, but I had not frozen. I had taken off my jacket, shirt, and long johns, and lain back down, determined to do a good job of it, and ice had embraced me. It melted a little under me and closed over me. I lay feeling it over me like a blanket, holding me in what I was certain was false warmth, and my mind slowed; I could feel my thoughts calming and crystallizing. Ice held me while I watched the short day fade and the stars blink into being in the dark sky. Later, when Pop came out of the house, calling for me, nothing in me had frozen. I sat up out of crackling ice, brushed a film of ice from my face, dressed, and went back to the Venture.

I had never told anyone. I was pretty sure it had been a dream. Still, when I touched the lake, I felt a quickening inside me, and when I went swimming in it, I dove down and stayed down for longer than I could hold my breath, to remind myself that something strange was going on. I liked it.

I touched my wet fingers to my face and straightened. I wondered what Evan was thinking. He seemed wholly wolf, though, so I didn't ask. I headed for the path instead.

After yesterday's heat, the morning's cool felt wonderful. The blue of the sky was clean scrubbed, not dusty the way it got later in the day when people drove around kicking up clouds. I took some deep breaths. No sound but birds and crickets and bees and the conversations pine needles have with themselves when there's a touch of wind. Our footsteps didn't make much noise on the fallen needles.

My thoughts drifted to who I was going to spy on today. It occurred to me that this might be awkward. How much did Evan know about my habits? Maybe more than I thought.

"Were you watching me yesterday morning?" I asked Evan.

"Yes," he said.

"While I was watching Willow."

"Yes."

"But you didn't do anything."

"Neither did you."

Studying him, I walked.

He said, "If you had tried anything—*anything*—toast, buddy. But all you did was watch."

"That's all I ever do."

"Not last night."

I thought about kissing Willow. "That was different. It stopped being a watching thing. We moved past it."

We traveled a way in silence. He said, "What was strange to me about yesterday morning was that you could see Willow at all. She was warded against the sight of outsiders."

"She disappeared, Evan."

"You weren't supposed to be able to see her even before that."

Lauren had mentioned second sight, something I had even heard of, unlike a lot of the weird words with which Evan and the others peppered their language. "Where did she disappear to?"

"I don't know." For a while we walked. "That was a woman's mystery; I don't understand it."

We were approaching Lacey number five. I sat down in the path and looked at Evan, face to muzzle. "So," I said, "this is where I sneak up and see what they're up to."

He laughed.

I said, "I was thinking. There's lots you could tell me about what goes on here."

He blinked at me, then slowly smiled.

"Or you could tell me to get out of here and stop watching them. And you know I would."

He looked up into a nearby tree. He yawned, tongue curling.

"Or you could just sit there and let me do what I do. Want to give me a hint, here?"

"Or I could turn you into a snake and you could slither right up to the cabin. How about that?"

"A snake?" I said. "I don't think snakes can hear very well. Let's go with the chihuahua."

"All right," he said, dipping his nose.

"Uh—no, I wasn't serious."

He laughed. "Sooner or later, Nick. Sooner or later."

"Later, I guess." I shuddered. "I have to open the store pretty soon."

"Well, you do your watching; I'm going to see if anything is stirring that I can eat. Usually I hunt at night." He vanished into the underbrush with hardly a rustle.

It felt strange to be alone. Even though I couldn't figure out when he was teasing (and if he wasn't teasing, I felt apprehensive about what he had said), I liked having him with me. This was what I had been missing since Mom left and maybe before, someone to be with me; jeez, even someone I could just touch without worrying about it too much, although I hadn't asked him if that was all right; it just felt right. Which was probably what rapists said afterward. I had better ask him next time.

I walked quietly until I came to the quirk in the path that let me see the cabin from the cover of the forest. I ducked down and looked past underbrush. The two boys stood on the porch facing the lake, holding out their arms and saying words. I watched carefully, but I didn't see any extra light or anything else.

They stopped chanting and knelt and dipped their fingers in the water. It spooked me completely, despite what Willow had said last night about kinship. They rose again, holding wet hands toward the sun, and chanted something else.

I backed away and continued past cabin five to the rest of the Lacey's; but it was so early only Ms. Tommassetti was up, wearing nothing but a white robe, and doing tai chi on her porch. She was a retired librarian who had inherited money late in life. We'd had some fun talks about books when she came in the store. Sometimes she brought me good ones she'd found at yard sales and library book sales. I only watched her for a minute. Her movements were smooth and graceful as a wind blowing across a field of grass.

I gave Lacey number five a moment's study as I headed back toward the store. The boys were still chanting to the sun, and nothing that I could see had changed. I felt frustrated. So these people stood out on the porch and addressed something I couldn't see in a language I couldn't understand, and achieved ends I couldn't fathom. Was watching them getting me anywhere? I had my wolf and my girlfriend now. I probably didn't need anything else from these people.

What was I thinking? I always needed information. My credo.

When I turned back to the trail, I came face-to-face with Aunt Elissa. "Boy," she said.

"Ma'am," I said, backpedaling. She was wearing a black bodysuit, and she had nightshade flowers and berries twined in her red hair. *Poisonous,* I thought.

"Boy, I respect your right to lead your life as you wish, and normally I leave *Domishti* strictly alone, but the fact is, you are interfering with our work."

"I'm sorry," I said.

"The *skilliau* are shy, and your watching us makes them hesitate to respond. We have given ourselves a certain amount of time to do what we need here, and it is taking too long. You must stop watching us."

"I—"

"Will you do that?"

"I—" *Could* I stop watching them, now that I felt like I was part of the family in some weird way? You had to watch your family. You had to know when to jump, and how high. More important still, you had to have some idea of when they were going to jump and where. On the other hand, I felt like I was part of Willow and Evan's family, a subset of the larger group; I could stop watching the rest of them, I supposed, and I could stop watching Willow and Evan because they were letting me see them anyway. "I—"

Her mouth firmed. She held up her hand in front of my face, muttered some words in the other language, and gestured with her fingers.

The world went dark.

I rubbed my eyes, opened them again, and saw ... nothing, just blackness. I could still hear the wind and the birds and, distantly, the boys chanting.

"When we have done our work and are ready to leave, I will lift the blindness," said the woman.

"Ma'am—" I said, my voice too high. "Ma'am, no!" How could I work like this? "No, please!" How could I live without being able to see? My whole life depended on observing. "I won't watch! I won't even come over here at all! Please, ma'am, I promise. Please . . ."

I heard her steps moving away. I stumbled after her and tried to catch her. "Just a moment," she said. The crackle of a branch breaking. I reached toward her and tripped over a root. I hit the ground on knees and one elbow, tried to remember what I knew about falling, tucked and rolled, fetching up against bushes, crushing pungent leaves. A little bramble branch scratched my cheek. Panic grabbed my breath away. I had to catch her. I had to make her take this back. . . . I had to stay where I was, because I couldn't see where I was going. I groaned and sat up, then got to my feet, thinking about which way was up. I was all turned around. Usually my directional sense was so strong I knew where things were in relation to myself, but right now I didn't know which way the store was and which way led to Lacey's.

Despair tasted like warm syrup, thickening my throat. I listened and listened, finally heard the distant roar of a motorboat to my left, and the shush of little pebbles being moved by tiny wind waves in the lake fifteen feet from the path. If the lake was to my left, then home was behind me. Knowing which way home was made me feel marginally better.

Words muttered a little way off. I wanted to run and catch her, but I knew I would only fall again. I closed my eyes and hoped, wished, prayed that when I opened them the world would be there, blue and brown and green, light and shadow. I opened my eyes and saw soft black and nothing else. Muffled footsteps approached. She touched my hand, pressed the rough bark of a stick into it, closed my fingers around it. "This will lead you," she said. "I have put an eye at the tip of it to watch ahead of you and help you."

I dropped the stick, grabbed for her, and managed to close my hand around her forearm. "Ma'am. Please."

"Release me," she said. Her voice wasn't soft and promising like Willow's; it tasted of vinegar, and command gave it harshness and weight. Before I knew it I had let her go. She put the stick back into my hand. "Stay away from us," she said, command still girdering her voice. Then nothing but the sound of her light footsteps, traveling away.

I closed my eyes and opened them about six times, hoping that the result would be different, but every time it was the same. I tightened my hand around the stick, wondering how it could help me, or if it would. Maybe I'd just be here, lost within sight of civilization, thrashing around until I drowned myself in the lake or fell over one of the little dropaways in the woods.

The stick thrummed in my hand. I stood with my eyes closed, touch-listening to the stick, wondering if there was really an eye at the end of it, and how that would help me. I remembered seeing blind people feeling their way forward with white canes, sweeping them back and forth. I faced toward the store and swept the stick in front of me. I felt a strange humming pitch in my hand. I lowered the stick to the ground and the thrum intensified. I raised the stick and the vibrations eased away. I swept it to the side, and felt a strong hum right before I whacked a bush.

Tapping the ground with the stick, I took a step, and then another. I swished the stick slowly right and left. It vibrated harder just before I touched something with it. Trusting the stick, I walked slowly in the direction I thought led home, turning my head, listening for birds and wind and waves in the lake, hearing squirrel chatter, crows cawing, the hum of bees in the thimbleberry blossoms. I kept my eyes closed. It would be awful if something flew into them before I could blink. How would I ever get it out again? I felt my watch. No way to tell what time it was now. Probably way too late.

Pop was going to regret giving me my freedom.

Couldn't run the register, couldn't stock the shelves, hell, couldn't even make meals. Well, maybe I could learn. The stick was already feeling like a natural extension of myself; I was walking faster now, and the ground was solid under my feet.

"Nick?"

I stumbled. The stick supported me so I didn't fall.

"Evan," I said. I had forgotten about him. I realized how tense my shoulders had been because they started to relax. "Evan?"

"What's wrong?"

"I'm blind."

He yipped. Then he said, "I'm coming up to your left side. Stink! This stick smells like—"

I stood quiet, wanting to hug him, not knowing how to find him, not sure he really wanted to be hugged.

"Like my aunt," he said, his voice hollow. Then he said, "What happened?" This time he was mad.

I felt my way down and sat on the path, laid the stick beside me, reached out and found his fur. "Is it okay for me to pet you?" My voice had a wobble in it.

He pushed up against me and I put my arms around him. He was big and warm and furry, and he smelled like dirt and dog and herbs and blood. After a long moment he shook his shoulders and I let go.

"What happened?" he repeated.

"She told me she didn't want me watching them anymore because it was disturbing the skilly—skilly— you know what I mean."

He growled. It lasted for a while, and it expressed part of what I was feeling too, a spinning anger.

Then he said, "Let me smell your face."

I sat still and felt the little puffs of sniffs, heard the quick breaths, occasionally felt the wet touch of his nose.

"*Faskish!*" he said at last. "She can't do this to you! You're mine. *Kolesta y kiya, Sirella.*" He licked my eyelids. "Casting, begone from my fetchling," he muttered. He licked my eyelids again. "Open your eyes, Nick."

I opened my eyes and saw light, and colors, and fuzzy blobs. "Oh, God," I said, blinking. Slowly things came into focus. Evan stood just in front of me, his eyes wide and amber yellow, his head cocked to one side. "Oh, God. Thank you," I said. "Thank you." I touched his cheek and he leaned his head against my hand.

"You're welcome."

"It was awful. I was really scared." I would never have said that to Paul or Jeremy, maybe not even to Junie, but somehow I could say it to Evan. "I didn't know what I was going to do."

"That's one of the reasons I don't like them. She's mean."

I rubbed my eyes.

He said, "And not even thinking mean. We may have been snots at home, but we thought through some of the consequences. And we knew we shouldn't be mean, even when we were. Mama and Papa saw to that. Aunt Elissa's mean, and she thinks she's not. She thinks she's righteous and everything she decides is correct, no arguments."

He gazed toward the forest and away from the lake for a long moment. Presently he said, "Listen to me carefully, Nick."

I straightened without thinking about it and stared at him.

"Take this deep inside you."

I felt as if a well opened up inside, waiting for what he would fill it with.

He said, "It comes from me, and I mean it. Anything she tries to do to you won't work on you, because you belong to me. It will slide off you without hurting you. *Kolesta y kiya,* according to our covenant." He licked my face.

"Salt between us," I murmured.

"What?" His ears stood straight up, openings toward me.

"Something Lauren told me."

"You know Lauren?"

"Mmm. She introduced herself to me."

"And said 'salt between us'?"

"Mmm. I gave her French fries."

He laughed. "So Aunt is three ways wrong." Then he said, "Did you hear me, Nick?"

"Yes," I said.

"Let these words take root in you. Aunt Elissa cannot hurt you. Uncle Bennet cannot hurt you. Uncle Rory cannot hurt you. You belong to me."

"Yes," I whispered.

"Take my breath."

My thinking mind didn't understand, but some part of me did, because he leaned close and I leaned close; he breathed out and I sucked it in, tasting things that weren't very appetizing (his hunt must have been successful), but breathing in deep and long anyway.

"Now I'm in you," he said, "and I will protect you." He licked my cheek. "Now you're in me, and I will protect you, *kolesta y kiya.*"

"*Kolesta y kiya,*" I said, tasting words like old iron.

"Okay," he said. "I think that should do it."

I took in a deep breath and let it out in a sigh. Why did I trust this wolf when I didn't even know him? Maybe I didn't have a choice. On the other hand, he had already been the best friend I had ever had. I made a few distant friends every summer, working in the store, but I had never felt this way about one of them before.

Working in the store.

I checked my watch. It was nine-thirty, and I hadn't seen to Granddad, hadn't stocked the till and opened the store. . . .

"Uh-oh," I said. "Pop's going to kill me!" I scrambled to my feet. I hadn't come very far along the path with the aid of the stick—the stick; I stooped and grabbed it—but running all out, I could be back at the Venture Inn in about six minutes. "Come on," I said.

Evan laughed and we ran.

"I'm sorry, I'm sorry, I'm sorry," I said as we burst through the door. "I had an accident."

Pop was sitting in the chair behind the counter, his arms crossed over his chest, his face blank. "Better have been a good one," he said.

"I ran into a tree branch and knocked myself out."

"Evidence without pain," muttered Evan. I felt something trickle down my cheek, put up a finger to touch it, and found blood. My stomach went cold. I looked at him sideways. He cocked his head and looked back.

"Gaw dang, I see it," said Pop, rising and coming around the counter. "You need Doc McBride?"

"I don't know." I pressed my hand to my left temple, where I discovered my hair matted with wet. "It doesn't hurt. I think I just need to clean it up. I lost half an hour, though. I'm sorry, Pop."

"Okay," he said. "Get back here fast as you can. Give a yell if you need medical attention."

Evan and I raced upstairs, where I washed blood off my head and watched the reddened water swirling down the drain. "Where did that come from?" I asked him.

"Your head."

"How?"

He yawned.

I parted my wet hair, looking in the mirror for a wound, but there was nothing. No more bleeding, either. I ran a comb through my hair. "Evan . . ."

"You can spare a little blood for a good lie, Nick."

"You say bleed and I bleed?"

"Yep."

"You say sleep and I sleep. You say wake and I wake. You say see and my eyes are opened."

"Mmm."

I washed my hands and dried them on a towel, watching him. His eyes were half open.

"What if you say something I don't want to do?" I asked after a moment.

He glanced toward the door, panting, tongue hanging out a little, then looked at me, ears up.

"I mean, something I really don't want to do," I said. "Anything I can do?"

He lay down, nose on front paws, forehead wrinkled. "Tell you what," he said. "Unless it's urgent, you can question my orders. Permission, Nick. Put that where you know it."

"Thanks."

"Doesn't mean I'll change 'em." He jumped up. "I know I'll regret it. You're fun to tease."

"Another goal I've always had," I muttered, heading for the stairs. "Fun to tease. Feh."

My next bad moment of the day came when Aunt Elissa walked into the store.

It was approaching eleven-thirty. Evan was sleeping behind the counter. I was checking to make sure the right video was rewound and in the right box, and listening to two preteen girls chattering among the teen magazines, but I knew somehow the instant Elissa put her hand on the door, and I had already gone cold inside when she came in. She was wearing something almost normal this time—an orange sun dress with a red sash—and she didn't look my way; she focused on the food aisles. I nudged Evan with my foot. He made an irritated dog groan and tucked his nose further under his paw.

One of the girls came up and offered me a *Sassy*. I sold it to her without even looking at it. I was watching Elissa in the antitheft mirror. The girl moved over to get into my line of sight, smiling and showing me her mouthful of braces and colored rubber bands, and I blinked out of my terrified trance enough to smile back and murmur thank you to her, at which point she blushed and darted out of the store, magazine rolled up in her hand, friend rushing after her with a ring of bells.

When I looked up, Elissa was standing before me, holding out a jar of bay leaves. Her eyes were wide and her face was pale.

I could feel the blood seeping out of my face, prickling as it went. In my mind I knew that Evan had told me she couldn't do anything to me, but I still remembered the primal terror of losing the world because she said a few words and waved her fingers at me. Nobody should be able to do that to someone else.

I reached out for the jar, and she dropped it almost before I got my hand there. I caught it, though. "Dollar seventy-nine," I said, setting the jar on the counter and punching cash register keys.

"What did you do?" she demanded, the vinegar strong in her voice.

Evan stirred beside my feet, stood up. I glanced down at him. His eyes were wide, his face solemn.

"Tell me," she said. I could feel her words trying to slide inside and order me around, but they slipped off, just as Evan had said they would.

"Dollar seventy-nine," I said again.

"What did you do? How? Tell me!"

"Lady, leave me alone and I'll leave you alone, okay?"

"What . . . did . . . you . . . do?" Her words sounded like rocks grinding against each other. My stomach did some gyrations. I could feel her words trying to sand down my will.

The bells rang behind her. Lauren walked into the store. She was wearing a blue shirt and shorts, and her feet were bare and very dirty. "Hi, Nick," she said. "Mama, Daddy says hurry."

I said, "Hi, Lauren."

Elissa reached across the counter and gripped my shoulder, her fingers digging in. "How do you know my daughter?"

"Salt between us," I said.

Her face leached even paler. She let go of me and looked behind her at Lauren.

"Daughter, is this true?"

Lauren kicked the floor, scraping her sole against the hardwood, staring down, then flicked a glance at her mother and nodded.

"You shared salt with this stranger? This particular one? How could you?"

Lauren's voice came out very small. "He gave me some food. I didn't know it had salt on it." Her gaze was fixed on the floor.

"He tricked you?"

"He didn't know about salt. I had to tell him."

Elissa's eyes went so wide I could see white all around the irises. "When was this?" she asked.

"Yesterday," whispered Lauren.

Elissa stared at me for a long, uncomfortable moment. "I have violated a covenant between us, but I did not know. I hope you will forgive me."

She scared me more at that moment than she had before. "Uh . . . sure," I said.

"Without your forgiveness I lose the good favor of the Presences. I regret what I have done."

"Okay," I muttered. I glanced at Evan, whose eyes were narrowed. I wished I knew what to do. I didn't like this woman focusing on me any more than I liked it when Pop paid real attention to me. The end result couldn't be good.

Then again, last night Pop had surprised me.

"I won't make that mistake again," she said. She stared at me. I could feel her gaze like a hot breeze against my face.

"Okay," I said, since she seemed to be waiting for something.

At last she looked away. She fumbled at her waist, pulling out a small woven purse tied to her sash with strings, and fished a couple of crumpled dollar bills out of it. I made change and handed her coins, bay leaves, and a receipt, and she turned and left.

"Sorry," Lauren said in a wobbly voice, and followed her mother out of the store.

As soon as the door closed behind them, I looked at Evan and said, "What? What? What was I supposed to do? She's mad at me now!"

"Because she was wrong," he said.

"That's not my fault!"

"I know."

I stooped so I was looking him in the eye. "Why didn't you help me?" My voice came out higher than I meant it to.

He licked my face. He said, "Anything I did would just have made her more angry. You did fine, Nick. Remember: she can't do anything to you."

"I . . ." I looked away, toward the place under the counter where we kept paper bags and cleaning things and a box of lost-and-found objects. "I don't know if I believe that."

"She can't do anything to you, and if she tries, I'll fix it. She knows she was wrong, Nick. She knows she did something the Presences would object to. I don't think she'll compound that error."

"I hope you're right," I said, as the bells rang.

"Hey?" said someone.

I stood up.

"Wow, magic," said Megan, the girl I had met at the dance last night. She was wearing a green halter top and black short shorts, and she was tan all over. Her dark curly hair was tied into a loose ponytail at the left side of her head. Strands had escaped the rubber band. She looked relaxed.

"What?" I asked, startled. How had she known what was going on?

"Well, it was like you were invisible, and then suddenly you appeared. What were you doing back there?"

"Talking to my wolf," I said.

"What?"

"Hey, Evan, this is Megan," I said. He rose on his hind legs, his front paws on the counter, and looked at her. "I met her last night at the dance."

"Yikes!" she said.

"*Uuf,*" he said.

"Megan, this is Evan."

"I, uh," she said. She sucked her lower lip into her mouth for a second, then took a couple steps closer. "Pleased to meet you," she said, edging up and holding out her hand.

"*Ruf!*" He grinned at her and extended a paw, and she grasped it, then released it, her eyes wide. He blinked at her and she blinked her turquoise eyes back, then looked at me.

"I never met a wolf before," she said, her voice low.

"Bet she has," said Evan. He dropped to the floor and walked out from behind the counter to sit neatly facing Megan, smiling at her.

"You're beautiful. You're so beautiful," she said, crouching and reaching to stroke his head.

"*Arou,*" he said. "She's cute."

"He thinks you're cute," I said.

She glanced up at me sideways, her grin impish. "Why, Nick, I thought you told me last night you already have a girlfriend."

"But I—"

Evan laughed at me.

"That wasn't a line, Megan. He thinks you're cute. Well, you are." I stopped, confused. I usually didn't foul myself up in quite this fashion.

"You can understand what he says?" she asked.

"Yeah."

"Ask him if it's okay if I kiss him."

"What?" I said. Did she know somehow about Evan?

Evan licked her nose. She kissed his nose right back, then said, "Eh! Do something about that breath, fella, or this relationship is going no further!"

He laughed, then asked me, "What could I do about my breath?"

"I don't know. Mouthwash or brushing your teeth, I guess. Or suck down some flavored water? I don't know if your mouth works the same as ours."

Megan laughed. She reached for a roll of breath mints from the candy display on the counter and showed them to Evan. "If you're really motivated, you could chomp on a few of these," she said.

"Anything for you, babe. Hey, Nick, who is this woman? I've never met anybody who responded to me like this, at least not while I was this shape. It's very odd being tame. I used to just scare people. Who is she?"

"I don't really know," I said.

"What did he say?" said Megan, standing up and reaching into her tiny purse for an even smaller wallet, handing me a one-dollar bill.

I raised my eyebrows and she waved the breath mints at me, so I rang up the transaction and gave her change. I said, "He asked me who you were."

She pulled the strip to open the roll and handed Evan three mints off the top. He chewed them, then said, "Yuck!"

"Probably not your favorite thing," she said. "Thanks for suffering for me."

"What if they make him sick?" I said. I remembered a vet had once told me you could make a cat sick with aspirin; remedies that worked for people didn't necessarily translate for other animals.

Evan muttered, "I can stand them, but they sure taste awful. Next time I'll just chew up some real mint."

Megan popped a mint herself, then said, "So you want to know who I am?" to Evan.

"*Ruf!*"

She glanced at me.

I shrugged. "That was a yes."

She sat down so she was face-to-face with him. "Well," she said, without looking at me, "I'm the leftover girl—you know, the one who's best friends with the prettiest girl that everybody's interested in. They dance with me when they can't get to her. But their focus is always somewhere else."

He licked her face.

"I'm sorry," I said.

She looked up. "No, I didn't mean you."

"But that was—"

"At least we had a real conversation," she said. She was stroking Evan's fur without paying attention. "Which reminds me. About that bathing suit . . ."

"Oh, yeah." I went to the rack with swimwear on it and pulled out the suit I'd told her about last night. It was sexier than I had remembered, French cut high on the hips and with a daring dip in back, with black crisscross straps. Not a very big scrap of material.

"Wow," she said, eyebrows up.

"Yeah," I said, turning it. The Lycra rainbow swoosh sparkled. "Maybe not what you had in mind?"

"I think I'll try it on," she said. "You have a fitting room?"

I showed her into the downstairs bathroom next to the kitchen, where there was a decent mirror. It wasn't too much of a mess, just a few of Granddad's things— his shaving equipment and some of his medicines on the counter.

When I went back out front, Evan was standing at the door and looking out. "You want out?"

"Look."

I peered out in the direction he was staring and saw

a dusty maroon Kharmann Ghia pulling into the motel driveway. "So?"

"Strange energy," he muttered. "Trouble."

The car drove back toward the office and out of sight. We heard the engine turning off.

"Let me out, Nick."

I opened the door and he dashed out. After a glance toward the back where Megan was, I followed Evan around the edge of the store, watching the car.

A woman was wrestling a suitcase from the backseat. She got it out onto the asphalt, then slammed the car door and straightened, smoothing a hand down the small of her back. I ducked around the corner and peeked from the safety of the storefront.

Her dark hair was short now, and she was skinnier than I remembered, but I knew her. Mom.

5

❦

Shocks to the System

I edged away across the storefront from the corner and sagged down onto the varnished wooden bench between the newspaper vending machine and the door, my hands pressed against my stomach, my eyes not tracking.

I had always figured that if I ever saw Mom again it would be by my choice. When I was ready, I would study all the letters she had sent me, triangulate the postmarks (there was never a return address on the outside of the envelope, never even a name, I suppose because she thought Pop would censor the mail, which he might have done if he knew she was sending letters; but the mail came when either I or Mariah was watching the store—a good thing, because Mom's handwriting was as recognizable as ever), actually read the contents in case she put clues to her whereabouts inside (I assumed there wouldn't be a return address inside, for the same reason—Pop might track her down), and detect where she was. I would go to her community, establish myself in some secret identity—dye my hair, grow a mustache, get colored contacts—and study her life from a distance, deciding for myself if I ever wanted to talk to her again. I would be in charge. I could be bitter and angry and removed if I wanted to, and sneer at her; or I could decide I'd let her know I was okay and that I'd finally gotten away from Pop, if she even cared.

The depth of preparation in this scenario surprised me. I hadn't realized I had made these plans, but they had the bittersweet taste of thoughts often cherished in anger.

And now, of course, my choices were gone.

I don't know how long I sat there.

"Snap out of it, Nick," Evan said. I blinked and looked at him. My hand was cold. I glanced at it and realized it was wet, probably with his spit, so he'd been standing in front of me for a while and had tried other ways of waking me.

My stomach still hurt. I let go of it and worked my fingers. They were stiff.

Evan said, "She's checked in."

"What?" Panic wavered my voice.

"She went into the office, and a little while later she came out, grabbed that suitcase, and took it to room four, which she unlocked using a key with a metal dangle. She checked in, wouldn't you say?"

"Oh, God."

"Who is she, Nick?"

"My mother."

"How very interesting," he said. "She's warded."

He had said something like that about Willow yesterday, and Lauren had used that word too. I remembered that Lauren had defined it, but I couldn't remember exactly how. "What does that mean?" I asked.

"Means that the surface she's presenting isn't what she really looks like. I don't think she'll expect you to recognize her. Unless she knows that you can see more than most people . . . how long since you've seen her?"

"Four years." If she looked different to most people, that explained how she could check in and not alert

Pop to her being here. My mother, in disguise. Just like I had planned to be when I caught up to her.

My mother.

Evan asked, "How old are you now?"

"Seventeen."

He cocked his head, studying me. Then he looked away. "She may not know you can see through things like that. So don't let her know you recognize her."

I felt a little snick in my head. *You say bleed and I bleed.* Somewhere in my brain I was preparing to act as if I didn't know my own mother.

Served her right.

"Nick? Nick?" The voice came from inside the building.

I jumped to my feet and went into the store with Evan on my heels.

Megan was wearing her clothes and holding the swimsuit.

"God, Megan, I'm sorry," I said. I had forgotten she was there.

"It's okay," she said. "I had to study it for a while before I decided I could stand it. It's a new look for me. Doesn't feel quite right."

I stopped thinking about Mom and let store mode take over. "Did you want a second opinion? I didn't mean to leave you all alone in here, but we had to check on someone who drove up to the motel."

"Stop by the pool this afternoon and give me an opinion then, you and Evan both. And you better wear a suit, too, and not one of those three-piece-with-vest types. What do I owe you?"

I told her and she pulled more cash out of her tiny purse and paid me. She stooped and kissed the top of Evan's head, then breezed out of the store.

"You going to take her up on that?" Evan asked.

"I don't know," I said. "I don't—what about Mom? What is she doing here? How could she be . . . warded? Do you think—" Did she want to come home? Did she want to take care of me and Pop and Granddad again? Why would she be disguised if that was what she wanted? What else could she want? What was I going to say to her?

The morning she had left, I woke myself up because I couldn't breathe. I didn't even know Mom was gone, but I could hardly breathe. Pop had to call Doc McBride. The doc had had to shoot me up with a tranquilizer before I could breathe normally again, and I had still felt like somebody cut my chest open and scooped something important out. By the time Pop told me Mom was gone, it didn't surprise me.

"I don't know what's going on. I have to watch Mom. I can't think of . . ." I was having trouble breathing again.

"Calm down, Nick. You're okay. Take a couple deep breaths. You're fine."

I took a couple of deep breaths and felt calm, okay, and fine. "This afternoon is my day off, Evan, but—"

"An afternoon is a day? What language is that?"

"The language of Pop."

"You work all the other days of the week here?"

"During the season."

He growled. "When do you play?" he said.

"Most of the winter. At night. In the morning. Saturday afternoon."

Evan growled again.

The bells rang and Mariah breezed in. "Sorry I'm late. Take off, kid—ai-yi-yi!" She clapped one hand to her sternum and stared at Evan.

"Mariah, this is Evan," I said quickly. "He's somewhat tame."

"He's growling," she said in a swallowed voice.

I stroked his head and he stopped growling. "Evan, this is Mariah."

"She smells like turpentine and oil paints," he said.

"She's an artist. She spells me when I take my lunches and covers for me on my half day off."

Evan sat with his tail curled around his forepaws and grinned at Mariah.

"You are a beauty," she said, "and you know it, don't you?"

He yipped.

"I'd love to paint you."

He laughed.

"Nick, where'd he come from?"

"He's my dog," I said, and noticed a waver in my own voice. Silly. I had practiced lying, and ought to be able to do it better by now.

"Where does one get a dog like that?"

"I found him in the woods," I said, and that part came out smoothly, maybe because it was true.

"Good God," said Mariah, "what makes you think he's the least bit tame?"

"Well, he is," I said, continuing to stroke him. The hair on top of his head was the softest. I scratched behind his ears, and he turned his head against my hand, pushing for more.

"What kind of name is Evan for a wild beast?"

"It's his name," I said.

"Let's get out of here," Evan said.

"We've got to go," I told Mariah, suddenly worried that Mom would come in and I would have to figure out how to not recognize her. And how not to collapse.

"Have a good time," Mariah said, smiling. Evan yipped and we brushed past her and escaped into the out.

I ran until the breath burned in my lungs and I could hear the blood pounding in my ears and we were almost to the Lacey's. Then, remembering my last encounter along this path, I slowed and veered up into the woods, Evan at my heels. Father Boulder's clearing was up this way, but I wasn't ready to take Evan there, so I headed for another place I knew, where a forest giant had toppled, leaving roots reaching for the sky, some sheltering a big hole in the ground whose floor I had smoothed and covered with dead bracken several years ago. It was one of my first forts. Occasionally I went back and renewed the floor covering and cleaned out the cobwebs among the roots, but it had been a long while since I had been there.

Evan and I flopped down on the dusty dried fern. For a time I just listened to the breath moving in and out of me, sliding past my roughened throat. Evan lay beside me, nose on paws. After a little while I could smell the dried, crushed bracken under me, and the earth and pines. The sweat on my back and face cooled. I rolled my head and looked at Evan.

He lifted his head, cocked it.

I opened my mouth and words fell out. "She left. She didn't even tell me good-bye. She never said why she was leaving. She sends me letters, but I don't read them. We spent all our time together. I didn't know how to live without her. Then she left. At first I didn't even know how to see without her. It hurt. It took me a long time to get over it. What the hell is she doing here, Evan? I don't want her here. I got used to her being gone. I want to kill her. I want to talk to her. I want to ask her why she left, but I'm afraid her answer won't be good enough. How come she knows some of the same magic as your family does?" My breath was getting short again.

"This is upsetting you."

"It's driving me crazy. I have to find out—I have to, but I don't even—I wish—I can't—" I clutched at my chest, wheezing, struggling for air. If I strangled, Doc McBride would never be able to find me out here.

"Stop thinking about it. Give it a rest. We can work it out later. Forget her for now, Nick."

Click.

I blinked up at the roots above me, sucked in breath, let it out. I closed my eyes. I opened them. I glanced over and saw a wolf sitting near me, watching me.

After a minute I recognized him. I lifted my arm and looked at my watch, which told me it was about twelve-thirty on a Saturday afternoon. "It's my day off," I said to Evan.

"That's right," he said. "Your half day."

"What do you want to do?" I asked him.

"What do you usually do?"

"Go places and look at things," I said. "I thought . . . I thought if you were going to turn me into anything, this would be the best time for me. I don't have to be anywhere until suppertime." Sometimes he sounded like he would consider my wishes, and sometimes I wasn't so sure if he would, but mostly he seemed friendly. It would be a load off my mind if I knew he would restrict his playful ideas about me to a time when it wouldn't interfere with my regular life. Thought I'd at least give him the opportunity.

"Close your eyes," he said after a moment.

I closed my eyes, wondering what it would feel like to turn into some other creature. It always looked so painful in werewolf movies, hurting and slimy. I wasn't sure why movie monsters always had to be covered with slime, or at least be drool factories. Did it have anything to do with the real world? Would shapechanging hurt?

I put my hands on my stomach, wondering if it mattered. What if it hurt so much I couldn't stand turning back into myself? Nobody would know where I was. Pop would be plenty upset. He would start asking questions. Maybe other people would too.

They could ask all they liked, but I would be a poodle somewhere, maybe out in the wild woods, maybe in the pound. Nobody would ever figure it out. I scratched a bug bite on my shoulder. All I felt was the breath of a breeze tweaking my hair, and the solid earth below the mat of leaves I was lying on.

"Okay," said Evan.

I blinked and looked at him, because his voice

sounded the same but different. And instead of a wolf, there was a tan, muscular, naked man sitting there, his face angular and strangely young, as if he had never tried out any expressions, his eyes lemon colored around their dark irises, his hair like heavy white-gold thread falling about his shoulders, his tan body furred faintly all over with silver. He had dark eyebrows that peaked at their outer edges. He didn't look quite human.

"Yikes!"

He grinned and cocked his head. I closed my eyes because I could tell he had been the wolf, and it was too weird to think I had scratched behind his ears not a half hour earlier.

"Wake up, Nick," he said.

I opened my eyes reluctantly and looked at him.

"Come on," he said. "Let's go swimming."

"Evan?" I said.

He rose and reached down, grabbed my hand and pulled me to my feet. It required about the same effort as a shrug, apparently. His hand felt rough and hard against mine. He was half a foot taller than I was. "Come on," he said again, and brushed a broad, long-fingered hand over my head, dislodging bits of dead leaves. "What's the matter?"

"My brain has trouble with this."

He hooked his elbow around my neck, stared into my eyes, and said, "No, you're fine. I change from one thing to another, and you can relate to everything I change into and feel comfortable with it. It's an expanded relationship. You can handle this, even though it's new to you. You have a good brain, Nick, and a good heart." He let go of me and mussed my hair. I felt caramel and vanilla and smooth melted chocolate changes flowing through me, warm and sweet and comforting. I blinked.

"Hey, you need a swimsuit," I said. I assumed he wanted to go over to Lacey's and take a look at Megan in her new bathing suit; and though there were beaches on the lake where you could skinny-dip, the pool was a suit-oriented place.

He glanced down at himself and frowned. "Yeah," he said. "Where am I going to get one?"

"We have them at the store," I said, and shivered. There was some reason why I wanted to avoid the store this afternoon. I looked at Evan again. There was a white scar on his shoulder—a bite mark—and the scratches of other scars like random graffiti on his arms, legs, and torso. For a second I thought, *I don't know this guy!* Then I thought, *Sure I do, he's my best friend, there's nothing weird about this.* Then I thought, *You say bleed* . . . "Evan?"

"Yes?"

I gripped my head. "You did something to my brain."

"Yes."

"I don't know if I . . . I don't know if . . ."

"Do you want me to undo it?"

"I don't know." I felt like I knew him, and it didn't bother me that he was some lion-maned naked guy in the woods; but at the same time I could remember how I would have felt yesterday running into someone who looked like him—I would have thought, *This guy is nuts* and run the other direction. Mix in the fact that I knew a wolf and that the wolf and this guy were one person—I could spend days being confused about it. I wasn't sure I wanted that confusion back. I just didn't want to lose who I was because Evan said so, any more than I wanted his aunt Elissa to be able to make me go blind in a couple of seconds.

Maybe what I wanted didn't count. There were lots of times when it didn't.

"Look," he said. He squinted and glanced toward the sky for a minute, then looked back at me. "It wasn't like I changed your mind around. What I did was speed up something you would have done naturally. Like the healing."

When he put it like that, it didn't bother me anymore. "Okay," I said. Eyes closed, I pressed my hands over my face for a moment, waiting for my mind to settle. I took a breath, let it out.

He nudged my shoulder. "Okay?"

"Okay," I said again, looking at him. He grinned, and I smiled back, feeling that I knew him and that was all that mattered. Knowing even as I thought it that it wasn't really true. Oh well. "Suit," I said. "I don't want to go in the store right now." I usually didn't want to go back to the store once I had a legitimate reason to be away from it, but there was something, some extra reason today.... I frowned.

"'S okay. I'll ward myself and do it. What about you—you want to swim?"

"Yeah, I guess." I had swum in Lacey's pool last summer once or twice, when Jeremy had invited me, but usually I made do with the lake. The pool didn't embrace me the way the lake did.

"I'll get us both suits. Size?"

"Medium."

"Want to wait here or come with me?"

"I'll wait," I said.

He slipped off through the trees, not toward the path, with only a little rustle of underbrush. I sat and thought about sanctioning shoplifting. If I saved the tags, I could pay for the swimsuits later. My regular one was getting old, anyway; the pockets had holes in them and the lining was torn.

I had to wonder if this warding stuff would actually work. What if Mariah looked up to see Evan, naked, in the store? How would she react? I was wondering more about Mariah than I had before, since we had actually talked. I wasn't sure anymore that I could guess what she would do.

I wondered if Willow ever used the pool. Maybe she would be out communing with the wood spirits. I would like to watch her do that if I could be sure she didn't know I was there. Maybe even if she knew. What a weird idea. I couldn't remember the last time I had watched somebody do something secret when they knew I was watching. I wondered what Willow would look like in a bathing suit, even though I had already seen her without one.

I lay on the ferns and thought about Willow for a while. Presently I noticed there was something bumpy and warm near my leg. I sat up and patted the ground, groped through the dried ferns until I closed my hand around a water-smoothed rock about the size of an egg. It was warm, as if it had baked in the sun for a while. I opened my hand and looked at it. River gray, nothing to set it apart from a million other rocks. I touched its surface to my cheek, then my forehead, and felt calmer, almost sleepy. I slipped the rock into my pocket and curled up.

"Wake up. Maybe that energizing command this morning was a bad idea," Evan said.

He was squatting beside me, two pairs of navy trunks dangling from his hand. I smiled up at him and stretched. From the direction and length of the shadows and sun speckles I knew some time had passed. I felt totally relaxed. I rolled and stood up.

He rose and stared at me, his brows lowered. "You smell strange," he said.

"Mm?" I lifted an arm and sniffed my armpit. The earlier dash through the woods hadn't defeated my deodorant, as far as I could tell.

"There's a—never mind. Here." He handed me one swimsuit and stepped into the other one. I changed, slipping the new rock into the suit's pocket. It made a lump. This wouldn't work. I would have to put it back in my pants pocket, and for some reason that bothered me. Evan put his hand near it, his brow furrowing. "What is this?"

I shrugged. "It's a rock."

"No," he said in a distracted voice.

"It's a rock."

"It's *skilliau*."

I slipped the rock out of my pocket and held it out to him. "This is what you're looking for? Why?"

He held out a hand to the rock, pulled it back. "No," he whispered, "we must approach with the proper respect."

I cupped my hands around the rock, wondering if I had done something wrong by just picking it up. It still felt calm and warm. "What the heck is this skilly-whatever, anyway?"

Evan looked away from me for a moment, frowned, and then turned back. "*Skilliau* is the soul of a thing, the spirit of a thing, the energy of a thing; or it is something like that that was put there by a Power or a Presence or by the life of the thing; it is what you can wake up in something, and then it can work with you. Sometimes it wants you to work with it. It is a . . . a potential that waits to be addressed. It can do many different things. *Skilliau* can enrich soil and waken seeds and sweeten ovens. Some can bring you luck; some will take a personal interest in your life and help you through troubles. Some keep your cattle healthy or make fruit and vegetables grow bigger. Some aid in powerworkings. That one might be a relaxation aid or something else. Here at the lake there are different kinds. We found this place by consulting a *krifter* in Southclan, and we are here to find some *skilliau* and request that they come home with us to enrich our household and aid us in our efforts to make things happen. Or to enrich Aunt and Uncle's household, at any rate. Mostly they want *skilliau* that will help with crops and animals. Not a project *I'm* particularly interested in.

"It's here for us. We just have to find it and wake it and instruct it or request things from it. But . . ." He stared at the rock in my hands, then looked up at my face, his eyes the color of melted butter. "If we do it wrong . . ."

I touched the rock to my cheek. It felt drowsy as a kitten's purr and as warm. I couldn't see how there could be anything wrong with that.

"Where did you find it?" he asked.

I knelt and patted the fern-covered ground. "Here."

"I didn't sense it when we arrived or when I left. You woke it, Nick."

I shrugged. I went to the root mass of the fallen tree and scooped out dirt in a crevice between three small roots until I had enough space to plant the stone, then edged it into its new hiding place. I stroked it and said "Thanks." My fingers tingled. I made a mark in my memory, thinking that if my mind was troubled I could come here and the stone would calm it, maybe. I backed away and studied the roots; you couldn't see a stone was lodged among them—their shadows kept it safe. I looked at Evan.

He blinked at me, glanced toward the rock. "Nick?"

"Yes?"

"How did you wake it? It isn't angry. You must have done it right."

"I didn't do anything, Evan. Honest. It was warm and I picked it up."

"Give me your hand."

My hand was out even before he reached for it. He frowned, gripped it with one hand, and gestured above it with the other. The little ring of blue flame I'd seen the night before when Willow had done the same thing showed up again above my hand, not so striking in daylight, but there. He leaned over and licked it, then shook his head. "*Eauch,*" he said, more a breath than a word. "Don't know quite what you are, but you're something, all right, something air." The circle of light faded.

"Willow did that to me last night. How do you make it happen?"

He cocked his head. "It's a dialogue, or kind of a greeting. A way of talking without words."

"What's yours look like?"

His brows rose. He released my hand and gestured above his own, drawing up a yellow spiral—not a cone like Willow's, but a curling staircase of glowing strands.

"Pretty," I said.

He smiled and flicked the lights away. Then he nudged my shoulder with his. "Come on." He glanced toward the hidden stone, then gave me an open-mouthed grin that reminded me of his wolf grin. "I'm so glad I fetched you. I mean, you smelled interesting right from the start, but I don't know if I would have found out how interesting any other way." He roughed my hair, then gripped the back of my neck and headed toward the path, pulling me with him, his hand warm and hard.

"You don't have to lead me. I'll come quietly," I said.

"Huh?" He blinked at me, stared at his own hand, then let go. "I'm sorry. I forget I'm not a wolf anymore. Lead the way."

We detoured through the woods when we reached the stretch of path near Lacey number five, and came at the pool from the direction of the driveway.

"Nick?" Adam Lacey said, venturing out of his office.

"Megan invited us to the pool," I said.

"Megan? Which one's she?"

"Cute little brunette. Friend of Kristen's. Couple inches shorter than me with brown curls. Cabin nine, I think. She came by the store earlier to buy a swimsuit and asked me and Evan to join her at the pool."

"I'm not doubting your word," he said, lying.

"This is Evan," I said. "Evan, Adam Lacey, your host."

"What?" said Adam.

"Evan's staying with the people in number five. . . ."
I glanced toward number five and saw Willow strolling
up the road toward us, wearing a green dress that barely
came down to her thighs. Her legs looked incredibly
long and tan and muscular, even though she wasn't that
tall. She smiled at me, then spotted Evan, and her stroll
turned into a run.

"Evan?" she said, breathless.

He grinned at her.

"Evan? Nick? Evan?"

"This is my sister," Evan said to Adam.

Adam rolled his eyes. "Wait just a second," he said,
"and I'll get you some towels."

"What happened?" Willow asked after Adam had
disappeared into the office.

"I met this girl," said Evan.

"I wonder if she'll recognize you," I said. "Should
you use a different name?"

"No," said Evan. "She kissed me on the nose," he
told Willow, and grinned with his mouth open.

"Are you crazy?" Willow said.

"You know she'll believe it or she won't. It won't
matter," Evan said.

Adam reemerged from the office and handed us three
white fluffy towels.

"Thanks," I said, surprised. He'd never given me a
towel before, no matter who invited me.

His gaze slid to Willow and Evan and away again.
"Welcome," he said gruffly. He disappeared of-
ficeward again.

"What have you been doing to that man?" Evan
asked Willow, his voice light and amused.

"Nothing, really. I don't know why he's spooked. I
think it might have something to do with Aunt Elissa."

"That makes sense," I said.

"Why?" Willow asked.

"She scares me plenty."

"I told you not to worry about her," Evan said.

"Not in those words," I said. If he had told me not to worry, maybe I wouldn't have been able to worry. And even though he had told me he would protect me from Aunt Elissa, I still wasn't sure.

He considered it. "True. Well, you can worry if you want." He put his towel over his shoulder, glanced at me, grinned, and said, "Heel, Nick."

I didn't even know what the word meant, but found myself half a step behind him, pacing him, as he walked toward the pool yard. "Cut it out," I said as we entered the gate in tandem.

His yellow eyes glinted. Light bounced off his teeth. "Okay. At ease."

Willow gripped my arm. "Nick?" she murmured, slowing me down as Evan walked over to the redwood table with the picnic umbrella over it.

Her fingers were warm against my wrist. I looked down at her hand and it was outlined in golden light. I wanted to taste it.

"Are you all right?" she asked in a quiet voice.

"Huh?"

"I mean—he fetched you—are you all right?"

"I'm fine," I said.

"He makes you do things."

"Yeah, but it's okay. He likes me."

"*I* like you. I would never make you do anything silly."

"But—" I had a sudden uprush of contradictory feelings. Evan scared me every once in a while, but not in some life-threatening way. If I had been in the same kind of thrall with Willow that I was with Evan—how would I ever have been able to think of her romantically? Unless she told me I had to. And that would feel different, wouldn't it?

Maybe she never would have made me do anything silly. Maybe she would only tell me to love her; maybe my heart and hers would beat together and I would know what she was going to do next without her having to say anything, and she would learn what I knew, effortlessly.

Something about that felt exactly wrong. If I were Willow's, I thought, I would disappear—turn into her shadow. If I were hooked to her, every move would be part of a pas de deux. I couldn't see her letting me continue to run my routine—though maybe I was wrong? Whereas, as Evan's—I could continue to be me.

"This is much better," I said.

Her yellow eyes widened, her eyebrows rising in wounded crescents.

"Because," I said, and leaned forward to kiss her, "you know it's my idea when I do that. You can't make me if I don't want to." Or maybe she could, but we would both know if she used her voice on me. "Don't you think that's better?"

She kissed me again, blinking, then wiped a tear from her cheek. "Okay," she said. She looked away. She sighed. "I can't take you home, anyway. That would have been the point. I don't live at home anymore."

"What?"

"There was a prophecy. My little brother died, and I was going to find out who—I've never told anybody about this, but—"

"Nick," Evan said.

I surfaced and looked at him. For a second I wished we had never gotten tangled up with each other. I wanted to hear what Willow had to tell me. I wanted to be my own person for half an hour.

Evan stood in the shade of the umbrella, his face blank, his poise gone. Megan lay on her back on a chaise beyond the pool. A fashion magazine lay open over her face, and the rise and fall of her chest was slow as sleep. The white blonde of Kristen's hair spilled over the edge of the neighboring chaise, where she lay motionless on her stomach. Both their bodies looked oiled and tan.

He was a wolf. He didn't know how to strike up a conversation. He was my wolf. I might not be an absolute master of social arts, but I could help him.

I glanced at Willow. "Later," she said. "It's all very old news."

Taking Willow's hand, I went to Evan and nudged him with my shoulder. "Come on," I murmured. I led them around the pool and tossed my towel on the chaise next to Megan's. I sat Evan down on the chaise, glanced at Willow. She slid her hand out of mine and stretched out on a neighboring chaise.

I leaned close to the fashion magazine and whispered, "Megan? Hey, Megan?"

She startled and sat up, the magazine slipping to the ground. "Oh. Jeez, Nick."

"The suit looks great." It wrapped her body in promises, drawing the eyes and heating the blood. I had had no idea she was shaped like that.

She crossed her arms over her breasts and hunched her shoulders. "I don't know," she said. "I feel weird in it."

"You look terrific."

Kristen stretched her arms above her head, then turned her face away from us.

I sat down beside Evan. Megan glanced in his direction. Her eyes widened. Her knees came up, hiding her stomach.

"Megan, this is Evan."

"What?" she said, her voice high.

"This is my friend Evan."

Evan held out his hands to her. She blinked, then reached her hand out. He took it between his and kissed it, his lips resting against her skin a moment. I felt like I should nudge him or something.

Megan's shoulders shuddered. After a moment she tugged her hand free of Evan's. "Kind of a mean trick," she said, her voice low, her arms tight across her chest again, hands buried in her armpits. "I had thought better of you, Nick."

Evan looked at me, his face blank except for the worried lift of his dark eyebrows.

"It's not a trick," I said. "Evan's his name."

"So where's your wolf?"

Kristen turned her head toward us and pushed blonde hair out of her eyes, stared at Evan, then frowned at me.

"I can't explain that."

"I don't think I like you anymore, Nick."

"Okay. I can explain it, but you won't believe it."

Evan reached out and stroked the backs of his fingernails up Megan's arm to her shoulder. She shivered. "I *am* the wolf," he murmured. "I like you very much. I wanted to talk so you could understand. But I will go back to being a wolf if you want."

She glared at him with narrowed eyes. "Please do," she said.

"Not here," I said to Evan. There hadn't been any slime the last time he changed, but who could tell? Maybe you only got slime when you were turning from a human into a wolf. I tried to remember that scene from *An American Werewolf in London*. It was gruesome enough on screen. I wasn't sure I could stand it in real life. Besides, Kristen was lying there watching everything.

Evan ran his hand across my hair, then nudged my shoulder, grinning open-mouthed at me. "What have I got to lose?" he said.

"Don't, Evan. Honestly. People will see you. It might upset Megan and Kristen. Adam might see you. He spies on people a lot. Could get your whole family in trouble. And somehow I have this conviction that everybody will blame me."

"I'll protect you," he said.

"*Please.*" I would have put my persuaders into it, but I wasn't sure how that would work, considering he was technically my master. It occurred to me that Evan didn't know I could use my voice that way, and perhaps it was just as well.

"My lady fancies me a wolf, Nick," he said. "Now be quiet."

My tongue lay still in my mouth. I put my hands over my nose and mouth to mask the sound of my breathing, which made it sound louder. I held my breath.

He cuffed me on the arm. "Not that quiet." I gasped and started breathing normally again. "Megan, do you promise if I go back to being a wolf you'll still like me?"

"If you're the same wolf I met at the store, sure. You're adorable." A second after she said it, she flushed bright red.

"Good," he said. He glanced toward the office where Adam Lacey had vanished. I looked too. No sign of Adam. Evan stood, stepped out of his trunks, handed them to me, lay on the ground between the chaises where he couldn't be seen except by us and then puddled, shimmering as though seen through mist, his blond human form melting down before his pale wolf form firmed into itself. It was very fast and there didn't seem to be any slime involved.

Megan clapped both her hands over her mouth. Only a faint voiced gasp came out. Evan sat, head cocked to one side, looking up at her. Kristen had jerked upright when Evan lay down, and now she sat staring, her hands gripping the edge of her chaise so tightly that her knuckles showed white through her skin.

"*Faskish,* Evan!" Willow said. "You spit on our ancestors!"

Megan slowly lowered her hands from her face. "Nick," she croaked, "tell me I'm dreaming."

I didn't know what to tell her; it was just as well I was still being quiet, as per Evan's last order. I dropped his swimsuit and looked down at him.

"This was a mistake?" he said.

I shrugged.

"You told me it would be," he said.

I lifted my shoulders, dropped them, sighed without sound. Strange how this silence felt safe in some new way, when I had learned lately to consider my voice my protection of last resort.

"What's he saying now, Nick?" Megan said, her voice raw as though she had swallowed screams.

I smiled at her and stroked Evan's head. It was still softest between his ears. He closed his eyes a moment and let me just stroke him, then looked up at me. "What do you think? Is she going to be okay?"

I looked at Megan. "Nick?" she said, more urgent. She gripped my arm, stilling me in mid-stroke. Beyond her, Kristen was breathing in short pants, her eyes fixed on a place where Evan no longer was. Worry stained my thoughts.

With my free hand I gripped Evan's muzzle, pointing it up toward me. When I was sure I had his attention, I tapped my throat twice. For a moment he was puzzled, then said, "Oh! Damn! Don't let me do that to you again, Nick. I wasn't thinking. Talk all you want."

"He thinks maybe it was a mistake," I told Megan. "Kristen?"

Her eyes didn't shift. Her knuckles were still white.

I stood up and went around Megan's chaise, sat down beside Kristen. I touched her cheek and she turned to stare at me. "Kristen? Listen," I said, and felt heat in my throat and mouth. Evan would find out about the voice trick, but this was more important than being secret. "Listen," I said again. It came out weighted with persuasion. Kristen blinked and focused on my face. Her breathing deepened and smoothed. "It was just a trick. A magic trick. An illusion. Okay?"

She blinked three more times, then nodded, her hands relaxing from their death grip.

"Pretty good trick, huh?" I said.

"Boy oh boy," she said. "You could take that show on the road."

"But Nick, you said—" Megan began. Evan licked her leg. "Hey!" She pushed his nose away. "But, Nick—"

"Ruh!" Evan said, nudging her thigh.

She looked down at him and her face crumpled. "Nick—Evan—" She stroked his face, buried her hands in the thick fur on his shoulders.

"Give me a minute, Megan," I said. "Kristen, you okay?"

"I'm fine. Why?"

"Thought you were a little ... sleepy," I said.

She yawned. "Now that you mention it ... edge over, Nick."

I slid off the chaise and she stretched out, resting her head on her hands, and fell asleep.

I stood, breathing hard, holding my hands down and away from me as though I were ashamed of them, even though I hadn't done anything with my hands. That had been too easy. What if I started doing things like that to people just to be mean, just to play with them, just because I wanted something from them, just because I *could?* If only Evan had stayed his wolf self I would never have had to face this situation and act on it.

But all these things had happened. I looked at Kristen, her face slack and innocent. Her chest moved up and down in the slow breath of sleep. I turned to stare at Evan. He stared back, then blinked and grinned. "This just gets better all the time," he said.

Willow sat hunched, scowling and hugging her knees, beyond him.

Megan looked at me. "Did you put a spell on Kristen?" she asked.

"Pretty much," I said. "Guess you could call it hypnosis."

"Are you going to put a spell on me?"

"Are you so upset you can't think straight?"

"I think I'm going crazy."

"Well, when you know instead of think, and if you want me to, I'll—I'll hypnotize you too."

"Oh, no. Don't. That's really creepy, Nick."

"You said it." I went around and sat down on the chaise facing her again, my shoulders slumping forward. "So what do you want to know?"

"Was it really a trick?" She looked down, realized she was petting Evan, let go of him.

"I don't know how he does it."

"But—I mean, he was a man, and then he's a wolf, and—I mean—is that real?"

"I don't know. I think it's real."

I remembered that Evan had had to do a mind trick on me to get me to accept this change, but Megan seemed to be working this out on her own.

"This is a werewolf?" Megan said, touching Evan's shoulder.

"Naw," I said. "Has nothing to do with the moon. Besides, does he look like some ravening beast?"

"*Ruh,*" Evan said, and licked Megan's leg again.

"Stop it! You're weird!"

"You taste like coconut," he said.

"Must be the tanning oil," I said. "I wonder if it's poisonous?"

"Tastes good," he said, licking her arm.

"Eww, stop it!" She pulled her arm up out of range. "I mean, if you're really a dog it's okay, but if you're a guy pretending to be a dog, there's—that's disgusting."

"It's confusing," I said. "I think he's really both. He's been a wolf for three and a half wolf years. I had problems with it too."

Evan jumped up, put his paws on my shoulders, and pushed me flat on the chaise, then licked my face. "I think I'm more calm about it now," I said, wiping my face with the back of my hand.

"Tell her I like her," said Evan.

"He likes you," I said.

"She sure tastes good. Tell her if she wants I'll turn back into the other form for her."

"Yes, but pick a better place?" I said.

"Tell her." He stared down into my eyes.

"He says if you want him to he'll turn back into his other form."

"Do I really want a boyfriend who's a dog?"

"It sounds different if you consider that he's a wolf," I said, though I wasn't sure if the connotations were better. "Besides, he's probably lots of other things."

"That's supposed to be reassuring?" Megan said.

I laughed. I had forgotten how she might take that, but now I remembered what Evan had said about chihuahuas and poodles. If he could turn me into those things he could probably turn himself into them, too. Spooky thought. Snakes—he'd mentioned snakes. What else could he accomplish? Owls? Seals? Bats? Elephants? What about—a different human being?

"Maybe he's got a career or something. Maybe he's got a future on the stage. Maybe—" I thought about what I had seen Willow's family doing since I had discovered them. None of it looked like anything you could make a living at. Maybe this was the wrong line of reasoning to follow. Or maybe they could make a living off whatever their magic was, only in some weird way I couldn't even imagine. Magic food? Magic money? Magic life-forms that didn't need what I assumed all humans needed? I felt the itch to spy on them growing inside me again. I hadn't seen the men do much, or Aunt Elissa—had only observed her torturing me, basically. I didn't even know what the boys had been doing when I watched them. If I could get Lauren alone again I was pretty sure I could find out a lot from her.

I said, "Hey, maybe he's going to college."

The thought of that staggered me as soon as I mentioned it. I imagined Evan in an MBA program and grinned. Imagine Evan wearing a suit and tie. Or how about law school? A guy who broke rules all the time and refused to obey authority. A laugh escaped me. No, definitely the arts. I could see Evan covered with clay, throwing pots he would personalize with a paw print.

"Hey!" he said. "Think I couldn't do college?"

"I was just trying to figure out what your major would be," I said. I wondered what my major would be if I could ever get away from Sauterelle. It had never occurred to me to think about college. My primary goal had been just getting away—at least, getting away from Pop and the store. I wasn't so sure I wanted to leave the lake and the forest. But if I did go—yeah, detective work. I'd figured that out a long time ago. Where did you study to be a detective? Something I should probably detect pretty soon.

Even though my feet were set in cement here.

Evan owned me, and that meant more than I had ever suspected. If anybody could get my feet out of cement, he probably could, if he were correctly motivated. But for the first time I was sort of worried about Pop. How would he manage without me? Maybe he couldn't. Maybe he'd have to sell the business, even though it was his dream to run it. Maybe he'd have to hire somebody. He couldn't afford that ... could he? The one thing he never let me do was the books.

But I had the inventory in my head. I could extrapolate from what he paid to what he charged. I could do that kind of math if I really wanted to. It wouldn't hurt me to know.

"I was good in school," Evan said.

He was still standing half on me and glaring down at me with fierce yellow eyes. His breath was hot against my face and smelled as if he had been chewing mint.

I'd never seen him defensive about anything before. Must be a sore spot. I filed that for later and said, "I never said you weren't. How would I know? It's not something we've talked about yet.''

He rested his head on my chest. ''I was good in school,'' he said, ''but I haven't gone since I left the Hollow.'' He moaned. I stroked his head.

''Akenar,'' Willow said. Her voice was relaxed, more fond than condemning, but I could tell it wasn't a nice word.

''Wurf,'' said Evan. ''I didn't see any human future, so why bother learning anything new? Animals don't need school. . . . Little did I know I would find people I would be interested in.''

''What are you guys talking about now?'' Megan asked.

''School,'' I said. ''If you're really going to be her boyfriend, it would probably be better if she could understand you,'' I told Evan.

''No, only family members and *fetchayim* and those with the gift of tongues can understand me,'' he said. He lifted his head, cocked it, and looked at Megan. *''Fetchayim.* You think—?'' He took his paws off me and sat on the pebbled concrete of pool skirting, studying Megan, who seemed to have forgotten she was embarrassed by her swimsuit and sat cross-legged on the chaise, gripping her toes.

I felt a stab of cold in my stomach. Scared for Megan's sake or just jealous? Or something else? A small wordless feeling from somewhere deep inside flashed through me in a dazzle of white sparks and orange splashes and was gone.

What language was that? Who, inside me, spoke it?

''Nick told me why it's a bad idea, fetching someone you might love,'' Willow said.

''He did? When?'' asked Evan.

''About twenty minutes ago, when we first got to the pool.''

''How many fetchies can you *kilia*, anyway?'' I said,

hoping I was being obscure enough. I couldn't remember the real words they had used.

"Fetchies!" said Evan, and laughed. He licked my hand. "Fetchies!"

"No limit," Willow said.

"Fetch? Kill? Are these the kind of dog commands you people use?" asked Megan.

"Or, I should say, one is limited by how much one can control. How much," Willow said, "or how many."

"They're not dog commands, Megan," I said.

Speaking to Evan, Willow went on, "Nick said if you get it mixed up with romance, you'll never know how the other person really feels about you."

"As *kolestyani*, I could just ask Nick how he feels," said Evan, "and he'd have to tell me."

"Try it," Willow said.

"Don't," I said. "Not just now."

"Nick, tell me how you feel about me."

"Don't, Evan."

He laughed. "How can you say no to me, Nick? What are you hiding?"

"I can say no because you told me before not to let you mess yourself up again, and I'm not hiding anything from you. I'll tell you later."

"What?" He jumped up and sat on my stomach, then glared at me as breath oofed out of me. "I never said any such thing. I would never give my actions over into your hands!"

I looked up into his eyes and tasted a syrup of sadness, because I had handed myself to him almost utterly—was counting on him in ways I didn't even know yet—but he was saying he wouldn't return the favor. I had a clearer idea of where I stood in his regard. Not the almost-equals I had assumed. I closed my eyes and sighed.

"Hey," he said, pawing at my shoulder, "that probably came out wrong. What did I say that makes you think you can stop me from messing up?''

I sifted through my memories. I wasn't sure exactly what he had said, but I remembered feeling it gave me permission to question his orders when I thought they would get him in trouble. I remembered the specific instance from that morning, when I had been wide open to his words because he had told me to be, and he had said I could ask questions if I didn't want to do what he told me to; but this was something even more specific, something he had said in the last little while.

''What was it, Nick? Tell me.'' This time his voice had that hot edge to it I had heard in my own voice and in Willow's when we were persuading people against their wills.

I opened my mouth. '' 'Don't let me do that to you again, Nick.' '' Megan jumped. It was eerie. Evan's voice was lower than mine, but it sounded like Evan's voice coming from my mouth.

''Do what?'' Evan asked.

''Something stupid that will get you into more trouble.''

''I never said that part.''

''I guess I assumed that was what you meant.'' I remembered: he had rendered me dumb and then undid it, and I had assumed he meant I should stop him from making me do things that would make him look foolish. This introduced a new element to our relationship: creative hearing.

I wanted to stop doing everything else and just think about that for a while, but Evan said, ''Why is it stupid for me to want to know how you feel?''

''Because we're not alone,'' I said.

He sat staring down at me for a long moment, then gazed away across the pool. Presently he turned and licked my nose. ''You fascinate me,'' he said.

''I wish I knew what you were talking about,'' said Megan.

"You would be able to if you could deal with him turning back into a human," I said. "On the other hand, I'm not always sure what we're talking about, and I can understand the words." I looked at Kristen. She was still peacefully asleep. I looked toward the office. Adam Lacey was nowhere in evidence, which didn't mean he wasn't watching.

"If he changes into a human, is he going to keep kissing you?" Megan asked.

"Nick, say this to her: a lick is not a kiss. A lick is just a way of getting reacquainted."

I grinned and said it out loud, then added, "Of course, he hasn't said he'd turn back into a human, anyway."

"I'll do it for the rest of the afternoon if she likes. After that ... it depends on what happens."

"The Friday night dance," I said.

"Make Nick teach you how to dance," Willow said.

"Megan can teach him. More fun for both of them."

"It is really a wonderful thing, Evan," said Willow. "You get to hold the other person, but the music sings through both of you. It's a good way to live inside music."

"Get off me." I pushed at Evan until he jumped down off my chest. "Megan, you want to try this again?"

"All right," she said. "I'll close my eyes."

Evan lay down between the chaises. This time I sat up and watched him, but I still couldn't understand what I was seeing. The white wolf stretched out on the cobbles, laid his head between his front paws, and shimmered and pearled and *shifted,* and then there was a tall muscular man with wolf-bite scars and a blond mane. He rolled over and stretched his arms up in the air. "Ahhhh."

I tossed him his swimsuit and he pulled it on. He sat up. "You can be my valet," he said.

At the sound of his voice, Megan opened her eyes and smiled.

"As long as you only have one pair of shorts, I think I can handle it. Megan, this is Evan. Evan, this is Megan. I hope you like each other."

Megan reached out a hand, and Evan took it and licked it. I nudged him with my foot. "Stop it! Shake her hand."

"That's stupid," Evan said. "Your tanning oil is making me hungry," he told Megan.

She put her feet flat on the ground and leaned forward until her face was close to his. She stared into his eyes. He stared back. She reached out, slowly, and touched his hair, snagged her fingers in it, and he leaned his head against her hand and closed his eyes.

"It's a trick?" she whispered.

He moaned like a contented dog, high in his nose. She brushed the hair back from his face, and he opened his eyes and smiled up at her, his open-mouthed grin.

She gripped his head between her hands, then stroked her hands down over his shoulders. He stretched up and laid his head and arms on her lap, and she continued running her hands down his head and shoulders and arms.

I was feeling hot and pleasurably uncomfortable just watching them. "Let's go somewhere else," I said to Willow.

"In the water," she said. She stood up and pulled off her short green shift, revealing an orange suit that was more like a short-sleeved leotard; it covered her except for legs, arms from the elbows down, and neck and head, but it was skintight, and she looked just as great as she had looked and felt the night before.

She grabbed my hand and pulled me up off my chaise and into the water. The shock of cold against my body solved my tent-suit problem. At least I had grabbed a good breath before we jumped in. I made for the bottom of the pool.

Willow followed me down and kissed me. I wondered if she had been getting as stirred up watching Evan and Megan as I had, and then I didn't wonder anything at all, not even how to breathe.

When I opened my eyes I realized we were drifting toward the surface of the water, which was just as well, since my lungs were telling me I was out of air, and pool water didn't sustain me the way lake water sometimes did. Willow let go of my head just as we broke surface, and both of us gasped for breath. She still gripped my shoulder. Her orange leotard had darkened in the water, and it clung even tighter than it had before. I glanced down at her through the distorting magnifying lens of the water, then smiled and glanced away, peeking at Evan and Megan, who weren't talking, but were communicating. I looked at Willow again. She was looking at me. I wanted to finish our broken-off conversation about her baby brother from before, and I wanted to kiss her again.

"Evan!"

Willow and I jerked. I felt my heart speed. The tall muscular man I had only seen through a window at the store and a doorway at Lacey number five stood on the concrete, not too far from where Evan and Megan had been sitting side-by-side and somewhat wrapped around each other on the chaise. Evan turned and rose, stepping between Megan and the speaker. Red flushed his cheeks.

"*A lyllya veshoda,*" the man said, and began a long harangue in the other language. Evan lifted a hand, pushed it against the tide of words, flinched, wilted. Megan stood behind him, her hands against his back to support him, her face showing confusion.

"Hey!" I yelled, pulling myself out of the water onto the lip of the pool. Willow grabbed me, tried to shush me. I shook her off. "Hey!" I said, walking up to this guy and getting in his face.

The man looked through me with his silver-flickery eyes, and continued to speak.

"Hey, cut it out!" I grabbed his arm, pulled on it, trying to get him to shift his attention.

He spat out a few more foreign words, said, "Worthless *nazgar!* You've slacked long enough! Pull your weight! Earn your keep!" in Evan's direction, clicked his teeth together, then stared down into my eyes. The green and blue flickers among the silver drew me in again.

When I woke up this time, I was at the bottom of the pool, my mouth open, trying to breathe water.

My throat was raw by the time I finished coughing up the water, and I felt soggy and tired. Willow stroked my head while tears dripped from her face onto my chest. Evan knelt at my other side, with Megan beside him. Megan had given me the actual mouth-to-mouth; it wasn't something Willow or Evan knew. Megan's face wore no expression.

Willow glanced up at Evan. "How could you let this happen to him?" she said in a small hard voice. It had an edge to it that sliced—at least, I felt it. "He was in your care. How could you?"

Why was she blaming Evan? How could he have stopped it? It had happened so fast.

He had told me I would be safe from his relatives. I had wanted to believe him, but I never really had. How could you stop a snake in midstrike?

Evan looked hollow-eyed and exhausted. He stared back at her. "I didn't stop it," he whispered. "I should have."

Willow gripped my hand hard. "Not again, Evan," she said. "Can't lose him."

"No," he said. He touched Megan's cheek. "Thank the Powers you were here. You gave us grace. Thanks." She stared at him unblinking.

He lifted his hand and laid it on my throat. It was

warm. "Heal," he murmured. He ran his hand over my chest. "You are refreshed. You repair yourself. You feel fine and energized."

I closed my eyes and just breathed in and out for a while. His hand was warm against my chest, almost tingling with a heat that radiated outward, chasing the deep chill out of my blood. I could feel the soreness fading, though the hurt wasn't evaporating instantly this time the way it had before. In a little while my throat didn't feel as though I had swallowed broken glass. I opened my eyes and looked up at Evan.

He said, "Nick. Listen. Take this in. Don't get in front of Uncle Bennet, okay?"

"But he was hurting you!"

"Hey. I'm supposed to protect you, not the other way around. I should have stopped him from—I was too shaken up and couldn't think in time to—don't risk yourself for me, Nick. I mean it."

I could feel that command trying to take hold of me the way his other words had, but it didn't lock in. I tried to figure out why. "Well, I couldn't—I didn't—I don't know, it wasn't like I knew I was going to—" I tasted wolf, remembered how we had exchanged breath that morning, and said, "You're in me."

He patted my chest three times and looked across me at Willow. She wiped her eyes.

"Besides," I said, "*you* didn't hurt me. Your uncle did. It's not your fault. It's not his fault," I told Willow.

She touched my face, my mouth, my chest. She shook her head. "I didn't do anything either," she whispered. "I couldn't think fast enough."

"I'm okay now."

Willow looked across me at Megan. "Thank you. Thank you."

Megan finally blinked. "Once a lifeguard, always a lifeguard," she said.

I said, "Thanks, Megan. I owe you."

"No problem."

"I owe you, too," Evan said to Megan. "Willow's right. Nick's my responsibility." He sighed. "And that's more important than what was happening to me. . . . Nick? I can't be your dog anymore."

"What? I—What? Why?"

"Because I was stupid. As long as I stayed a wolf he couldn't do anything to me. The change web protected me. But I relaxed my web, and he locked me into this"—he thumped himself on the chest—"and took my change web away. Dad give Uncle Bennet a sliver of my snow crystal, and he used it on me." His yellow eyes narrowed as he stared in the direction of cabin five. "I can't shift shapes—my own or anything else's—now. And that is the part of my power that I treasure, the part I use." He shook his head slowly. "This isn't what Mom and Dad meant to happen when they sent us to be with Aunt Elissa and Uncle Bennet. I know it isn't."

"No," said Willow. "You haven't exactly been behaving the way Mom and Dad expected you to, though. I've been doing what they tell me to, and they've been okay to me." She shook her head. "But Uncle Bennet should never have done that to Nick."

Evan looked off into distance, then stared down at me, his mouth grim. He touched my chest. He said, "I told you they smelled wrong, Willow. They're not supposed to hurt people. Let alone Uncle Bennet violated the covenant of salt! You could have died, Nick. Stupid *paragar*. Didn't even think it through. This is wrong."

"Yes," Willow said.

Evan patted my cheek twice. "I am crippled, Nick, but this much I can do. Introduce you to the family and tell them you have shared salt, that they have to leave you whole and well. Megan, eat something with us."

"Oh, no," she said. "No."

Evan sat back and looked at Megan. She crossed her

arms over her chest. "No. I just saw that guy stare at Nick, and Nick jumped into the water and nearly drowned. I like you, Evan, but I don't want to be where you are. I mean, that shapechanging thing was almost too much." She shook her head slowly. "This web stuff, and crystals and all that . . . I'm sorry, but I can't take any more of this."

He reached out and put his hand on her shoulder. "But—" he said.

"No," she said. "No, I . . . no." She got to her feet and walked away, pausing briefly to look at sleeping Kristen and pick up her towel and magazine.

Evan watched her go. When he looked back at me, something had gone from his eyes. "Come on," he said, rising and pulling me to my feet. "Come meet the rest of us."

6

Family Matters

I had left my clothes back by the fallen tree. Without them I didn't feel exactly ready to meet the rest of the family, but Evan was waiting, so I wrapped my towel around my shoulders. He patted my head. "I'll tell them right away about the salt," he said. "Then they should leave you alone."

I glanced toward Kristen, who was still asleep. "Just a minute," I said, and went over and knelt beside her. "It's okay to wake up now," I murmured. "You've had a nice nap and everything's okay." I touched her shoulder gently. She sighed and woke up, smiling at me, then frowning.

"You're not Ian," she said.

"You've been asleep. Didn't want you to sunburn."

"Oh." She yawned, stretched. "Thanks, Nick." She glanced past me at Evan and Willow, and for a moment her pupils snapped wide, then irised down to pinpoints.

"These are my friends Willow and Evan," I said. "Willow you met last night."

"Yes," she said in a toneless voice.

"We have to go."

"Okay."

"You okay?"

She closed her eyes. A single worry line split her forehead. She looked at me and said, "I guess."

"I'm sorry," I said.

"Why?"

I bit my lower lip. I remembered when all I had wanted was for her to look at me, to give me a chance, to maybe take me seriously even though Pop had said it wasn't possible. Now I knew I could tell her to fall asleep and she'd do it, and who knew what else she might do if I told her in just the right voice? I had plenty of ideas left over from nights of staring at the sloping ceiling above my bed and thinking about her. She might even enjoy some of them. Who knew?

"Just am," I said. I had told Willow we were better off not ordering each other around, and I was pretty sure I had meant it. What if I told Kristen to do something and she did it? How would I know whether she liked it? What if I didn't even care?

What if I ordered Pop around the way he had been ordering me around all this time?

"Okay," Kristen said and sat up. "Where'd Megan go?"

"Back to her cabin, I think. We had sort of an argument."

"Wow, I was really out of it." She gripped her forehead as if trying to squeeze knowledge out of it.

I stood up. "You going to be okay?"

She lowered her hand and glared at me. "I feel fine," she said.

I shrugged and went to join Willow and Evan.

Granddad's creel was sitting on a low table in front of the living room fireplace in Lacey cabin five, surrounded by bits of flora—leaves, flowers, pine needles, a rubbery gray-green piece of lungwort, and a moss-covered branch with a small shelf fungus on it—and other weird objects: a clouded crystal as big as my hand, a small brass bowl holding a flickering fire that gave off spice-scented smoke, a slender green glass vase with liquid in it, small bones from I couldn't tell what kind of animal, and tangled woven stuff that reminded me of bird nests and macramé.

The wood-veneer walls of the cabin were draped in silver-gray webs that looked almost spidery but much too big. The webs even hung across the French doors that led out to the porch above the lake. Things that winked and glittered hung in the webs.

All of the other furniture that belonged in this room was gone. Nothing here but a lot of people, the cluttered table, the fireplace, and a bunch of webs big enough to trap toddlers.

Evan's hand rested light and warm against the back of my neck. Willow stood to my right. Everyone else faced us: Aunt Elissa, in something long and black and almost translucent; Uncle Bennet, bulky and ominous in the clothes he had worn to the pool, pseudojeans and a blank white T-shirt; the third grown-up, whom I saw clearly for the first time, a tall thin jeans-and-flannel-shirt-wearing man with sandy hair, sleepy blue eyes, and smile lines, just the sort of man Mariah would have been attracted to if she had met him; pale redheaded Lauren disguised in dirt, staring at Evan as though she had never seen him before, which maybe she hadn't—at least in human shape; and the two stair-step boys, their features blurred mirrors of each other, both dark-haired, the older my height and gray-eyed, the younger a few inches shorter and green-eyed.

"I told you to work, Evan," Uncle Bennet said. "What are you doing here? Why did you bring that?" He stared at me. I didn't want to get trapped by his gaze again. I closed my eyes, turned my head toward Lauren, opened my eyes, and studied her. She looked small and scared, but she offered me a shadow of her tiny smile, an instant of expression and then gone.

"Uncle Rory, I respectfully request hearing," Evan said.

The sleepy-eyed man straightened and crossed his arms over his plaid-shirted chest. "Powers and Presences, aid us and guide us. Evan Seale, I recognize you." His voice was deep and full.

Evan put his hand on top of my head. "This is Nick Verrou. Lauren gave him salt privilege yesterday. I submit that Bennet and Elissa have violated that covenant grievously though unknowingly and in three different ways. First, they have both hurt him; they have not respected his salt privilege. Second, Elissa blinded him; she has not respected his personhood. Third, Bennet came close to killing him! They have not respected his life."

"Bennet and Elissa, how say you?"

Elissa said, "I have acknowledged my error and made my plea for forgiveness, which this person said he accepted."

"Nick Verrou, is this true?" Rory asked.

"Yes," I said. Elissa's gaze was on me, and I could almost feel the burn of her regard. I wished she would forget that I existed.

"Elissa mentioned some boy had salt privilege, but I didn't know it was this one," Bennet said. "All I have ever done to him was put the wander-eye on him. Hardly murder or attempted murder."

"Evan?" said Rory.

"Because of Bennet's wander-eye, Nick wandered into the pool and nearly drowned," Evan said, his voice low and hot. "If not for the help of a *Domishti* girl, Nick might have died."

"Nick Verrou, is this true?"

"Yes," I whispered. I touched my throat, remembering the crushed-glass feel after I had coughed up the water.

"I gave him no direction toward the water," Bennet said.

"*Akenar,* water was the only direction away from you!" cried Evan, his fists rising.

"Evan!" said Rory.

Willow's hand crept into mine.

Evan stiffened. His hands opened and sank to his sides. "I submit," he said and took a breath. "I—my words were not well thought out. I apologize. I submit that Uncle Bennet did not knowingly try to kill Nick, but that thoughtlessness is its own kind of violation."

"Nick Verrou, do you require healing?" Rory asked.

"I don't think so," I said. "Evan healed me." I wished Rory wouldn't keep talking to me. I didn't like having Bennet and Elissa staring at me the way they were.

"Nick Verrou, do you wish restitution?"

I wondered what restitution might involve—treating Bennet and Elissa the way they had treated me? A cash prize? Or what?—but before I could ask, Evan said, "What we ask is that Nick be left alone, as is his clear right by salt privilege."

Rory closed his eyes. He murmured something that sounded like a prayer. We all waited.

The air tightened. The fire in the little bowl flickered a sign that looked like writing in Hebrew or Sanskrit to me. Nobody else was looking at it. I glanced at Willow. Her eyes were wide and watchful, her gaze fixed on Rory's tranced face. Evan was staring at Rory too, his eyes hot and yellow. I wondered if I should say anything, but thought probably not. I watched the fire some more. A little face flickered above it and smiled at me. I shrugged. It stuck its tongue out, then vanished. I looked around the room. Lauren put her index finger in front of her lips. I figured she hadn't seen the fire doing tricks.

No one spoke.

The longer I stood there, the worse I felt about the whole thing. I had thought we were just going to come and tell these people to leave me alone and get out of here. This was way too involved for me. Meanwhile, outside, Saturday afternoon was ticking away. The ironic thing was that if I were watching all this stuff through a window and it was happening to someone else, I would have been fascinated. At least at first.

Finally Rory opened his eyes and looked around the room, even though as far as I could tell, nothing had changed. "I do not perceive any clear leading from the Presences and Powers. Does anyone else? Do any have more to say in this matter?"

"This boy is interfering in the collection of *skilliau*," said Elissa, my fan club. "I wish him no harm, but I wish him at a distance."

"I submit that my aunt speaks in ignorance," Evan said. Willow squeezed my hand.

"How dare you?" Elissa cried.

"What evidence do you have?" said Evan.

"This boy has been spying on our invocations and enticements, and seeing more than he should be able to—he is one of those *Domishti* with extra sight, it seems—and even though we use the forms that for years have succeeded, this time the *skilliau* resist us. Give me another explanation."

Willow glanced sideways at me, her eyebrows rising. I tried to remember if I had ever discussed spying with her. I thought probably not. I looked down at our clasped hands; she didn't pull her hand away.

"I don't have another explanation yet," Evan said slowly. "I'm working on a really great one."

"I'll stay away," I said. "I won't watch anymore. I'll leave you people alone."

"I don't know if we can permit that," said Rory.

"What?"

"You know too much. We will have to make a decision about how to deal with you."

"Hey!" said Evan.

"I don't know anything! I don't know your language, I don't know what you people are doing when I *do* watch you, I don't even know where you came from. I'd like to know, but I really have no idea."

Rory smiled at me. Mariah would have melted if she saw that smile. Lots of nice teeth in it. "I sympathize, Nick Verrou. We don't know anything about you either. I don't think what I need from you is anything serious or painful—just a minor binding that wouldn't even violate your salt privilege."

"Stop it," said Evan. "No one binds or unbinds Nick but me."

"This is a family matter," Rory said. "I am glad you brought it to our attention. You have not been acting in the best interests of family, however, and you have no authority here, Evan Seale."

Evan's eyes widened. He stepped forward, sliding half in front of me. "I have fetch right," he said.

"What?" Bennet said. His voice held thunder.

"We do not recognize that right," said Rory. "This changes the whole complexion of the problem. It is you, Evan Seale, who have violated salt privilege."

"I have done Nick no harm, nor ever intend to."

"The very existence of fetch-bond is abomination enough," said Rory, "and demands an unbinding, unless you release it of your own will. I would advise you so to do."

Evan turned his head so I could see his profile, and looked me in the eye. "Nick, do you want me to unbind you?"

"No," I said. Evan had said he would protect me from these people, and that he wouldn't hurt me himself. So far the only one he'd protected me from was Willow. Maybe the others would think twice now that they knew he and I were linked, or maybe they wouldn't. Even the chance that they would think twice was something.

Anyway, I didn't want to lose my connection to Evan. If I lost my connection to Evan, I would fall back into my own life, and that wasn't where I wanted to be, given a choice.

If I lost my connection to Evan, I didn't know where

our friendship would go, and I was worried about that. Also about how I would relate to Willow.

Rory made a series of gestures with his fingers. "Say again, Nick Verrou, and this time, clear of compulsion. You may speak freely, without fear of retribution."

"No, I don't want Evan to unbind me," I said. Sky blue flame shot from my mouth as I spoke. I clapped my hand over my mouth, only worrying that I might burn myself when it was too late, but I couldn't even feel the fire.

"Truth," whispered Rory. Blue flared from his mouth, bigger than the whispered word.

I dropped my hand. "I wish the rest of you would stop messing around with me," I said, still spitting blue fire. "I never did anything to you." This time the fire was a little more green.

"Watching is doing," said Elissa, in blue.

"Oh," I said. Blue with a streak of white through it. "What is this stuff, anyway?" White flame edged with blue.

"Truthspeak, a power of air," Willow said in blue. "Blue is true."

"Quiet!" said Rory, blue laced through with black. I don't know what the others felt, but after he said that, my tongue was locked in place the way it had been earlier when Evan had told me to shut up. Rory made a series of gestures again. The people around him relaxed. "We need to deliberate," he said. His words had no color in them. Now I knew why people had relaxed. Evidently truthspeak was not a real popular power. "You may speak and consider."

I could move my tongue again, and I was relieved. I decided to get as far away from these people as I could. Orders from Evan intrigued me, but orders from a room full of hostile strangers—

Rory said, "Nick Verrou, go to sleep."

My eyes fell shut and my balance wavered. Evan caught me before I collapsed. I blinked at him, remembered him telling me that other peoples' words would slide off me. Though the "quiet" one hadn't. Maybe other people's orders could get to me if I thought they could. I took a deep breath, and stood up. "Stop it," I said to Rory. Fear and anger simmered inside me. I thought of Mariah's pink unicorn. I wanted to go back and beat myself up for selling it to her. I thought about Kristen, sleeping by the pool because I had told her to, and I wavered. Going to sleep was better than going nuts, wasn't it? "Deliberate all you want. I'm leaving." I slid out of Evan's grasp and stomped out of the cabin.

The instant the door slammed behind me I wished I had grabbed Granddad's creel while I had the chance, but then I thought, *Those are scary people in there,* and, amazed that I had managed to walk out on them, I ran.

I wasn't ready to go home to the store, though I couldn't figure out why not. I ran to the fort instead. I changed out of the wet swimsuit and into my clothes, hanging towel and suit on some outreaching roots. Then I sat holding the calming rock in the shade of the root fort for a while, trying to figure things out.

How had it gotten to the point that all these strangers felt they could boss me around? Did they do this to everybody, or was I a special case? Did I invite this stuff? Because I said yes to Evan, did that make me a target for the rest of them? Should I maybe talk to the Laceys' produce driver and leave Sauterelle right now?

Presently I stopped wondering about anything and just cradled the gray rock between my hands, occasionally touching it to my forehead. I breathed. I tasted air and watched shadows and sun move across the forest floor. All the tension drained out of me. I felt unreasonably calm and cheerful.

Small flashes of memory came when I touched the stone to my forehead. Mom taking me to a clearing in the woods when I was very small—some other woods, because we weren't living at Sauterelle yet—and playing "find the stone" with me. She would show me sixteen different little rocks, all of which looked the same, then ask me which one was different. I would touch the one that hummed—though it was a feeling hum rather than a heard hum: a silent hum. She would make me hide my eyes, and then she would hide the humming stone somewhere, and I would track it for her. She always laughed and touched foreheads with me after we played.

Sometimes she took the special green stone, the one that leaked light, and touched it to my forehead.

Strange. I hadn't thought about Mom's stone games in a long, long time.

When I looked up and saw Willow standing there, I smiled at her.

"What are you doing, Nick?" she said in a hushed voice.

"What does it look like?"

"Using *skilliau*."

I smiled again, stroking the rock. "Maybe," I said.

"Have you been laughing at us all along?"

"No," I said. "Definitely not laughing."

She took two steps toward me. "Where did you get that?" she murmured.

"Found it here." I held it out to her. "It's nice."

She knelt before me and reached out a hesitant hand, almost touched the rock, then lifted her hand away.

"Why are you and Evan scared of it?" I asked. "It's a rock. It's a nice rock."

"I must . . ." She kissed her thumb, then used it to sketch a sign in the air above the rock.

The rock started humming and grew warmer. "Wha—!" I said.

She murmured to it, a liquid string of sounds that sounded the way caresses feel. Radiant warmth flowed from the rock into my hands and all through me—not enough heat to be uncomfortable, which was odd, because the day was warm enough as it was; the rock made me feel as though I were wrapped in clean down quilts and sipping hot chocolate on a cold day. It was better than comfortable; it was a dream of comfort come true.

Willow, on her knees, edged closer. She said a sentence and made another thumb gesture, then waited. The warmth kept pouring from the rock into me. I saw when the comfort reached across space and touched her. Her face relaxed and her shoulders lowered. She held open hands out to me and I placed the rock in them.

"Oh, thank you. Thank you," she murmured. I figured she was talking to the rock and not me. I didn't care. The rock had me convinced that I was going to be warm and comfortable for the rest of my life; I could feel its energy even though I wasn't touching it.

Eyes closed, Willow touched the rock to her breastbone. "Thank you," she murmured. "Thank you, Nick."

"Me?" I said.

"Thank you. Thank you, Powers and Presences." She took a deep breath, let it out in a long contented sigh. Gently she set the rock on the dried ferns between us. She put her hands flat against the ground and asked a question in the other language. A second later I felt the answer, and it was yes.

Willow looked across the rock at me, her eyes alight. Then she leaned forward and kissed me. She tasted like clover flowers. Touching the rock, she said, "Look, I'll give this to them, and then maybe they'll lay off you and Evan."

I frowned. I had handed her the rock, but I didn't think that meant I had given it to her. I had thought I was just loaning it to her—if it were mine to loan to anyone, which I wasn't sure of. "And that's okay with the rock?"

She nodded. "It agreed to be moved," she said. She

picked up the rock and made a sign above its surface, smiling down at it like a woman looking at her own baby. "First piece of luck we've had since we got here."

"Luck had nothing to do with it."

I looked up and saw Evan standing at the edge of the smoothed earth of the fort.

"It's Nick," he said.

"What do you mean?" Willow asked, setting the rock down.

"The reason the Keyes can't find *skilliau* now. This is my theory, anyway. They've been mean to Nick, and the *skilliau* like Nick."

Willow stared at me, eyes wide. She flicked a glance at Evan, then back at me. "Nick, do you know where more *skilliau* are?" she whispered.

I couldn't remember other rocks that had behaved exactly like this one had. On the other hand, I had touched or picked up a lot of rocks around the lake over the years, and not always for reasons I understood. Some of them hummed silently, and some of them felt warm, and some of them just called to me somehow. Mom had always been interested when I found a special rock. She had hugged me, but she hadn't touched the rocks themselves. I remembered hiding some of them, throwing some of them into the water, taking some of them home and having Pop throw them away because they were "clutter." "I'm not sure," I said. "Maybe. I want to learn how to do what you just did, Willow. It made the rock stronger, even more awake. . . . What happened after I left?"

Evan dropped to sit beside us. "Lauren got in trouble for sharing salt with you. I was chastised for fetching you. I'm supposed to know better. As if they never noticed that I don't do anything they tell me. They're sure that Willow has made mistakes, too, though they don't know what those mistakes might be. Aunt Elissa still wants to punish you for making her wrong. Uncle

Rory isn't my favorite person, but he's more fair than Aunt Elissa or Uncle Bennet. He's not sure what they should do. He did some more guidance queries, but there were no leadings. It really bothered him. Bet they wish they had a *krifter* with them now. Still, they're paying attention to all the wrong things.''

"What should they be looking at?" Willow asked.

"Elissa and Bennet were warded, and Nick saw them. Elissa dismisses it as extra sight—doesn't that mean anything to her? Lauren was warded and Nick saw *her*. Lauren is intelligent and curious. But shy. Maybe that's why she didn't tell them about you and the salt privilege before or ask any questions.''

"Lauren said maybe I had second sight," I said.

"Second sight? What's that?" Evan asked, frowning. "Extra sight. Second sight. I haven't heard of this before."

I said, "There are all kinds of stories about people with second sight. Never thought I was one of them. They can see fairies and stuff like that."

"What's a fairy?"

"It's a small magical being that—heck, I don't know. I always thought they were made up, anyway. Maybe not." I looked around. The only magical being I had seen besides this family was the face above the flames at Lacey number five. There was a lot of vocabulary I didn't have yet.

"I don't know about second sight, but you can see more than most people. Why aren't they concentrating on this information? If we were home, everybody would notice this stuff. They'd call a *krifter* and see what they could find. Uncle Bennet could have sent to Southwater for a *krifter,* if he were only curious instead of condemning. Anybody could check Nick's signature, but so far only you and I have done that, Willow. The Keyes just keep wondering how they can make Nick shut up and go away."

Willow frowned. "You can see people when they're warded, Nick?" she said.

"Uh-huh."

"And you've been spying on us."

I stared at the ground for a moment, then looked up at her. "That's what I do," I said. "Or did." I hunched my shoulders and looked toward the forest. "That's what. . . that's what you do if it's no fun at home and you don't have people to talk to. That's what you do if you really, really need to know what makes people tick. That's what you do if you don't want things to happen without warning, like people acting like everything's normal and then leaving without telling you." I touched my lips, wondering where these words had come from and if they made sense. I couldn't remember if I had always wanted to be a detective or just since Mom left.

The trees I was watching weren't moving much. I glanced at Willow.

Willow stared at me, not frowning, not smiling. I remembered how beautiful she had looked, naked in the morning light with the water shining on her skin. "Where do you go when you disappear?" I asked.

She blinked. "I disappear?"

"Evan said it's a woman's mystery."

For a moment she stared at me, frowning. Then her eyes widened and her face flushed. "You were watching me yesterday morning?"

"You are so beautiful."

"Rrrr!" She put her hands around my throat, but she didn't squeeze. Having some idea of her strength, I was grateful. "Don't do that again!"

"I won't." I cleared my throat. Her hands were warm against my skin. "I didn't even know you then." So much had changed, so fast. . . .

"Rrrr!" Her fingers tightened a fraction. "You . . . were . . . watching me, and the Presences didn't . . ." She let go of my neck and sat back on her heels, resting her hands on her thighs. She stared at the *skilliau* rock between us. "Presences didn't warn me."

"See what I mean?" Evan said.

She picked up the rock. It spoke comfort. She held it out to Evan, who sketched a sign with his thumb and accepted it. His face relaxed. I moved my thumb the way Evan had. It didn't look quite right. Maybe later they'd show me. I wondered if I could get a thing like that to work.

Willow said, "Nick, you have voice. And vision. And now—some kind of *skilliau*-speak. What else?"

I shook my head. "I don't know what any of these things are, except the salesman thing. Voice."

"Wish I knew how to *krift* beyond signature," said Willow.

Shadows had stretched until there was almost no sunlight left where we were sitting. I fished my watch out of my pocket and looked at it, then strapped it on. Almost five-thirty. I should be home by now, figuring out what we were going to have for dinner. "Evan?"

"Mmm?"

"The meeting—did they come to some sort of decision about how they plan to treat me?"

"Rory gave Aunt Elissa permission to cast a silence on you," he said. "So I want you to remember what I told you, Nick. Whatever she casts at you will slide off. She has no power over you. You're mine."

But that hadn't saved me, not when Rory told me to speak truth or be quiet. On the other hand, once I remembered about it, I had been able not to fall asleep. "How can I figure out what Elissa's doing in time to remember that you told me it won't work?"

"You shouldn't have to remember. It should just work."

"But it didn't."

His pupils flashed wide. For a second I thought he was mad at me. It occurred to me that that could be scary, considering the hold he had on me. "It didn't," he said slowly.

"Blue fire came out of my mouth."

"Yes," he whispered.

"Maybe the bond is different because Nick is *Ilmonish,*" Willow said after a moment.

"So we don't know what it does, really," Evan said. "And we don't have time to experiment. They will be casting an unbinding at us. It's just the sort of moral decision they would make, without regard to the people involved. They know what's right. And they're strong in their disciplines. Maybe I should loose you now." He pressed the rock against his forehead.

"No," I said. I had an awful vision of many things unraveling. If he freed me, would everything he had done to me while I was his come undone? Would my throat be glass, my hands scuffed? Would my head be confused about who he was and how I could relate to him? Would the energy he had gifted me with that morning evaporate? Would the strong thread between us break, leaving us strangers? I didn't want to find out.

Evan sighed. He lowered the rock. I reached out and touched it. It calmed me. Evan said, "This morning I thought there was nothing they could do to us. I didn't realize Uncle Bennet had a piece of my snow crystal."

"What's a snow crystal?"

"It's a . . . it's hard to explain. It's, well, it starts out as—I mean, it's this, it's something your parents make for you when you're just born, or some parents do, anyway, and they, it's, you have it with you and it collects some of your, well, your *skilliau* maybe, and then you can use it later."

"Or it's a well of memories," Willow said.

"Kind of a . . . soul diary, maybe." Evan sighed again. "Most of the folks at home don't make them for their kids much anymore because they can be used to hurt you if you don't keep them safe."

"But Mama and Papa . . ." Willow looked at Evan,

and he looked back. "When we were little, things were different. People weren't scared of each other the way they are now. I was almost glad we left when we did, except I didn't get to"—she looked at me—"I didn't get to do what I meant to. Chapel Hollow just got scarier and scarier. Say what you will, Evan, South-water Clan is cleaner, the way it works between people. If somebody does something to you, at least you know why."

He said, "Have they been using your snow crystal against you, Willow?"

"No," she said. "I've been trying to do the right things. I don't know if Papa gave them a piece of mine, anyway. You were the problem child."

"What?" he yelped.

"I heard them talking. Mama and Papa were worried about you."

"You're the one who was always fetching people, bringing boys home, letting them loose, making trouble!"

"I had a reason for that. . . . You're too old to be animaling all the time. You never would learn how to talk to people, except babies, and that was forbidden. Babies have to know they're alone so they'll learn to talk like people. You can't keep making them feel like it's okay for them not to understand other grown-ups."

"Babies need to be protected," he said. "You know that, Willow."

She stared at him. "Oh," she whispered. Her face crumpled.

Evan handed her the calming rock. She pressed it to her chest. After a moment her breathing evened out again. "I never knew that was why you—"

"You had a reason for all those boys? You never seemed to know what to do with them once you got them home."

"Great-aunt Scylla was teaching me just before she died. She gave me a prophecy. She said a man would come—a woman would bring him, as a fetch—and then we would know who killed Kenrick.'' She put the stone down. ''Our baby brother, Nick,'' she said. ''The sweetest little child I ever knew. Somebody killed him.''

''Killed him?'' said Evan, his face going pale. ''I thought he fell. I didn't want any of the others to fall.''

''On Farewell Night Scylla and I talked to Kenrick's Presence, before he went back to the Source. Someone pushed him down the stairs.''

''Oh, Willow! Why didn't you tell me this before?''

''Scylla told me not to tell anybody. It only hurts. Nobody could have had a reason for doing that, not one we could understand. I thought if I could just find the right fetch . . .'' She touched my hand.

I wanted to be a detective. I wasn't sure I could detect anything in their home environment, though. Too many new rules. ''How long ago did this happen?''

''Ten years ago,'' said Evan. He looked at Willow. ''*Faskish*. If you had told me at the time, I could have sniffed out the truth.''

''Ten years ago, you were too young to change into a wolf. And the prophecy didn't say anything about *you* finding the truth. I kept thinking *I* would do it. Anyway, everything switched around. I'm not sure when they'll let us go home now, if ever. Maybe I'm not the woman in the prophecy. Somebody else will do it. We *will* find out. I probably shouldn't be telling you now. Except . . .'' She touched the *skilliau* stone. ''It's all right. It's finally all right to talk about it. Evan, Kenrick was okay before he left us. He was with other Presences who were taking good care of him.'' She swallowed.

''You're sure?''

''I'm sure. I could let him go after that. He was ready to go to the next place.''

They sat quiet for a while. Willow stroked the comfort stone, then handed it to Evan. I tried to imagine what it would feel like to know somebody had killed your little brother, and decided it would be horrible. I tried to figure out whether there was anything I could do to help or to change things for either of them, and I couldn't think of a thing.

At last Willow sighed and said, "So I don't know which of us was the problem child. It wasn't just you with the babies. Mama and Papa were worried because you weren't growing up yourself or taking responsibility for anything. You weren't strengthening the thread that binds the bones, or even thinking about wife-seek."

"That's ridiculous!"

"Think about it," Willow said.

Evan shook his head. "I don't see why everybody has to start a family right away. There ought to be time to play and explore."

"Anyway, you figured out how to do that, by going wolf before Uncle Bennet could stop you."

"And then I changed back. I can't believe I was so stupid," he said, looking down the length of his human body as if he'd like to stab it.

Willow reached to make a sign above the rock. Waves of comfort rolled from it. Evan's shoulders relaxed and so did mine. "You didn't know," she said. "You didn't know Uncle Bennet had the snow crystal."

"I think I knew . . . something. I knew it wasn't safe to be human. Not around these people."

"That's not fair," Willow said. "We hardly knew them. They've been good to me. How can you expect them to be good to you when you defy them at every turn? They want to help you, but you won't let them."

"They smell wrong." He growled. "Look what they did to Nick."

"It was awful, but it was an accident." She touched my arm, touched a pulse point in my neck. "He's okay."

"I don't want them messing with me. I think they're

accident prone. You didn't even see what Elissa did to Nick."

"No," Willow said. "I didn't even know, except what you said during the hearing."

"She took away his—"

"Listen," I said, climbing to my feet. "I have to go home now and fix dinner." I didn't want to talk about that morning. I was glad Evan had helped me. I would rather Willow didn't know just how scared and helpless I could be.

Evan said, "Anyway, I don't think they're very wise, and I don't trust them."

"I'll be more careful," Willow said. She glanced at me. "I don't trust them either, not anymore."

I studied Evan. Pop was going to wonder what had happened to my dog, I thought. A mourning ache lodged in my chest for another dead dream. "Why don't you just call your parents and tell them you don't want to live like this?"

"We don't have phones at home," Evan said. He took Willow's hand and placed the rock in it, then rose. "I don't have the skill to contact Mom and Dad without going home and seeing them face to face."

"There isn't some sort of crystal ball thingie you guys could do?"

Willow smiled at me. She shook her head. She stood up.

"Write a letter?" I asked.

"Could," said Evan. "Probably that wouldn't get anything to happen fast enough. Maybe I should do it anyway. You never know if a letter's going to make it, though. The postman doesn't like going to our house."

"How far away is home?"

"Two hundred miles. You got a car, Nick?" asked Evan.

I shook my head. "I wish. So you're stuck?"

"I'm not going back," Evan said. "Stuck I may be, but I'm not going back to that cabin."

I said, "I don't know what Pop will say if you come home with me."

"I can sleep in the woods. This is a good place right here."

I looked at him. "You don't have clothes. You don't have food. This is stupid."

"I can hunt."

"How?"

He grinned at me, his eyes alight. A few seconds slipped by while we all thought about it, and his grin faded. *"Faskish!"*

"Come on. I've got some clothes you could wear, even if your ankles stick out the bottom. I can get you food. You could at least come to supper. I'm pretty sure I could sneak you into one of the rooms in the motel, too."

"Faskish," he muttered. "I've got skills. I could . . . *faskish.* I could manage. I don't like being inside."

"Come on," I said, nudging his shoulder with mine. "Figure it out later. Willow? Is it safe for you to go back?"

"I'll be fine," she said. "I'll give them this." She held up the rock. "I'm going to see if I can get Evan's crystal back from Uncle Bennet."

"Don't make him mad at you," Evan said.

"I won't." She grabbed my shoulder, pulled me close, and kissed me. "Catch you later."

"So," Evan said as we headed down to the trail. "We're alone."

"Yep."

"God, it's irritating not to know what's going on."

"What?" I had thought that was my line. All these people speaking a foreign language. Even when they defined things for me I didn't understand them. And they had foreign skills nobody could have guessed at, and foreign priorities. Usually I had a much better idea of what was going through people's heads.

Now I had some inkling of his family's plans, but I guessed we wouldn't know what they were really up to until we felt the effects, and that bothered me. If I were already a detective, I could have left a listening device in cabin five. Going back to spy on them seemed way too risky—okay, so I could see them when they were warded, but they somehow knew I was watching, too. At least, Aunt Elissa had known.

I remembered telling Rory I would stay away and not watch them anymore, but he hadn't accepted my promise. And I hadn't known then that watching them might be necessary to survival. The need to know burned hotter in me than it ever had.

Evan said, "The air is full of smells and sounds, but I hardly know they're there. I would know who, where, and what right now if I were myself. What everyone is cooking for dinner, who's out wandering around, and half the time, why, and who they're with. I'd be hearing every little creature in the brush. They would smell like dinner. I'd smell where anything had peed and I could tell who they were and what they had eaten and drunk. I feel deaf and scent blind. Half the world has gone invisible."

"Wow," I said. He felt just like I did, in a weird way.

"Eh," he said, shrugging. "So anyway—tell me how you feel about me."

"I love you and I worry about you," I said before I thought. Then I thought. Then I felt the heat flush my cheeks, and I walked staring at the ground.

"Ah!" He touched my neck. We kept walking. "Nick, do me a favor."

"What." My voice came out low.

"If I tell you to do something, and it's going to mess me up or make me look stupid, don't do it, okay?"

"What if I can't tell?"

"You don't have to be prescient. Wait a sec. I wonder if you are prescient. Do you have prophetic dreams?

I wonder if I'm already totally screwed up because I fetched somebody who's not even *Domishti*."

"I don't think I have prophetic dreams." I had had strange dreams while sleeping on Father Boulder, but they hadn't predicted the future.

"Doesn't matter. You're a student of human behavior. If you *can* tell, when I order you to do something, that it will make me look stupid, it's okay for you not to do the thing. You were right about this one."

"You're not as embarrassed as I am."

"I'm not embarrassed at all, but it might have confused Megan. Look, Nick. I chased you first."

"What?"

"I spied on you before you spied on any of us. I went into the store to find you because you smelled so interesting. I don't even want people, but I wanted you. I think the Presences had something to do with all this. I didn't know I wanted another little brother until I found you."

The air was cooling as the sun seeped away. I looked at him in the fading light, and he smiled. He roughed my hair. "I wish I knew another kind of binding."

"There's something I know." I felt much calmer now that he had redefined everything so it was safe. The fierce wild love I felt for him had confused me. It was completely different from the way I felt about Willow, but it was just as strong, or stronger. I knew it was mostly about relating to him as a wolf, and I hadn't been able to figure out how it would translate into relating to him as a human person, until now.

Blood brotherhood. That would work.

"Really?" he said.

"I'll explain it to you later." We had reached the road. I looked at the store. The neon beer signs glowed bright as dusk settled around us. There was a CLOSED sign in the front window of the store.

"Wait, Nick," Evan said.

"What? I have to start dinner."

"Sit down."

I dropped to the dirt, and he squatted beside me.

"It's time to remember now what I told you to forget before."

"What?" He had told me to forget something? And I had forgotten it! Maybe this wasn't such a hot relationship after all.

"Your mother's here."

It came back to me. I remembered the spinning panic I had felt, dizzying as the whirl of a top, when I couldn't stop long enough to make sense.

He gripped my shoulder. "Listen. You're safe. You're okay. You're still mine, at least for now. Whatever it is about her that scares you, I'll do my best to protect you from it, okay?"

"Scares me?"

His eyebrows rose. "What would you call it?"

"Scares me," I said, tasting it, trying it for a match with what I felt. "Why should I be scared of her? All she did was leave."

He stared at me a moment, then pulled me into a clumsy embrace, startling me. What? What? He pushed me back before I could tell him to cut it out. "I wish we still had that *skilliau*," he muttered. "It was a good one for calm. Remember to breathe, okay? I'll be there."

"Maybe we won't even run into her," I said. I pushed to my feet and he rose beside me.

I led Evan around back of the building and peered in through the window in the kitchen door. The lights were on, and so was the radio; I could hear country-western music faintly through the door. Granddad was sitting at the table, studying that morning's paper. Pop was nowhere in sight.

I glanced toward the motel and saw that a dusty station wagon was parked next to the office. Someone checking in for the night; Pop would be busy. I opened the kitchen door and held it for Evan.

"Hi, Granddad," I said.

He looked up and smiled at me. "Have a good day, son?"

"Mostly. Granddad, this is my friend Evan."

Granddad held out his hand. "Pleased to meet you," he said.

"Thank you, sir," said Evan, shaking hands with him. "Likewise."

Granddad held his head sideways and stared at Evan for a long minute. Evan stood quiet under his scrutiny.

"You have a look about you," Granddad said.

I examined Evan sideways too. He looked like a wiry guy—plenty of muscles, but not bodybuilding muscles, flatter and tighter somehow—pretty tall, maybe chilled, though his swimsuit was dry and he didn't look goose-bumpy. In this light his body hair wasn't as bright or apparent as it had been under the sun. His face still looked something other than strictly human. His eyes were spooky looking, the yellow of goats' eyes or cats' eyes. He raised his dark brows as if asking a question.

"A look of what, Granddad?" I said.

Granddad's gaze wandered. "A boy needs a dog," he said. He shook his head and looked at the newspaper.

Creepy. "I'll be right down to start dinner, but I need to find Evan some clothes first. You hungry?"

"Got rats gnawing in my belly."

I wondered if Mariah or Pop had given him any lunch. Come to that, it had been a long time since breakfast, and Mom's arrival had spooked me out of getting myself a lunch. I had rats gnawing in my belly too.

I got a bag of potato chips out of the cupboard, poured it into a big stainless steel bowl, set it in front of Granddad, then got him a can of Coke from the fridge. "I'll get you something hot real soon, Grand-dad." I grabbed a handful of chips, threw them into my mouth, and chewed them just enough so they would fit down my throat. I grabbed a second handful and offered some to Evan, who shook his head.

Granddad ate some chips and nodded, looking back at the paper. He was still nodding gently as we went up the stairs.

I led Evan up to the attic. Pop hated waste; he saved everything he had ever owned. He was taller than I was, and in earlier years had been skinnier than he was now. There were trunks and suitcases and boxes that held clothes in the attic. Maybe some of Pop's castoffs would fit Evan better than anything of mine could.

I pulled the chain on the hanging lightbulb and looked around. Evan lifted his head and sniffed, his eyes wide. Dust was heavy everywhere except near one big steamer trunk with a bowed lid. I knelt and looked at footprints that made a trail through the dust. Bigger than mine; bigger than Granddad's. Must be Pop's. Curious, I headed for the trunk, tested the lid. It was locked.

"There are things in there," Evan said.

"Eh?"

"Things," he said. "Strange things." He stretched out a hand, held it above the trunk a second, then pulled it back.

"How strange? What kind of things?"

"Something with a touch of *skilliau*," he said. "A pledge, I think."

"Pop has something with magic in it?" I thought about that for a minute. It didn't make sense. "I wonder when he comes up here," I said. Maybe while I was minding the store or maybe after we had all gone to bed.

Imagine Pop having a secret and me not even knowing about it. I didn't spend much time watching Pop because I figured I knew him so well that nothing he did would surprise me. Now I was surprised. I wanted to open the trunk and see what made him tick. How could he have something with magic in it? I had been thinking this over, and I was pretty sure my magic heritage came from Mom. Even though Evan wouldn't touch the trunk, I reached for the latch again. There might be some way I could tease it open. Maybe if I talked to it in the right tone of voice. Failing that, I could straighten a paperclip and—

Then I had a strange thought. Pop had a secret. Maybe Pop needed a secret.

"Leave it," I said to Evan, but mostly to myself.

I opened one of the other trunks where I vaguely remembered having looked when I was younger, probably right after Mom left. I had been looking for traces of her then, thinking that something horrible must have happened to her. Something or someone had stolen her. It was the only explanation I could understand, at first. I had thought maybe she left a note or a map or something. I had searched. In this trunk I had found only abandoned clothes, but that was good enough for right now. The trunk with strange things in it was new.

I found some bib overalls. I had never seen Pop wear overalls, but he must have at some point. These ones showed wear at the knees, some dark oily stains on the stomach where it would have been natural to wipe your hands off after doing a dirty job, and hand-stitched repairs near the pockets. He must have carried a lot of heavy awkward things in his pockets. I pulled the overalls out of the trunk and held them up to Evan, who was still stroking the air above the locked trunk, his eyebrows lowered in a frown of concentration. The overalls looked like a decent fit.

"Come on. Try these on. I have to make dinner."

He looked at me, one eyebrow up, a faint smile quirking his mouth.

"Please," I said. "Look, Pop just started trying to trust me, and I've already let him down. I really need to get downstairs."

He took the overalls and slipped into them, with some confusion about how to fasten the shoulder straps, so I did it for him, and showed him that he could close the buttons at the sides if he wanted to.

"I like these," he said, pushing his hands down into the pockets. "They don't bind anywhere."

They looked odd on him; maybe that was just because I still felt like a boy dressing his dog in a sweater, or maybe anything normal would look odd on him. I closed my eyes for a second and then looked at him from a fresh perspective. Decided I was right: anything normal would look weird on him. He might look all right if he was in a black body stocking with spiky silver armor over it, or maybe in one of those bright, wild ski outfits athletes wore in the Olympics. All right, but never normal.

"What?" he said.

I shook my head. "It'll have to do."

"I like it better than most clothes." He studied the bib, popped open a snap on one of the tool/pencil pockets. "Lots of places to carry things," he said.

"Yep." I turned back to the clothes trunk, dug out a worn plaid flannel shirt. "Here's a shirt, for if you get cold. You put it on under the straps."

"How?"

"Take the straps down. Come on." I tossed him the shirt and headed for the door, let him out first, went back and turned off the light, then clattered down the stairs after him toward the sound of country-western music.

When we reached the kitchen Pop was still not there. A tightness in my chest loosened a little. Granddad had eaten all the potato chips, and he still looked hungry. I gave him a banana, starting the peeling process for him. I checked out the fridge and the cupboards even though there was nothing I hadn't put there yesterday. Couldn't make sandwiches two days in a row, but I needed something quick. I got out spaghetti noodles, put a big pot of water on to boil, and dumped a jar of marinara sauce into a saucepan to heat. I checked the freezer and found some sausages, started them thawing and frying. Turned around to find Evan watching me.

"What?" I said.

He gave me half a smile and shook his head. "What else do you do?"

Like there was something special about cooking? Or maybe he was talking about something else. I glanced at my watch. It was almost six-thirty. We usually ate around now. Where was Pop? Not that I wanted him to show up any faster than he was going to, but what would he say about Evan? What if he said, "Another mouth to feed? Forget it!"

Whatever time Pop arrived, he'd be expecting dinner, ready. Thinking about speed healing, speed mind-altering, I asked Evan, "Can you make water boil any faster?"

"Sure." He came to the stove and put his hands on the sides of the big pot before I could yell at him not to.

"It's hot!" I said.

"Sure," he said, rubbing the metal. I didn't smell burned flesh. Suddenly the water was boiling, great domes welling up from the bottom and bursting at the surface.

"Uh," I said.

Evan let go of the pot and smiled at me. "Sign fire."

Like I knew what that meant. I swallowed. "Thanks." I opened the package of noodles and dumped them into the furious water, set the timer for eight minutes. I rinsed and chopped up lettuce and to-matoes for salad, added canned olives and grated cheese. The sausages sizzled and smoked and smelled delicious. I turned them over with a fork.

Granddad had left his banana peel on the table among the newspapers. "Gotta do setup," I told him. He backed his chair away from the table and I cleared it and wiped it clean, then put down place mats, silver, napkins. Got the guest chair from the closet and un-folded it.

The back door opened and Pop breezed in, followed by Mom.

My throat tightened. I set the chair at the table and tried to smile at my parents.

"Smells good, Nick. I hope you're making lots. I brought company," Pop said, then glanced at the table. "Oh, good. How'd you know?"

I pointed a thumb at Evan.

Pop's eyebrows rose. "Oh! Who's this?"

I swallowed, and said, "My friend Evan." My voice squeaked. How was I going to not recognize Mom? And what if Pop kicked Evan out? I had never brought a guest to dinner before. Neither had Pop, at least not since Mom left.

"Evan, again?" Pop glanced around.

"Yeah. Weird, isn't it? We left the wolf in the woods for now."

"Interesting coincidence," he said. He cleared his throat. "This is Susan Fox. She's staying at the inn. Just thought I'd offer her an alternative to Mabel's. Susan, this is my son, Nick, and his friend Evan."

Susan. Mom's name was Sylvia. I held out my hand and she stepped across a distance and gripped it, and a million memories flashed through my brain—I was nine and her hands stroked my back after I'd coughed and coughed, her fingers warm and her voice singing something that touched my throat more than my ears and relaxed it; I was five and wanted to chase a ball across the park because I hadn't caught it when she threw it, but I ran toward it and smacked into a wall that wasn't there and fell, and when I turned around, I realized I was too far away from Mom, a hundred feet, a year away, farther than I'd ever been before: I had to wait until she came closer before I could go after the ball; her hand against the side of my face after I'd drawn a picture, at six, of our family, with her outlined in yellow and Pop outlined in green and me without any colored outline at all; I was three, and she held me in her lap and stared into my eyes a long, long time, until I felt like she had stared me right inside of her; my hand cupped around the green rock and her hand curled around mine, and her whispering, "Hold on tight, hold on tight," until light leaked from our nested hands; the press of her lips on my forehead in a good night kiss, night after night, and the whispered words, "May the night hold you gently"; the first time she took me down and introduced me to the lake, dipping her fingers in, touching them to her mouth and then mine; the tight grip of a hug after I had fallen down on asphalt, my bike spinning out from under me, my arm and elbow scraped and bleeding. . . .

"I'm so pleased to meet you," she said. Her voice hadn't changed. Now that I was sensitized I realized it had an element of push in it—not a push for me to do something much, just a little push for me to believe her.

The questions rose up in me like bubbles in boiling water: Where have you been? Why did you leave? How could you do that? Don't you even care about us? What did I ever do to make you leave me? What can I do to make you come back? Could I stand it if you did come back? Do you know how much you hurt us? They rose and faded, and I said, "Pleased to meet you." My voice came out flat. I let go of her hand. "I better get the other chair from the store."

Mom's smile faded a little. She shook hands with Evan, murmuring something nice.

Pop gave me a stern look, letting me know I wasn't behaving quite right. He said, "Susan, this is my dad, Leo Verrou."

Would Granddad remember Mom? I had been about four when he first came to live with us. Nine years he'd spent in the same household with her, and sometimes I thought Granddad saw things none of the rest of us did. Then again, Pop had lived with Mom fourteen years, and he didn't seem to sense anything.

While Mom was reaching for Granddad's hand, I

slipped through the hall to the store to grab the chair behind the sales counter. Evan followed me after excusing himself. "Look," he whispered as we stood in neon-tinted darkness, "forget what I said before about not letting her know you recognize her. That's none of my business. Let her know you know, if you want."

"I don't want to." I closed my hands around the top of the chair and gripped hard.

He waited a moment. "I didn't give you a chance to talk about this before. You just seemed so close to some edge. I hope it didn't hurt you that I took that away from you for a while."

"It's all right," I said, though I wasn't sure. The afternoon had been full of enough chaos. If I had been thinking about Mom on top of all that . . . well, maybe things would have happened differently. I would never know.

He murmured, "How come she left? What happened?"

"I don't know. She never said."

He roughed my hair. A moment ticked by in silence. "Maybe she'll tell you now," he whispered. "Maybe there was a really good reason."

I shook my head. "She's alive," I said. "She could have said something." Maybe she *had* said something, in all those letters; but that was too late. How could she leave me after making herself the only thing that mattered? She had stolen my very breath.

I didn't want her to do it again.

The timer went off in the kitchen. I lifted the chair and took it down the hall to the kitchen table, then grabbed a fork and tested the pasta, which was ready. Got out the colander, drained the noodles in the sink. Put the salad and a bottle of dressing in the center of the table. Cut up the sausages and dropped them into the marinara. Glanced over my shoulder at my mother, who had taught me to cook, here in this kitchen. "I had to learn this out of books," she had told me. "Except my roommate from before I married your father taught me a few things, but mostly how to make dishes that your father doesn't like, like tofu and eggplant. It's more fun if somebody teaches you.''

She had taught me while she was teaching herself, and it *was* more fun. Pop wasn't so pleased when Mom started teaching me to cook, but he eventually relaxed about it. I had loved those hours after school with her.

After she left I had wondered if it had all been part of her plan: how to take care of Pop without having to be there. Soured me on remembering how much I had liked being in the kitchen with her, listening to the music she loved (mostly classical), reading around in cookbooks, mixing things up, kneading dough, cutting out cookies, experimenting sometimes if we had made a trip to the valley and found strange vegetables or spices or cuts of meat Pop didn't carry in the store.

Mom was staring at me, her smile trembly. Evan had gotten out another place mat, napkin, and set of silver, and he edged one of the other mats aside to add it to the table.

''Anybody want anything to drink?'' asked Pop.

''Soda,'' said Granddad.

''Wine, Susan? Beer?''

''Fruit juice?'' she said.

Pop opened the fridge and got out the orange juice, and another can of Coke for Granddad. I took plates and cups from the cupboard, filled a glass with water, and handed it to Evan. He swallowed the water and handed the cup back to me, so I filled it again. Pop took a cup from the collection on the counter and poured juice for Mom. I had a weird flashback of him doing that morning after morning while she cooked breakfast for him. She thanked him just the way she always had. How could he not know it was her?

Feeling a little dizzy, I dished up some spaghetti and sauce for Granddad and set it on the table in front of him. ''Serve yourselves,'' I said, ''please.''

"Ladies first," Pop said.

Mom helped herself and I stood and watched, with Evan beside me, his hands in his pockets, his whole self somehow dimmed. I had an intense feeling of longing: Mom belonged here. Things were finally set right.

Be realistic. She'll leave after supper. The ripples of this will fade. Things will go back to non-Mom normal.

I couldn't let them go back to Mom-normal. I couldn't take the chance that something would hurt me that much again.

"Evan?" I said when Mom had filled her plate.

He hesitated. Then he served himself. "Salt," he said.

"Oh, yeah," said Pop, fetching the salt and pepper shakers from the stove and putting them in the middle of the table.

"Salt," I said. "Thanks, Pop." Evan had never eaten anything with me before. I hadn't even thought about it. How could salt between us be any more intense than breath between us? I got the Kraft Parmesan from the fridge and put it on the table.

"Enough salt for everybody," Evan said, watching Pop as he dished up spaghetti and sauce for himself, then glancing at Mom. Evan licked his upper lip. He made a pass above the food that reminded me of the way he had signed above the *skilliau* rock that afternoon and murmured a few words.

Oh. Salt between Evan and me, salt between Evan and my parents. What had Lauren said about that? You couldn't hurt people you had shared salt with, couldn't be enemies with them. And it extended to their whole families.

I wasn't sure how Evan defined family. Didn't salt between Lauren and me mean Evan had to respect my family already? Apparently not, or he wouldn't be worried about it. Maybe he no longer thought of Lauren as family.

Probably just as well if Evan and my family had salt

between us. Only I wondered what this would mean if it came down to a tug-of-war between Pop and Evan as to who really owned me. Technically, taking me away from Pop might hurt him.

My stomach growled. I got supper and sat next to Evan at one side of the table, across from Pop, with Granddad on my right, Mom on Evan's other side. Realized I had forgotten to get something to drink, and fetched myself a Coke.

"So, Evan, how'd you and Nick meet?" Pop asked after a period of forks and knives scraping plates and people chewing and swallowing, and Mom's murmured, "Delicious, Nick," another throwback to old times that made me wonder how long Pop could continue to ignore the fact that Mom was Mom.

"Evan is Willow's brother," I said.

"Willow's the little gal you took to the dance last night? And never really introduced me to?"

"Oh. Sorry. Yes."

Mom smiled, almost sparkled. The tightness in my chest moved up into my throat. She was wonderful when she sparkled. She could convince you that whatever you were doing was the most exciting thing you had ever done, even if it was just a walk in the woods. She could make you believe that your picture or your rock or the song you sang was the best one in the world. She could give you a glow that would carry you through a cold night.

"Your folks staying at Lacey's?" Pop asked Evan.

Evan nodded.

"Different from the usual Lacey's folks," Pop said, looking at Evan's overalls, then squinting his eyes and looking closer. "I could swear. . ."

"I got them in the attic," I said, before he could swear anything. "Evan forgot his suitcase."

Pop's eyebrows rose. I could see him thinking about making an issue out of it, but then he glanced at Mom.

She was also studying the overalls. She wore a faint smile.

I wanted to ask her what she was remembering. She probably knew Pop when he was still wearing things like overalls. The questions were percolating through me again till I couldn't even taste what I was eating.

Mom looked up at Pop with such a smile, her eyes tender. It was as if she were saying right out loud how she remembered him, and how she remembered loving him.

Pop's eyes widened. He cleared his throat. "We should talk about this later," Pop said to me.

"One man's trash, another man's treasure," said Granddad.

I chugged some Coke, said, "You were saving them, Pop, but for what? Were you ever going to use them again? Why not let somebody who really needs them use them?"

"Later, Nick," Pop said, going a little red. He slid a glance toward Mom.

Later, when there were fewer strangers and/or relatives around. Then he could yell. Maybe he was like Old Faithful, had to let off steam regularly. I put down my fork and studied him, wondering why I'd never had a thought like that before. Until this moment I had kept hoping that if I just did everything right, he wouldn't yell at me again. But it occurred to me that he always did yell, eventually.

The last time he had yelled at me—last night, before Willow and I went out—I had defied him, and both of us had survived.

"Susan, what brings you to these parts?" Pop asked, smiling at Mom. I studied that too. He really looked charming. How could Pop look charming?

Mom stared down at her half-empty plate. "I . . . uh . . . I was up here one summer a long time ago, and I wanted to see if it was still the same." She looked up, uncertain, maybe a little scared.

She was scared of him. I didn't remember that. I thought back. I could remember Mom and me doing things, but Pop wasn't in the picture very much. He was there at meals. He said silky loving things to her and touched her often. She smiled and pressed against him. She made little gestures in the air all the time. I had thought of it as dancing. It seemed like she waved us closer to each other, an air nudge here, an air stroke there, a soft humming you had to lean closer to hear, until Pop and I were part of her dance, moving in and out between Mom's movements, all of us harmonized. Scared had never entered the picture.

"What do you think?" Pop asked. "Are things still the same?"

"Oh, no," she said, with a sideways glance at me. "Everything has grown so."

Pop glanced out the window toward the night. "It's beautiful here," he said. His voice had a tiny wobble in it.

That surprised me again. I'd never seen Pop cast any but darkling looks toward the forest and the lake. He never swam. He never hiked. His idea of a good time was satellite TV, and driving down to the valley to shop for bargains. He was glad other people had outdoors interests, since it kept the store alive, but he never . . . that wasn't quite true. He did fish, and he shot, mostly at targets. I had always had the impression that nature spooked him, though. Which was another reason why I liked running around in the woods.

"It is," Mom said cautiously.

Pop took a deep breath and roused himself. "Evan, what are you doing in these parts?" He said it friendly, as though he had forgotten that Evan was sitting there in Pop's own pilfered overalls.

"Looking for rocks and some other local things," Evan said. "There's a lot of power in this landscape."

"Interesting," said Pop. "Nick used to collect rocks. He kept getting ugly ones that all looked like each other, though. Not like a regular collection, one each of really pretty things. He picked up a lot of brown and gray ones."

"Maybe they were valuable in another way besides just looking nice," Evan said.

"What other way is there? You think they might have been ore samples? S'pose there's uranium up here?" He sounded curious rather than confrontational. "Nick, what were you doing with all those ugly rocks?"

"I don't know, Pop. I just like picking things up."

Mom was watching me, her eyes wide.

"And saving them," Pop murmured, "just like your old man." He glanced at Evan's overalls and then at me. He smiled. "I'm sorry I threw them out."

I shrugged. "I didn't know what to do with them, anyway." If I had stroked them and murmured to them and gestured at them the way Willow and Evan had with the afternoon's rock, I wondered what things I would have wakened in them. I could have used comfort. But I hadn't known to think at the rocks.

"I was afraid you'd throw 'em at cars or something," Pop said.

"Why?" I was almost startled into a laugh. "Did I ever?"

"It just . . . looked like you were stockpiling 'em upstairs. That was the only reason I could think of for doing it."

I shook my head. "There was no planning involved."

"Huh," said Pop. He looked up, realized everyone was listening, smiled. "Well, I'm sure there are more interesting things to talk about than a kid's rock collection," he said.

"Dessert," said Granddad. He had cleaned his plate long before.

I laughed and got out the Tin Lizzy Special ice cream.

*   *   *

"Can Evan spend the night?" I asked Pop as I cleared the table. Granddad had turned on the TV in the living room half of the kitchen and retreated to his wicker rocking chair, and Evan and Mom were sitting on the sofa, watching a rerun of "Roseanne" with him. Mom had slipped into her old place near the lamp, where she used to do cross-stitch while she watched. Evan sat where I usually sat. He was staring so hard I wondered if he had ever seen a TV before. After all, he came from a home with no telephones and not much mail.

Pop was still sitting at the table, nearer to me than the others. He sipped from his coffee mug. "Where would he sleep? The motel's full."

"He can sleep on the floor in my room. He's used to roughing it." I loaded dishes into the dishwasher.

"Tell me true, Nick. Is he really staying over at Lacey's? If he is, why doesn't he go back there?"

"He's feuding with his family. He can't go back, Pop."

"And he doesn't have any clothes."

I got a mug of milky coffee and sat down across from Pop.

"But he has darned nice manners," Pop said. "All right, he can stay. You can even give him some more of my old clothes, if you want."

"Thanks, Pop," I said, surprised.

"No matter how I feel about my backhoe days, chances are I'm not going back," he said. He watched the back of Evan's head. "Somebody might as well get some use out of my old rags. Guess I was saving them to paint the house in, but there's more. Not sure they'd fit me anymore anyway. And we got fifteen-year paint on the house right now. Might last us eight or nine years." He smiled. There was that surprising charm again. "What do you think about that Susan, eh?"

"She seems nice," I said.

"Nice? With cannons like that?" He wagged his eyebrows at me.

I stared at my mother again. She looked way too skinny to me, and almost flat in front. I needed to ask Evan some more questions about warding.

"Nice," I said.

He patted my head. "You're so young." He got up, carrying his coffee mug, and wandered over to sit in his easy chair, where he could watch Mom and the TV at the same time.

I sipped coffee and watched my family from behind as they were transfixed by images on a small screen. This was like old times, with Evan standing in for me. Could we actually return to the way life used to be? Everything was so calm. Where was the fear and panic I had felt?

Mom turned to look at me. Her eyes were shadowed and looked like tunnels. I had stared into her eyes more than once until I got lost in them, not because they were silver and animated like Uncle Bennet's, but because I knew all she saw was me and all I saw was her. I had never needed friends while she was still living with us. She had been everything I wanted and needed.

Panic was right there, waiting. I stood up, turning away from her gaze, and said, "Night, Granddad, Pop, Susan. Evan, I'm going upstairs now. Pop says you can stay." My voice was a little high.

"Thank you, sir," Evan said to Pop. He rose. "Good night. Pleasure to meet you all."

If I had had wings, I would have flown up the stairs.

7

Trouble Breathing

I started feeling sick just as I finished brushing my teeth. One minute I was leaning over the sink, glaring at my foam-mouthed face in the mirror, occasionally staring at the reflected images of the biplanes on the brown-and-white shower curtain over the tub behind me, tasting the mint in the toothpaste and trying to ignore the mildewy scent the bathroom still had after a long steamy winter of showers with the window closed. The next minute I felt a theft of breath that left me dizzy and weak, and my stomach cramped. I spat out toothpaste foam and rinsed my mouth, hoping that would help, but it didn't.

I wondered if I had done the perfect thing, cooked a meal that would give my parents food poisoning; but the expiration date on the marinara sauce had been years away, and I knew the pasta and the sausage were fine. I hadn't eaten anything else since breakfast besides a handful of potato chips, and I'd never heard of potato chips making anybody sick. Maybe I had the flu. Which would just make things more difficult. Pop didn't cut me much slack for sickness.

Hadn't Evan told me to be well? How long did commands like that last? I would have asked him, but I was feeling too sick to even leave the bathroom.

I was wheezing. It was just like the day Mom left. My chest burned. My lungs labored. I lay on the fuzzy brown rug on the bathroom floor, sweat rolling down my face. I wished I were dead.

Evan staggered in through the open door and knelt beside me. His face was gray and wet with sweat. "It's happening, Nick. They unbind," he whispered, shutting his eyes tight. His cheeks were taut with strain, and tendons stood out in his neck. He gripped his head with both hands.

"Fools, they don't even know what they're doing!" Evan said in a harsh whisper. "Nick, bind!"

Breath whistled on its way into me. I didn't understand him in my head, but something in me understood, because I sat up, dug my Swiss Army knife out of my pants pocket, opened the smaller, sharper blade, and pulled his hand away from his head. I cut across my thumb and across his, said, "Blood brothers," and pressed my cut to his.

He opened eyes burning and golden and repeated it, then said some words in the other language. The constriction in my throat eased. I gasped in air. It tasted cool, refreshing as ice water on a hot day. My stomach settled and I started feeling normal again.

Keeping his thumb pressed to mine, Evan gripped my hand and drew it toward him. He touched his lips to our joined thumbs. Gently he released my hand, easing his thumb from mine, then licking the blood away from his wound with just the tip of his tongue.

"Taste," he said.

I waited a beat just to see if I could.

His power to command me had vanished.

I sucked the blood off my thumb. It had an undertone of salt.

"Now I'm in you and you're in me," he whispered.

"It's not the same," I said, feeling muted shades of

disappointment, sharper fear, and sadness. For the first time since Mom left I had found somebody whom I actually wanted to take care of me, and now that was over. It had barely lasted twenty-four hours.

"It's not the same, but it's something," he said. "Without it, we might have died. *Akenari*. They know they're right, but they've never dealt with a fetch bond before. They chose the wrong unbinding. I should have loosed you myself."

I got up and splashed cold water on my face. I filled a glass with water and offered it to him. He drank most of it, splashed some on his face too. I slumped down across from him, my back against the cupboards under the sink; he had his back against the tub, and we propped our feet up on each other's backstops.

Evan said, "So what is 'blood brothers'?"

"A way to choose your relatives. Something best friends do. Not a big formal thing like what you did to me before."

"Something they won't know to unbind," he said, "at least not yet. I don't understand why the Presences allowed the Keyes to unbind us. . . . I thought I was doing the right thing when I fetched you. Maybe there just aren't enough Presences here in this strange land to influence us one way or the other."

Thinking of the moment back in Lacey five when all the Keyes had gone silent, asking for guidance, listening, not hearing, I said, "What is a Presence, anyway?"

"It's . . . it's complicated. Those who have gone before are Presences, and then there are other sorts—creatures and beings that live with Powers. Some of them know a lot; some of them know only a little; some sleep deep and some sleep lightly, and some are always awake and watching; some come because they want to and some come because we call them. Some are strong and some are barely there. At my real home there are a lot of them, but they're pretty quiet. At the

Keyes' home I haven't noticed many. Here, none have spoken to me at all, but I thought maybe that was because I have cast myself out from the family. Once you cut the thread, the Presences abandon you, or so people say." He studied his cut thumb a second, then glanced sideways at me and offered me a small smile.

"Are these Presences supposed to actually guide you through your daily life? How do they talk to you?"

He thought for a moment. "Well, I guess first you have to practice your disciplines. Sometimes the Presences don't talk very loud. Disciplines help you hear them. I was never very good at my disciplines. Second, you have to decide you want to listen for the Presences. You look around and see if there are signs. You make a space where they can contact you—there's all kinds of ways to do that, with fire, water, earth, air, with *skilliau* or spiritspeak, or other things. I was never any good at that either. I'm not interested in having outside things telling me what to do. I don't know if you noticed that."

"I noticed."

"Third, you have to figure out how to interpret the messages you get. Actually, I'm pretty good at that part. I like puzzles. And fourth, you have to decide whether you want to follow the directions you've been given. That's the tricky part. If you don't actually perceive any of the directions, you don't have to follow them—that's my theory, anyway. If you actually figure out what the Presences and Powers want you to do, you can get in terrible trouble if you don't do it."

"You prefer flying blind."

"No. Not flying," he said. "If I'm a bird, I'd just as soon see where I'm going. But acting on my own, yes. So. Blood brothers, whatever that means." He frowned and stared down at his hands, which lay palms up on his knees. "Saved us, anyway. We were too bound together to survive being separated without preparation. Thank you, Nick."

"You're welcome," I said. I wondered if I loved Evan with the same intensity now that he wasn't a wolf and my master. I could still remember the orders he had given me, about accepting him no matter what shape he chose, about how his relatives' curses should slide off me, about how I should be comfortable. I looked at him. He raised his eyes and met my gaze. The instant overwhelming feeling I had gotten before from just looking at him was gone. I knew I didn't know him very well, and I could think about that now. Everything I knew about him, though, I liked.

He gave me an open-mouthed grin. "Different," he said.

"When she first saw me with you, Willow thought I put a spell on you."

"You did."

"She said you hated everything."

"I did."

"How could I put a spell on you? The only magic I really know is talking, and I hardly even talked to you."

"You spelled me just by being so interesting. It's a spell of fascination. Before I discovered you, I wasn't interested in anything except woodsrunning, exploring, and hunting." His eyes narrowed. "And there was something else about you. An opening. An asking. A place that needed something. Willow saw that too. We both had the same thought. We both wanted to connect with that place in you. But I got there first."

I wasn't sure I understood him. It sounded really eerie. I put my hand on my chest, remembering the scooped-out feeling I had had after Mom left. "Was it like a wound?"

"A wound?" he said. He frowned. "N-no, it was like a flavor, or a beckon, a, maybe half a melody asking for its other half. I'm no good at explaining stuff!"

"I don't know. You're better than no explanation at all, even though I don't always understand you."

"Why would you think a wound?"

"A big ... unbinding? What Mom did to me by leaving."

"Huh." He leaned forward and touched my chest too. "Huh." He sniffed his fingers. His eyebrows drew together. "I don't think ..."

There was a tapping on the door, tentative, un-Pop-like. I glanced over and saw my mother standing on the threshold. "Nick?" she said.

My hand on my chest closed into a fist. "Yeah."

"Could I talk to you?" She glanced at Evan. It was the sort of look that invites a person to leave. He smiled at her instead. "Alone?"

"Why?"

"Just because."

She had always said that when I asked "why" one time too many. Sometimes it worked and sometimes it didn't.

I wanted so much just to look at her.

Then again, I sort of wanted to kill her.

I said, "Evan's my bodyguard. He knows all my secrets."

"All of them?"

Her voice was so familiar it was strange. I felt it stroking me. I knew she had a laugh just under the surface. Part of me wanted to tease it out of her the way I used to, and part of me wanted to run.

"Lots of them, anyway," I said. "Some that I don't even know myself."

"Do you need him to protect you from me?" She sounded uncertain.

"I might." I scrambled to my feet, and Evan got up too. As I turned toward Mom, I saw an image in the mirror over the sink and jumped. There was a busty woman with a lot of wavy blonde hair, wearing a pink dress trimmed with white lace. She had killer fingernails polished pink, and she was wearing nylons and high heels. I blinked and looked back at my mother. Short hair, nearly flat chest, a sensible turtleneck in olive green, bare, bitten fingernails, a dark skirt that reached to mid-calf, gym socks, penny loafers. "Jeeezus!" I felt blood tingling in my cheeks.

Evan glanced at the mirror, at my mother, at me. "Hah," he said.

"What is it?" Mom said, and now she sounded worried.

I pointed to the mirror. "Tha—" I squinted at the image. Its lips were bright pink, and it was wearing silvery lavender color above its large blue eyes. "What the—"

Evan said, "It's the warding, Nick. I'll wait just outside the door. Yell if you need me."

"Don't—"

He nudged my shoulder with his knuckles and edged around my mother, shutting the door with her inside the bathroom.

"Warding?" She looked pale, even though her mirror image looked very healthy. I turned my back on the mirror, leaning against the sink counter.

"Mom?" I said.

"Nick? Oh, Nick!" She came toward me, her arms held out.

"Don't," I said, putting power into my voice, stopping her where she stood. I crossed my arms over my chest, tucking my hands into my armpits and hunching my shoulders. "What are you doing here?"

She lowered her arms and stared at me with wide eyes. "I had to see you."

"Why?"

"I miss you so much."

"No."

"Yes." She blinked. A tear ran down her cheek.

"If you missed me, you wouldn't have left."

She stared at the carpet. "I shouldn't have left. I should never have left."

"Why did you?"

"I had to leave." She rubbed the tear away with the sleeve of her shirt, and looked up at me again. "I tried to explain this in my note. Did you understand any of it? I know it was difficult stuff for a thirteen-year-old."

"What note?"

Her eyes got big. "Oh, Nick." She touched her cheeks with her hands. "You didn't get my note?"

I shook my head.

"I left it in the note spot on your dresser."

"There was no note," I said. The note spot was where she had always left notes to tell me of the day's plans. She had always wanted me to know where she was, and she had always wanted to know where I was.

"Oh, Nick. Oh, God. I didn't know ... I thought at least we'd have that much connection left. I left a note."

I thought about the morning after she left. The morning I couldn't breathe. Maybe there had been a note. Maybe Pop or Granddad or the doc had wandered off with it; I had been too far out of things to know. "I never got it," I said.

"Did you get any of my letters?"

I hunched my shoulders. The thought of the unopened letters in the bottom dresser drawer nagged at me.

"Not a single one? I thought maybe one would get through. I kept saying the same thing over and over. I hoped you would get one."

"Tell me now," I said, and bit my lip.

She sat down on the edge of the bathtub, gripping the lip with her hands until her knuckles paled. "You remember what I told you about growing up in my family?"

She used to tell me stories about her family. I had thought she made them all up. I had always thought everybody in her family must be dead, because she never said anything about us meeting them. She never called her parents my grandparents, or her sisters and brothers my aunts and uncles. She didn't have their names written down anywhere, no addresses or phone numbers for them. And she had never told Pop about them. He had mentioned to me once that he thought she must be an orphan.

She had told me about her brother Rick and his hunting with a bow and arrow, how he could sing the animals to him; and her sister Helena, who could make anything out of clay, so real you thought a clay baby might cry or a clay crow caw; how once Helena gave Mom a clay bunny and it came alive at night and cuddled with her when she was scared. There were other brothers and sisters, and each of them had a talent. She made the stories sound as if they took place long ago, in a faraway world. I had never believed they were true.

She chewed her lower lip for a little while, then ran a hand through her hair and looked up at me. "I grew up in a cage, Nick. In my family they give you a pattern and you're supposed to fit right inside, and if any of you doesn't fit, they just cut it off. I had too many pieces they wanted to cut off. I ran away. And then, after I'd been gone for a couple years, I realized there were some things about my family that I didn't know how to live without, a kind of closeness and belonging and always knowing someone would be there for me—but once you run away from that family, you're dead to them. I couldn't go back.

"I found your father instead. He had some of the right things about him. He gave me what I needed. . . . No, I'm not telling this right. Do you remember what I told you about the memory stones?"

I frowned. It sounded familiar. Something in one of her stories.

"These are stones passed down from one generation to the next. They carry the skills. When I was born everybody decided I was supposed to have the skills of the seamstress, so they took the seamstress stone and pressed it to my forehead every Sunday, training my mind. I grew up with that mindprint, and everybody else had some other mindprint from the memory stones. It was all planned out before we were even born.'' She took a deep breath and then let it out in a frustrated rush. ''Nobody ever asked me what *I* wanted to be. When I found out I would rather be a painter ... no, this isn't explaining it, either. I don't mean to keep making this about me. Remember the wolf tree?''

''Yeah.'' We had found the wolf tree on one of our walks by the lake. The wolf tree was a big tree standing in a place where no other trees grew close. It had long bushy limbs all the way to the ground. It looked like a giant shaggy Christmas tree. I hadn't visited it much since she left, because it reminded me of her. She had always liked to stop and study it.

She said, ''You asked me why I left. I left to save your life, and mine. I loved you so much, just the way your father loved me, that I was rooting down into you, giving you only air I had breathed first, keeping you away from the world, stunting and shaping you to my convenience instead of giving you room to become whoever you might be. Because that's the way I grew up, too, Nick. Even though I was strong enough eventually to run away from home, that was all I knew about being a parent.''

She had been breathing my air for me. Yes.

And I had liked it.

''I was so deep in you I squashed you, and I lost myself, too. Trees that grow too close together never grow all the branches and thickness and height they could grow if they had more room. You've seen those stands where the trees are just tall shaded poles, all close, light-starved and skinny, all their green up at the very top where the sun can touch them. Not wolf trees.''

An image of her surfaced in my mind. She held out her arms to the wolf tree, dancing around it without ever touching it, stroking the air near it in a nontactile caress.

"I woke up one morning and realized I had been making you a memory stone. I wasn't using one that had been in the family for generations, but I was making you a memory stone, as though I could take your character and turn it into just another coded lesson that maybe I could use on some other child or grandchild. I was doing the very thing I hated most in my own parents, *and I never even thought about it.* I had to leave, Nick. I had to stop myself.

"Is any of this making sense?"

I curled my left hand up in front of me. "A green stone," I said.

"Yes," she whispered.

"You said, 'Hold on tight. Hold on tight.' And then light came out of it."

"Yes."

"What happened to it?"

She shook her head. "No, Nick. You don't really want to know. Look at you. You look wonderful. You look healthy and strong and self-possessed. You look like a wolf tree. I know you hate me now, but I think I made the right decision."

"What did you do with the stone, Mom?"

Her eyes brimmed with unshed tears. "I guess it can't hurt. You'll never find it. I blessed it and threw it in the lake."

I frowned and thought about that, about dipping my fingers in the water every morning, about ice kisses from the winter lake. I thought about Evan's snow crystal: was that something like a memory stone? And then I thought about Evan, who liked puzzles, and heard his voice in my head saying, "They're paying attention to all the wrong things." There was a heat in my chest and behind my eyes. I wasn't sure what it meant. I rubbed my eyes and tried to think of the questions I should be asking.

"I'm not a wolf tree," I said. "Here's Pop. Here's me." I held up my index fingers, close to each other, almost touching.

"Oh." It was a small sad moan. "I couldn't change that. All I could do was take myself away."

"Away to where?"

"Away south." She stood up. We faced each other across a space that was too small for a normal conversation. I was surprised to find that I was taller than she. "I went to San Francisco. I was very confused. I wanted so much to—" She put out her hand and pressed her palm to my chest. Shock jolted through me, followed by a wine warmth, bitter and sweet as a hard green apple, then finally just sweet as late afternoon summer sun, inviting me to bask. I breathed in her scent of tea and toast and breathed out the taste of myself, the taste of Evan's and my blood, fading. . . .

"Stop it!" I said. "Stop it."

She jerked her hand away.

It took me half a minute to stabilize my breathing. "Don't you dare make that connection, not if you're going to break it again." My voice was low and harsh. It hurt coming out.

"I'm sorry," she whispered.

"Talk to me. Don't touch me."

She put her hands behind her back. She perched on the rim of the tub again. "I'm sorry." She let her head fall back and just sat, breathing shallowly, for a little while. Then she straightened.

"I tore myself away from here," she said. She pressed her hand against her own chest between her breasts. "It hurt. I did it anyway. I went to San Francisco, because I'd lived there before, after I ran away from my family. And I found something wonderful." She dropped her hand to her thigh. "I found a relative I'd never met before. I was looking for a place I could belong without—without gluing myself to other people the way I had glued myself to your father and you, and I found this group of people living in a big house together, and one of them was Dru. There's a thing you can do—Dru taught me—where you—'' She held out her left hand and gestured above it with her right. Her motions resembled the ones Evan and Willow had made above my hand, above theirs. Threads of pale blue light shone above my mother's hand. She looked up at me. She was sparkling, her eyes dancing and saying, *Share this with me.*

"Yeah?" I said. "So?"

The light faded from her face and from above her hand. "When Dru did it, she had these beads of purple and red light. She said that was one way members of our family could recognize each other. Show me your hand, Nick.''

I shoved my fists into my pockets. "It's all right. Never mind.''

She lowered her hands to her lap. Her face went calm. "Dru has been teaching me a lot of things. Ways to exist without twisting myself and everything around me. I'm not very good at it yet, Nick, but I'm learning. . . . I know I let you down in more ways than one. You had to do your *plakyanish* all alone.''

"*Plaka*—huh?"

She frowned. "Did you get sick? Sometime soon after I left?''

I rarely got sick, and even days when I had a temperature or a cold Pop made me go to school. I thought back to being thirteen and fourteen. I'd had a pretty bad week in there somewhere, but I'd gone to school anyway, except for one day when I was running a temperature of 104°. I'd had some hallucinations that really delighted me. Ghosts had talked to me, some of them the ghosts of animals. Now that I thought about it, one was a white wolf, even. "Yeah," I said.

"It's a teenage thing. That's when you grow into

your powers. I wasn't sure it would happen to you, because your father's not—well, he is, a little, but mostly not—like me. But I knew you were like me. I should have been there for you. You needed a guide. It must have been horrible and confusing.''

"No," I said. "I was just sick, a little. Nothing happened.''

''I should have been there.'' She made a sound like a kitten's growl. ''But it's better that I wasn't.'' She clutched her head. When she let go, her hair stood up in little twisted spikes. ''I wish I could make it right, what I did, leaving like that, but I don't know how.''

Part of me wanted to forgive her, to say it out loud and make her feel better, get this whole thing over with and go back to thinking she was the most wonderful person in the world. Part of me wanted to spit fire at her and burn her to cinders and bones. Leaving her twisting had a certain appeal, too. I sat with the heat inside me, staring at her and wondering what I really wanted.

''Tell me what you need from me,'' she said, meeting my eyes, her face placid, her hair wild.

''What have you got?''

''I love you. I never stopped loving you, and I never will, no matter what.'' *Believe me,* her voice pushed, and because I wanted to, because I was no longer under Evan's protection, because it might be true despite evidence to the contrary, I believed her.

I slumped against the sink counter, for a moment unable to breathe. *She loves me.* I opened my mouth, but no air came in. *It doesn't have to hurt.* I coughed out fear. I tapped my chest with my open hand and my lungs remembered how to draw again.

''Are you all right?'' she asked, her voice tight and urgent, and I remembered what it was like to have a mother.

I coughed a couple more times. My breathing steadied. My face felt hot. I nodded.

"Because I can—I can—whatever you need—"

"I'm okay," I said. My voice was a little scratchy. I filled the water glass and sipped from it.

She watched me for a little while, her hands reaching, hovering, dropping. I had told her not to touch me. I could see it was difficult for her, but she honored my instruction. "All right," she said at last. "What else I could do for you is"—she touched one hand with the other, miming the gestures that summoned a light signature—"see what light you have, and try to teach you how to use it. Dru has been teaching me so many things. She's been teaching me how to raise a child without"—she bit her bottom lip; she curled her arms out in front of her, making a circle by grasping one hand with another—"without binding it so tight to you that it doesn't know how to breathe on its own." She dropped her arms. "I have a little girl," she said. "You have a little sister. I can let her run into the next room without following her right away. I'm learning."

I blinked at her. "Jeez, Mom. Jeez! How old is she?"

"Almost four."

Mom must have been pregnant when she left, then. "She's Pop's? And you never told him?"

She stared at her hands in her lap. "Dru says I have to. I am so afraid." She looked up at me again. "But that's not—that's for next time. Next time I have to come as myself, and I'll bring Anika. I'm not quite strong enough yet, but I'm getting there."

I glanced back at the mirror. "How can you come as not yourself?"

"Dru taught me."

"Teach me." If this warding stuff worked the way it looked like it worked—Pop not recognizing Mom in spite of spending a whole dinner with her, and her making stupid mistakes—it would be a great skill for a detective to have. I wondered if I could disguise my-

self as a tree. No. Not a good idea. You'd have to stand
still too long.

"You have to have a certain kind of light in your
hand. You have to be a green or a blue. Will you let
me look?"

"I'm a blue, I guess," I said. "But Evan's yellow,
and he can ward."

"What?" Wide-eyed, she glanced toward the door.
"You're blue? Evan—Evan? What? He said—oh,
Nick." She broke into a dazzling smile. "You found
family too?"

Was that what I had found? Blood brothers. "Yeah."

"Oh, I'm so glad. Oh, I'm so happy. Oh . . . Unless
they're like the family I ran away from."

"No," I said. Evan and Willow might have wanted
to own me, but neither of them seemed to want to box
me up and cut off parts of me.

"Oh, this makes it better. I knew it was bad that I
went away, for a lot of different reasons. You need a
chance to learn how all these things work. But I didn't
know all the good things when I left. I couldn't have
taught you how to disguise yourself . . . how did you
know it was me?"

I shrugged. "To me, you look just like you. Skinnier,
and your hair is shorter, and you look tired. But you're
you: you sound like you, you act like you, and you
even say some of the same things. Evan told me you
were warded and wouldn't expect me to know you. But
until I saw you in the mirror, I didn't know what he
was talking about."

"Oh, my. You mean, all during dinner, you
knew. . . ." She frowned. "Dru has names for these
talents. I wonder what she'd call it, that you can see
through my veil."

I pointed to the mirror. "Why would you want to
look like that?"

She smiled. "It's different, for one thing. For another
. . . oh, this is very odd . . . but before your father met

me, that's the kind of woman he liked. I wanted a chance to see you here at home, and I thought he might invite somebody who looks like that to dinner. When we first met, he was so confused. He didn't *want* to love me. I didn't look like his dream girl. But I . . . I wanted him, and in some ways I was stronger in my desires than he was.''

I had a very weird moment, thinking about big blonde Kristen and small dark Willow, and realizing maybe Pop and I had something in common.

Mom stopped looking over my shoulder at the past and came back to the present. ''Do you know how to talk to your light?''

''What?''

''The first thing you need to do is—''

Evan tapped on the door. ''The Pop is coming up the stairs,'' he muttered through the door.

I stared at Mom. I had forgotten there was a world beyond the two of us; and that was often the way it had been when I was younger.

''Susan?'' Pop called. ''Why didn't you use the downstairs bathroom? Are you all right? *Star Trek* ended almost half an hour ago.''

Mom and I looked at each other, and there was a quickening in the air, a conspiracy between us. I remembered that too. I didn't like it anymore. No wonder Pop and I never talked. Mom and I had treated him like some kind of enemy.

Still, I wondered if I should duck behind the shower curtain and let Mom leave the bathroom alone. Pop had always thought women spent too much time in the bathroom. He would just think Mom's delay was natural.

In a lower voice, Pop said, ''What are you doing here, son?''

Jeez! Could he see through a door? Before I could even frame an answer, Evan said, crystal clear, ''Waiting for Nick.''

"What?" Pop slammed the door open, nearly hitting Mom. She moved just fast enough to evade it. "What's going on in here?" he yelled.

I gripped the counter behind me and pushed myself up so I was sitting on it. "Just talking," I said.

"Talking! What do you have to talk about, huh?" He looked back and forth between me and Mom. "What the hell is going on here? Nick, did this woman do something to you? Susan? What are you doing up here alone with an underage boy? What kind of woman are you, anyway?" Each sentence was louder than the last.

"Nothing happened, Pop. Calm down."

"Don't tell me to calm down!"

"Calm down," I said again, and this time I meant it. He blinked. He stared at me. He breathed deep and slow. His face lost its bright red hue.

I looked at Mom to see if she would say anything. In a detective sense, I didn't want to blow her cover. In a Nick sense I really wanted her to let Pop know who she was. Mom had always made me feel special by telling me secret things we kept from Pop. I had hugged those secrets as though they could feed me. Some of them had kept me going even after she left— touching the lake, walking the woods, sneaking a listen to the classical music station when Pop was out of the house, things I had done with Mom but never with Pop.

For the first time in my life I actually wanted my parents to talk to each other and me, all of us together. I didn't want Mom to leave me with the secret of her visit, just another stone in the wall between me and Pop.

Mom looked at Pop. Her eyes were tender and sad, but her voice stayed silent.

"Good night, Susan," I said. "Say good night, Pop."

"Good night," he said in a normal voice. "Good night, Susan."

"Good night," she said, after a moment. She touched her mouth, staring at Pop, then glanced at me. "Maybe we can sort this out tomorrow." She edged past Pop and left, murmuring something to Evan before I heard her footsteps clattering down the stairs.

Pop and I stared at each other. "What are you doing to me, Nick?" he asked. "I don't want to be calm!"

"Nothing happened, Pop. We just talked. Honest."

"Sometimes just talking is worse than anything else.... Don't order me around, Nick. How can you? You can't tell me what to do. How can you tell me to do something and make me do it?"

"You do it to me all the time."

"That's my job. I'm the parent. And it's not like I tell you to do something and you automatically—this is different." He thumped his chest. "This is ... this is my involuntary muscles, Nick. My nervous system, my lungs. This is my vocal cords. How is this possible? This is bad. This is not right."

"I'm worried about your blood pressure. Your face gets red, and you yell. You yell all the time."

He closed his eyes for a long moment. When he opened them again he looked really tired. "I didn't used to," he said.

I thought about that and realized it was true. He had started yelling after Mom left.

"I don't like this, Nick."

"You keep going off half-cocked."

"Not from my perspective. From my perspective I'm getting more and more worried about you. Why are you late all the time? Why are you lying to me? What happened to the dog? Who are these weird friends of yours? What are you doing alone in a room with a woman old enough to be your mother? What the hell did she want with you? I just thought she was some-body lonely and nice, and here I find out she's—I'm not sure what. What did you talk about? Why ... why aren't things normal and comfortable anymore?"

"Comfortable for whom?" I said.

We stared at each other for a while.

"I'll try not to yell," he said eventually.

"I'll try not to boss you."

He squinted at me. "Gaw dang," he said. He shook his head. "*Gaw* dang."

"Good night, Pop."

He stared a moment more. "Night," he said. "Sheee-oot."

8

Business Affairs

"**S**o what happened?" Evan asked after we crossed the upstairs hall and closed ourselves in my room.

I went to my dresser and took the stack of Mom's letters from the bottom drawer. I flipped the edges, glancing at different stamps, differing postmarks, most Californian. One a month, none of them very thick, for four years, two months—with a few missing at the beginning of the sequence, lost to ashes and the wind. A steady forthcoming of some kind of connection, one I had not accepted.

"I was so scared of her. I was so mad at her. Now I don't know what I feel." I tried to remember everything Mom had explained to me about stones and trees and her family, but it all mixed together.

During dinner I had been looking at her and thinking, *There is everything I ever needed. There is the person who took it away.* While I talked to her, my thoughts about her kept shifting. She had changed from someone who filled the whole sky to someone who was a confused person who had done the best she could. I was still angry at her. She had hurt me. If I wasn't careful, I might almost understand why.

I didn't want to understand her. If I did I might start worrying about her.

Of course I wanted to understand her. Wasn't that what all this spying was about, trying to understand people?

There had to be somewhere between her breathing my air for me and her not being present at all, somewhere between my wanting to kill her and my not wanting to let her out of my sight. Maybe letters could do it for us. I didn't think so.

I slipped the most recent letter from the stack, turned it over, and looked at the sealed flap. I picked at one edge of it, and then suddenly I slid it back in with the others. I didn't want to know anything else about Mom right now.

I was starting to get a headache.

"I could tell you to go to sleep and let it all sort out in your dreams, but it wouldn't work anymore," Evan said.

"Thanks for the thought, anyway." I looked at my watch. Tomorrow was Sunday, when I could either sleep in an extra hour (the store didn't open until ten) or spy an extra hour. It wasn't even ten o'clock at night, and already I was exhausted. It had been a long day. "Even though you don't own me anymore, can't you use that voice thing on me the way I did on Pop? Say something like, 'You're not tired anymore' or something?"

"I don't do voice. Willow does voice. Elissa does voice. You do voice. Why would I need voice? In my natural state most people can't even understand me."

"What?" I stared at him for half a minute before I figured out he meant that his natural state was being a wolf. "God, I'm tired. Guess I'll go to sleep."

"Good idea."

Evan settled down to sleep on the floor, curled up under a blanket. It looked really uncomfortable, but he refused the pillow I offered him.

I put the stack of letters on the lamp table by the head of my bed and turned out the light.

Sometime later I woke, staring up in darkness. Something in my throat felt warm, a wet sticky heat. I coughed and switched on the bedside lamp. It was around midnight. Evan sat up, blinking, and looked at me. I coughed again and touched my throat. Hot. I touched my forehead. Cool. This wasn't like other colds I had had.

"What is it?" Evan said.

"Throat hurts." My voice came out in a croak.

He came over and sat on the bed beside me, flicked his fingers near my throat. I could see the light that leaked out under my chin in response to his gesture. It was sickly pale blue. "Silence," he said. "Oh! They are so sloppy." He touched my throat with his fingertips and murmured words in a soft two-tone song. Gradually my throat stopped hurting.

"Silence?" I whispered.

"So you won't tell outsiders about them."

"What? I can't talk at all?" I whispered. I coughed against the back of my hand and tried to vocalize. "I can talk," I said. To my relief, my voice came out of my mouth.

"Good. They're so sloppy I was afraid they overstepped. Tell me something about them."

"Huh? Oh. Ah—" I tried to say "Aunt Elissa" and nothing but air came out of my throat. "Weird," I said. Not as bad as blinding or unbinding. Not even crippling, as far as I could figure out. I didn't want to talk about them, anyway. Still, it was disturbing that they could decide to do something to me, and then do it, and we didn't even have to be face-to-face. "Eh—eh—eh . . ."

His eyes widened. He touched his chest. I nodded.

"Akenari," he said, disgusted. He touched my forehead with all his fingertips and muttered in the other

language, then said, "I am in your family, not theirs.
Willow is in your family, not theirs." His thumbs
moved against my forehead. Green light flashed for a
second, and I felt tension and release in my skull.
"Try again."

"Evan."

"Good." He muttered a few curses I couldn't understand, shaking his head. "These people, these people.
Their teachers must be terrible. No fine-tuning. You
okay?"

"I don't know." I felt fine, physically, but I was
starting to feel a little sick on a thought level. This
would teach me to watch interesting strangers. It had
always seemed like such a safe sport. I'd never considered possible backlash from those being watched.

"Anything I can do?"

"Not that I know of. Unless you can make this go
away." I touched my throat.

"I wish." Narrow-eyed, he stared out the window at
the night beyond. "They're powerful when they act
together. And they're raising the kids to work with
them. That's something these Southwater people do a
lot better than my more immediate family—work in
concert. Makes for better, stronger bindings; one's lon-
ers can't fight very well."

I looked out the window too, and saw nothing but
darkness.

I had forgotten to set my watch alarm the night before. I woke about seven anyway. Evan was gone. I
heard the shower running. I went through my regular
sets. By the time I had finished, he was back, wearing
the overalls again. His hair lay wet and flat and darker
against his head and neck. I went for my shower, wondering what came next. I wasn't at all in the mood to
follow my route today.

He was sitting on the bed looking at Mom's letters

when I came back to the room. "There's a feel to them," he said, "like what was in the attic trunk."

"Huh," I said. I picked up the packet and pulled a letter from the middle somewhere. I opened it and took out a single sheet of lavender paper, unfolded it, stared at my mother's familiar sloping handwriting, her unique way of making *r*s. "Dear Nick," I read, "I love you. I will always love you, no matter what. I'm so sorry I had to leave. . . ."

I folded the letter and put it back in the envelope, then put all the letters in the bottom drawer.

Downstairs, I got out Granddad's cereal bowl and filled it for him and turned on the coffee maker, then went up to the motel office to set out coffee and pastries. Evan followed me silently. I went down to the lake to touch fingers to it, glanced up toward Mom's room in the motel, then finished my ritual anyway. The lake felt warmer than usual. For a minute I thought about diving in and swimming down and staying. I enjoyed thinking about it. I let it go.

"Are you hungry?" I asked Evan.

"Yeah."

"Let's get breakfast."

Pop was yawning and mixing milk into his coffee when we came inside. I couldn't remember the last time I had had breakfast with him. Usually he got up after I had gone in to open the store. Granddad was studying the Sunday funnies. I wondered if they made any sense to him or if he just liked looking at the pictures. "Want eggs?" I asked Pop. Granddad never wanted eggs. He loved sugar cereal. I poured milk over the Frosted Flakes in his bowl for him.

"Sure," Pop said.

"Evan?"

"Sure," said Evan.

"Toast?"

Everyone said yes. I heated the skillet and set up for a family breakfast, feeling strange. When Mom lived with us, breakfast together was an everyday thing; since she'd left it almost never happened. Eerie.

"Pop, can Evan live with us?" I asked when everybody was sitting down and eating.

"Wha-a-a-at?"

"I mean, he really doesn't want to go back to his fa—fa— to, you know. Could he stay with us?"

Pop studied Evan, who put down his fork, sat up straight, and raised his eyebrows.

Pop frowned. "Nick," he said.

"I know you don't know anything about him, but I think he'd . . ." I couldn't figure out what to say that would recommend Evan to Pop. I hadn't asked Evan about this, either. When I started to think of the real-world ripples this could have, I got dizzy. Would Evan go to school with me? Would he mooch off us? Would he even consider helping us? He didn't seem to like helping his other family. Would he just keep sleeping on my floor? It might have worked if we were both ten years old, but we weren't. These questions wouldn't have come up if he were still a wolf, but he wasn't. And how did magic fit into the picture?

Pop drummed his fingers on the table for a minute, then said to Evan, "Son, would you be willing to pull your weight around here?"

"What does that mean?" Evan asked.

"Learn the business or get an outside job that brings in a little income—rent and food money. There's space in the attic; we could fix you up a room, if you really want to live with us. I know Nick's been lonely here, especially in the winters."

That surprised me. I had thought Pop didn't notice things like that.

"I don't know how good I would be at jobs," Evan said.

"Nick could train you how to run the store easy, if you wanted to learn. I'm not sure there's enough work here for three people, though. How are you on housekeeping? You know anything about boats or fishing? Archie could use some help at the dock. If you got any maintenance skills, people keep having little jobs come up—reroofing or fixing a step or painting. Any experience?"

"No," said Evan.

"Or you could make deliveries, or Lacey might be able to use you for yard work—you know anything about that?"

"No," said Evan.

"Where you been all your life?" Pop sounded intrigued, which I figured was better than irritated.

"I guess . . . nowhere," Evan said. He cocked his head.

"No special skills?"

"I can hunt, and I can track. I can do a lot of other things I don't think people know enough to want."

"Like what?"

Evan bit his lower lip. He lifted his left hand above the table, palm up, and danced his fingers above it until he pulled the yellow spiral of his signature up.

"Holy moley," whispered Granddad.

"Magic tricks?" Pop asked.

"Yeah," said Evan. He closed his hand and the spiral faded.

"You know any card tricks?"

Evan frowned. "Not yet," he said. "I could probably learn."

"Hmm," said Pop. "We might be able to put something together with Parsley, if you could work up a show. You done any magic professionally?"

Evan glanced at me, eyebrows up.

"Magicians put on these shows, where they perform for a big audience," I said. "They make things appear and disappear, people float, change people into animals. . . ." I didn't want to pursue that one. "Pull rabbits out of empty hats. People pay to see them."

"Really?"

"Yeah."

"I'm not good with crowds," said Evan.

"So you'd have to work up to it," Pop said. "Maybe next summer. Hmmm." He drummed the tabletop some more. "Tell you what. We'll float you for a while till you find your feet. Three rules. One: you have to be trying to find work—you get a job and give it an honest try, no slacking. You make it an aim to contribute to the household, and that means helping with the day-to-day, too. Two: you have to not steal anything—any abuse of our hospitality, and out you go. You're welcome to whatever you find in those suitcases in the attic, though, long as you check with me first. Three: no smoking, drinking, or leading Nick into wild behavior, though maybe he knows more about that than you do. What do you say?"

Evan folded his hands and stared at the tabletop for a little while, then nodded and looked up at Pop. "I say thank you."

Pop smiled and offered Evan his hand. They shook.

We all finished breakfast. When I got up to clear the table, Evan rose, too, and helped me, smiling the whole time at some inside joke. I ran hot water into the dishpan, thinking that Evan could probably make it hotter faster. "Pop, about what's in the attic. There's a locked trunk up there."

"Shee-ooot, I forgot. That one's off limits."

"What's in it?"

"Just things," he said. "Private things. Nothing you'd need. Leave it alone, Nick."

"Okay."

Pop checked the kitchen clock. Still only around eight-thirty. "I'm guessing you haven't got out much since you came here," he said to Evan. "Otherwise people would be talking about you. Nick, you got more than an hour before opening. Why don't you take Evan around and introduce him? Check if Archie still needs help. Show Evan to Mabel. Give things a feel. If nothing else suits you, Evan, I got work up at the motel you could do. You ever run a washing machine?''

"Nope," said Evan. He smiled.

"How about a vacuum cleaner?"

"Nope."

"Criminy," Pop said. "Like the wild man of the woods or something."

"Yeah," said Evan.

Pop was still shaking his head gently as we left.

"Is this going to work?" I asked Evan as we walked along the road. He was barefoot. "I mean, isn't this the same as Uncle Bennet telling you to get to work?"

"No," Evan said. He had his hands buried in his overall pockets, and he walked looking at the sky and smiling.

"Why not?"

"Because your pop asked me. He didn't tell me. He gave me a choice. *I* picked."

"Hmm." Pop had never given me a choice. Or had he? He'd never offered me the chance to not work. What if I just didn't get up one day? What if I completely screwed up at work? What if I just left the house and ran around all day without telling Pop or asking him?

The way Evan had with his relatives.

I thought about that. I wasn't ready for the kind of fallout I'd get if I defied Pop that way. But maybe someday I would be.

I introduced Evan around as my cousin and said he was spending the summer with me and looking for work. Everybody shook hands with him, and he smiled at them and they smiled back. Whenever they asked him if he had any experience, he said, "No, but I'm ready to learn." Nobody said they had work for him. I figured they needed to get used to him first.

We got home in time to take another look through

the clothes trunk in the attic. Evan tried on worn jeans that were loose around his waist, Pop having been bigger around than Evan even in the past. When I gave Evan a belt and he slid it through the belt loops and buckled it, he shook his head. "Too binding," he said. Without the belt the jeans slid down. We gave up on the jeans and found him a couple more pair of overalls and some loose shirts. I wondered what would happen when winter came.

We stowed his extra clothes in my room and went downstairs to open the store. Evan really liked punching buttons on the cash register; accounting would be difficult at the end of the day. I tried to save all the receipts from his playing around so I could void them out later, and I showed him how to restock stuff to get him away from the register, then how to dust and straighten, and how to use the pricing gun, which he also liked. Granddad watched us from his seat by the stove, nodding once in a while. People came in and bought things. Evan soloed on the register, made change, smiled at strangers. I stood at the magazine display, looked at him behind the counter, and shook my head. Maybe I'd get used to seeing Evan in mundane contexts someday.

"These tasks repeat and repeat," Evan said. He was lining up canned goods at the front edge of a shelf.

"That's right. Once you know them you'll get lots of chances to use them." I was checking our stock of soda and making up an order form for the vendors.

"Discipline," he said. "Don't you get bored?"

"I might, if I stopped to think about it. So I don't think about it. I have this model of the store as it should be in my head, and I try to make everything match that image. Keeps me busy. If everything's perfect, I read a magazine or play solitaire, but that doesn't happen often. It's a living." I listened to myself talk about work and realized I had never articulated my feelings about it to this extent before. Would this way of correcting things toward an imagined end translate to other types of work? I guessed detective work would involve gathering information to fix something that didn't work the way it should.

"A living," Evan said. "Hmm." He pulled a wadded-up gum wrapper from behind the cans. "Where'd this come from?"

"Somebody tossed it there. So many agents of chaos . . ." Well, you needed agents of chaos or you'd run out of things to do. Might be nice to try living without them for a while, though.

He frowned and tucked the trash into his pocket.

Mom came in and stood quietly beside the fishing rods, staring at me and Evan. Evan looked at her with narrowed eyes. "This is your mother?" he asked. I glanced at the mirror by the hat display and moved around until I could see her reflection in it. She looked like herself.

"Mom?" I said. I hesitated, then went toward her. Where was Pop? I was pretty sure he was up at the motel office. If he saw Mom being herself, what would he do?

"It is time for me to be brave." She glanced at Granddad.

"Sylvia," he said, standing up. He collected himself into being the person he had been when I was very little. It was strange to watch him shrug into awareness and intention as if they were a comfortable old jacket he hadn't worn for a while.

"Leo."

"Thought you were dead," said Granddad.

"In a way, I was. It's good to see you."

Granddad walked over and stood in front of Mom, peering at her, his head forward, his eyes wider than normal. "You staying?" he asked after studying her for a moment.

She looked down and shook her head slowly.

"We been missing you."

When she looked up again her eyes were tear bright.

"But," said Granddad, "better if you stay away. You're poison." He shuffled back to his chair by the stove and collapsed down into his current self, his eyes going blank.

How could he say that to Mom? Had he always felt that way about her? I tried to remember back, but mostly what I remembered was how it felt to have her close; I would only have noticed how Granddad treated her if he had hurt her, and I couldn't remember her telling me anything about him hurting her.

Mom blinked and a tear streaked down her face. She nodded at Granddad even though he wasn't looking at her. "I've been building my strength," she said in a low voice, "but I'm not strong enough to stay yet. Not in the face of that. Facing your father will be even more difficult. Nick, I love you very much, and I always will. But I have to go home now. I'll come back."

I tried to think about whether I wanted her to come back. Her presence confused me. I didn't want our old closeness back, and I wasn't sure what to want in place of it. I was glad to know she was doing so well and learning how to use whatever powers she had, and I was still mad at her for deserting me in such a clumsy way. I wondered if I could get Evan to teach me anything. Maybe if I asked him the right way . . .

"Here's my address and phone number," Mom said, holding out a folded piece of paper to me. I took it without touching her fingers. "If there's anything you need, or anything you think I can do for you, call me. Write me. Do you want me to call you?"

"I don't know yet," I said slowly. Suppose she called and Pop answered. He would know she was back in touch. There would be fallout from that.

She looked down. She looked up. Her eyes showed hurt. "You decide," she said. She touched my cheek, and for an instant I was deep in the center of her sadness, a place of unceasing warm rain and dark skies. It was paralyzing. The bell rang on the door as she slipped out before I could even come up for air.

Mariah arrived at noon, as usual, and stared at Evan. He put down the videocassette he had been studying and stared back, his face quiet. She edged closer and circled sideways, watching him. His gaze followed her. After they had exchanged stares for a little while, I said, "This is Evan."

"What?" said Mariah.

"This is Evan."

"But the wolf—"

Evan cocked his head at her and gave her an open-mouthed grin. She blinked. "No," she said.

He yawned, tongue curling, then smiled at her again.

"How can that be?" she asked.

"I think he's staying the summer," I said. "I'm teaching him how to run the store."

"How can you take a thing out of a fairy tale and stick it in a convenience store? This makes no sense," she muttered.

"Evan, this is Mariah."

"I know."

"Oh." I had introduced them while he was a wolf.

"Delighted to meet you again," Evan said to Mariah.

"I—oh, all right," she said, and took his hand for a second.

"We'll be back in about an hour," I said to Mariah, and to Evan: "Let's get something for lunch and take it outside."

"Okay."

In the kitchen I threw together a couple of sandwiches and put them in a sack with a bottle of water. We ran away, Evan letting me set the pace and the direction. I plunged off my path to Lacey's about halfway along, going to a place where big rocks stood in a flat-topped spine that ran from the shore out a little way into the lake. We followed the rocks out to the end and sat surrounded on three sides by water.

He wrinkled his nose at tuna, then bit the sandwich I gave him and chewed slowly, his eyes closed as though he were listening to the flavor. I looked out over the lake at the pines on the opposite shore. A speedboat towed a water-skier in the distance, trailing distant motor sound. Sun touched my head and shoulders, arms and legs, and drummed a ripe algae scent from the lake.

We ate in silence. Afterward, I said, "Do you think this is going to work?" Training him in the store had been difficult, not because he couldn't understand or perform the tasks, but because he had trouble focusing on them or taking them seriously. Mariah was right: how could you take a thing from a fairy tale and stick it in a convenience store?

"I don't know," he said. "I don't mean to be giving you trouble, Nick. I don't think my mind works like yours. All I really want to do is sleep and eat and hunt and run around in the woods, finding out everything that's going on. I'll try again. I'll try harder. How do you make it important?"

"It's food and drink, TV and electricity, home, heat, comfort, being able to shower, wash clothes, drive a car. Work is the fire that heats our stove, the furniture we sit and sleep on. It's what keeps us together."

"Huh." He frowned. "There are other ways to get all those things, but the other ways take work, too. Huh." He scratched his elbow. "I wish I cared about those things, but I really don't. Well, I promised your pop. I can learn to focus. I'm pretty sure I can."

"Hey!"

I looked toward the shore and saw Willow. She ran out along the rocks and sat down beside us. "Are you okay? They did an unbinding last night—"

"It hurt really bad. They did the wrong one," Evan said.

"I tried to tell them not to. They closed the circle without me and sent me to sleep."

"Still think they're just good people?" Evan asked her. "I'm not joking. It nearly killed us. If Nick hadn't known a counterbinding, I don't know what would have happened."

She reached across and touched my face, then looked at Evan, her expression troubled. "But fetch-bonding is wrong," she said.

"*Sirella!* What a time to figure that out!"

She closed her eyes for a minute, then looked at him. "Uncle Rory explained it to me," she said. "Nick explained some of it to me. I've been thinking about this a lot. I know I always want to—" She touched my face again and frowned. "I crave it. I have to try not to do it anymore. It's not respectful. You'll kiss me without it, won't you, Nick?"

"Anytime."

"Will you show me how to find *skilliau?*"

"Will you show me how to do some of this other stuff, like make those lights over my hand?"

She smiled. "Yes. Oh, yes. As long as I'm here, I'll teach you what I can ... when the Keyes go, I must go with them."

"Why?" I asked.

"Because family is more important than anything else," she said, without thinking about it. Then she blinked. After a brief silence, she said, "You aren't seeing the good things about them, Nick. I'm sorry it's so lopsided. There's a warmth about belonging, about being with, about always having someone to talk with who understands. About knowing where you're going and what comes next, about knowing what the right thing to do is, or having someone to ask if you're confused about it. About knowing that when you do things well someone will notice and give you praise and thanks, about knowing that the learning is waiting for you there."

I remembered a belonging warmth I had shared with my mother before she left. I remembered what she said about trees shading each other out, too. To breathe or not to breathe?

"Is their teaching as sloppy as their castings?" Evan said.

"What?" She glanced at him. "They don't have the fine control of our teacher in the Hollow, it's true, but I know fine control already. Rory and Elissa have been showing me new things, things Great-aunt never taught us about how to address the land and the water and life in general."

"Does any of it work?"

"Yes. A connection kindles. I know there's a sort of . . . waiting going on right now, that's why we don't get farther in our tasks. I don't know what the waiting is for. I'm trusting the Powers to let me know when it's over. But I'm touching and being touched." She dipped her fingers in the lake, lifted them, and sent droplets sparkling in the sun, arcing and hanging on air for too long, given gravity. She smiled at Evan.

His face wore a blank look I hadn't seen there very often. "I'm glad you're learning," he said after a little while.

"They would teach you too if you gave them a chance."

"No," he said. "What they have to teach I don't want to learn."

"Evan, if you don't come back—what if the thread is cut?" She gripped his forearm. She shook her head. "Don't let that happen."

"I don't want that," he said. He put his hand over hers on his arm. "I don't want to lose Mama or Papa or you."

"You better figure out what you do want," she said.

"That's harder than I thought, as long as Uncle Bennet has my snow crystal."

I checked my watch. "We better head back," I said.

Evan grinned. "Yes. I'm learning how to run a store, Willow. There's a lot of fine detail work in that, too."

"What?" She laughed. "Whyever?"

He shrugged with one shoulder. "It's a job."

"Are you serious?"

His eyebrows rose. He smiled again, showing teeth. "Maybe," he said. He stood up and stretched. I got to my feet too. We followed Willow back to land.

"Nick? Do you know where other *skilliau* are?"

"I don't know. Pop was talking about my rock collection last night. I used to pick up rocks all the time because they felt different from other rocks, but I stopped taking them home because Pop would get rid of them. Got out of the habit of picking them up at all, actually." I glanced around at the underbrush and tree trunks, trying to tune to rocks the way I had when Mom played rock-hunting games with me so long ago, but I had lost the knack. "I'd have to practice," I said.

"When do you get off work tonight?"

"Five."

"Would you practice then?"

"Quit pushing, Willow," Evan said.

"I want to know what Nick knows."

"The sooner you find *skilliau,* the sooner the Keyes will want to go home, and then we'll have to figure out a lot of things I don't want to deal with, like whether you leave and I stay, or what," he said.

"This isn't about you, Evan."

"Everything's connected."

I glanced at my watch again. We had five minutes to get back. We could make it if we ran. "I'll meet you after work, Willow. Come to the store," I said. I ran through bushes up to my path, rustling and crackling, and Evan came after me, making no noise at all.

Mariah was talking with one of those sandy-haired men she favored. She was smiling an awful lot. It wasn't until the man turned to look at us that I realized it was Rory.

"Evan," he said, and his voice was silky and warm. "We need to talk."

"We do?" Evan's face was blank again, and his voice sounded blank.

"Please," said Rory. He glanced at me. "Alone."

"Whatever you want to talk to me about concerns Nick," Evan said.

I felt a chill. I didn't have protection anymore, and these people had already done things to me without permission. I didn't want them noticing me. I looked at Evan. His face was perfectly still. But there was a hum to him, a silent hum, and its tune was fear. Maybe I'd better stick by him.

"What? How can that be?"

"Nick has given me shelter and salt privilege, and has offered me a—a living."

"A living? How can you live, away from us?"

"I don't know, but I'm willing to try it."

Rory studied me for a moment. He nodded. "What difference does it make? He has a silence on him. Come outside."

"Excuse me. I have to go to work now," I said, glancing at Mariah.

She waved her hand in a shooing motion at us. "I'll stay a little longer." She smiled at Rory.

We went outside and sat on the storefront bench by the newspaper vending machine, Evan in the middle between me and Rory.

Tug-of-war?

"Evan," said Rory. He stared across the road toward Mabel's. After a long moment's silence edged by, he looked at Evan. "We love you. We need you. You are precious to us. It hurts us that you distance yourself from us. I recognize that we have made mistakes in how we treated you; we're not used to dealing with one who starts out so far from us, who keeps such a distance, who doesn't value the same things we value. Come back to us and let us start over. Maybe we can learn a different way to care for you.''

Evan leaned back and turned toward Rory, so I couldn't see his face. The fear hum was still coming from him, growing stronger. "Thank you," he said. "Thanks, but I'd rather stay here."

"This is your last word, even though it may mean cutting the thread that binds the bones?"

"Can you do that? I thought only my parents could make that decision."

"They gave your care over to us."

Evan shook his head. "There was no real hearing about that. I know they were doing what they thought was right, but I am old enough to decide my next steps, and no one asked me."

"You never demonstrated competence."

"What?" He sounded shocked.

"Opportunities have been offered you, and always you took a choice that led you away from what was right," Rory said. "Lately you have actively chosen toward the wrong. Using fetch bond weighs against you. . . . We can understand and forgive everything, though. Return to us. Let us work with you."

Evan stared toward the forest, his face a mask. "Thanks, but no thanks," he said after a moment.

Rory rose. He looked at us. "We love you. We need you." He walked away.

Evan spent the rest of the afternoon focusing on work so hard that we ran out of things to do. I showed him all the inventory we had in various storage spaces, finding some stuff in the rafters I had forgotten we ever had. We did the Sunday afternoon cleaning when there weren't any customers, a job I usually reserved for after the store was closed. Evan had a way of chasing dust that worked better than anything I had ever tried. Some of the dust we used to have was positively historic, but it was all gone now. Evan's method had to do with the transformative powers of fire, he told me, but he didn't explain it.

Pop dropped in in the middle of the afternoon and seemed to have trouble believing how clean and nice everything looked. He swallowed several times. "You should have no trouble finding other work if you want it," Pop told Evan at last.

Evan thanked Pop without smiling. He had lost his easy air, and his intensity made me uncomfortable.

"What's the matter?" I asked Evan when we sat down near the end of the shift. Pop had gone back to the motel, and Granddad was snoozing in his chair.

Evan shook his head. "It's not over. Nothing's settled. They know they're right." After a minute he looked me in the eye. "They might be right, for anybody else. I don't know."

I thought about Mom telling me her family wanted to chop off parts of her. "There must be a—this isn't . . ." I thumped the counter with my fist. I hadn't even known I was planning to talk about the Keyes, but my tongue wouldn't work anyway.

Evan smiled half a smile, then tightened his lips. "At least I know now that I can work."

Willow never showed up after we closed the store. I wondered what that meant.

9

Dirt

At supper that night Pop asked Evan if he had learned all about the store, and Evan said he had learned a lot, but figured there was more I could show him that we hadn't had to deal with today. Pop asked Evan if he wanted to come up to the motel in the morning and see how it should be run. Evan said yes, thank you.

After supper cleanup, we watched television and went to bed early. Evan was distant and distracted. I figured I better get used to this side of him, too; things were going to be more complicated than I had thought.

It was close to midnight when Evan whimpered. I hit the light switch in time to see him snap upright. My thumb throbbed where I had sliced it open the night before. I stared at Evan as he jerked to his feet, his arms bent at the elbows, his hands rigid. He whined. I saw a wolf head on his shoulders for a second. He blinked and it faded.

"What?" I said. My whole hand throbbed, pain moving outward from the cut in my thumb, streaking up my arm.

"Have to . . . go," he said. His legs moved like rusty

mechanical things, walking him to the window, while his upper body stayed stiff and still. He fell out the window. I jumped up and ran to look. His fall was slower than gravity would account for. He thumped down softly, on his feet, and walked jerkily off toward my path to Lacey's.

I dressed fast and ran downstairs and outside. I caught up with Evan not very far into the woods, tugged on his bent arm. It was as stiff as stove wood. He kept walking. "What?" I said. "What?"

"Go back," he said.

"No!"

"Guess they love me too much to let me go. They laid pullers and compulsions on me. This is going to be bad. Go back before they start on you."

"But isn't this"—I coughed—"what they told you not to do to me?" Even saying "they" was an effort. "They say walk and you walk?" I coughed again.

"But this is for my own good," he said. His legs scissored. His arms stayed stiff and bent, hands forward, like the arms of a mannequin pretending to catch a basketball. I had to push myself to keep up with him. "For the good of the family, too, whatever they think that is. They think they need to straighten out my priorities. Work, wife, babies. They won't kill me. They won't even really hurt me, except in the spirit. There's nothing you can do except get hurt. Do me a big favor. Let me go. Go away, Nick. Go home." He strode on past me without looking back.

I ran into the forest. It was different in the dark. Underbrush clung to me, bracken tripped me, and dewberry and blackberry canes scratched at me. The trees seemed too close together. Everything was damp with dew. The smell of pine resin was strong, and so was the odor of vanilla leaf and the rank green of the damp plants I broke through. I fought upslope for a while, then sat down on mossy, plant-heavy earth, surrounded on all sides by short spiky plants, shapes and scents telling me they were white everlasting, goatsbeard, fireweed, thistles, with elderberry branches pressing against my back. My throat felt thick and hot and sore, and my arm ached and throbbed as though on fire. I buried my hand in the damp moss and felt a little better.

Presently I calmed. How could I help Evan? Sneaking up on cabin five, I might be more of a liability than an asset. And he had told me not to, anyway.

Without his *fetchkva,* I didn't have to obey Evan, though.

I contemplated Pop. I wished he could do something. He had been bossing me around for years. But he couldn't even see these guys if they didn't want him to, and if my voice, not even trained, worked on him, probably the Keyes could order him around with impunity.

I thought about Willow and Lauren. I figured if there was anything they could do on Evan's behalf they would have already done it. Or maybe they were working on something now. I couldn't think of any way to get in touch with them that didn't involve sneaking up on Lacey five.

I thought about Megan. I imagined knocking on the door of Lacey cabin nine, waking her up, and asking her to come with me to Lacey five and help Evan. Suppose she said yes. What could she bring? She could do CPR, and she had a pretty elastic mind when confronted with the unbelievable. That was cool, but it was hardly offensive capability. Probably it had been smart of her to bow out of all this before it got any weirder than what she had already witnessed.

There had to be something I could do to help. I wished I could think of it. I wondered if a gun would do any good. Somehow I doubted it, even though I knew where Pop kept the shotgun and some shells. The Keyes would probably make me shoot .myself.

Tired and discouraged and cold, I got to my feet and headed toward Lacey five. Whatever happened to me,

at least I would know that I had tried to help. I could
gather information, if nothing else. I had always thought
information could save me.

Just ahead of the final crook in the path, I dropped
to my hands and knees. The pine-needle-carpeted dirt
was cool against my palms, but not cold. I crept a little
way and collapsed, feeling strange, as if the ground was
pulling me harder than it usually did. I pushed up again,
wondering if this meant something, trying to work it
out in my head, coming up empty. I kept crawling,
wishing my second sight or whatever it was was something handier, like night vision. I put my hand on a
twig and winced as it snapped.

Slowly and carefully, I made it around the side of
cabin five to where I could see in through the French
doors into the living room.

They were all gathered around the table the way they
had been that afternoon when Evan introduced me to
them. They all wore dark colors this time instead of
their fake tourist clothes.

Evan sat hugging himself across from the fireplace
and staring up at Uncle Bennet, who held something
tight in his left hand and gestured with his right. Faintly
through the half-open French doors I could hear him:
he would speak a phrase, gesture, touch Evan's forehead. Each time he touched Evan's forehead, my cut
thumb throbbed in sympathy. Evan would blink each
time, and each time he opened his eyes afterward, they
looked a little duller, their golden dimming to brown.

At first, Willow cried "no" every time Uncle Bennet
spoke. Then Elissa went and stood behind her and put
hands on her shoulders and whispered into her ear, and
Willow settled into unnatural stillness.

I thought about rushing the doors. I thought about
how useless it had been Saturday afternoon by the pool
when I tried to interrupt Bennet while he was locking
Evan into human form.

Bennet kissed Evan's forehead, patted him. Evan closed his eyes and did not open them.

Hot fury bloomed in my chest. I stood up ... and ran back into the forest. This was the worst thing I had ever seen: it was like watching a car wreck from a distance, seeing people destroyed before my eyes, and not being able to do anything about it. In my years as a watcher I had never seen anything else I so much wanted to step into and change, anything else I had felt so completely incapable of fixing. I might as well jump in the lake now and not come up.

They wanted rocks? I would get rocks. I would throw them. Maybe that would mess things up. I ran upslope off my path to a place where a tumble of jagged rocks lay, grabbed some, hugged them to my chest, and tried to run back down to the cabin.

But the plants wouldn't let me through, and the rocks grew heavier and heavier while I held them. I kept pushing downslope and the plants kept walling up in front of me, until I ended up heading deeper into the woods, following whatever path the plants left open to me. At last I put the rocks down and just stumbled whatever direction was open.

Presently I realized I knew where I was going, and I walked faster. I came to the clearing and climbed little rocks up onto Father Boulder. Treetops oceaned in the night above me, and the stars looked small in the dark sky. I felt far away from everything that mattered to me, but I was too tired to fight the forest anymore. I wished I knew how to send my mind out and do something with it, the way the Keyes could do things long distance like unbind me from Evan and pull him back into their web. Willow had promised to teach me things, and Mom had offered to teach me things, but I hadn't had time yet to learn. Now even the forest was fighting me.

Maybe if I got some rest and waited for daylight, I could figure something out. I could hardly imagine falling asleep, though, I felt so angry and helpless. My mind raged 'round and 'round in circles, pushing at facts, not finding any give: the Keyes were stronger than I was and they could do what they pleased; I had no weapons and no armor.

I lay on the rough sandy skin of Father Boulder. At first I was really cold against this huge cool stone, but presently I started feeling warmer. Gradually my mind slowed and settled. The fire in my arm eased. I felt like I was sinking into a warm, gritty soup. I curled up and fell asleep.

In the dream it was night, and I was sitting neck deep in sulfur-smelling warm mud, talking to a looming dark shape that looked like a big unpopped bubble floating on the mud's surface. ''Do you know what you want?'' asked the bubble. Its voice was almost too low to hear and had a sandy, gritty quality to it. I couldn't figure out where the voice came from: nothing on the bubble's surface changed. Then again, everything was dark and I couldn't see well.

''What I want?'' I said.

''Do you know what you want? That is always the question.''

I had the feeling I had been hearing this question for a long time—years, maybe. At least as long as I had lived at Sauterelle Lake. The answer changed. When I was younger the answer might have been something like a package of Twinkies, a ride on a horse, a new bike. I could remember hearing the question, casting out a net into the blackness in my mind, and finally fixing on something or other. Often enough when I narrowed down the focus and said what I wanted out loud, the bubble would give me a feeling like a smile and say it couldn't give me that. For a couple years, what I had wanted was Mom. When I had said that, always hoping that the bubble had the power to give me what I wanted, it would answer me with sad silence, a communion of sorrow. The mud would hold me as though hugging me, and I found some comfort in that.

Did I know what I wanted? Even when I did know, the bubble hadn't given it to me. Maybe it was waiting for me to want the right thing.

I had the feeling that lately I had been answering the question with, "I don't know."

"Do you know what you want?" asked the bubble.

I closed my eyes and thought. And then I knew. Peering at the bubble, I said, "I want to rescue Evan. I want to get his snow crystal away from those people so they'll have to stop hurting him. I want him to be able to do what he wants. I want Willow to be able to do what she wants too, even if she wants to stay with them." I thought about Willow and Evan's dead little brother, and how the mystery of it had warped both of them so that they had to be sent away from home. I couldn't want for that never to have happened, because if it hadn't, I would never have met them. And anyway, I had the feeling that the bubble couldn't do a really big want like that, either. It hadn't been able to bring Mom back, and their little brother was a lot farther away than Mom had been. "That's what I want," I said.

"Ahhhhhhhh," said the bubble. It sounded deeply satisfied. The mud grew a fraction warmer.

"Can you help me? I don't know who else to ask."

"I can help you. You have to decide how much you want this, though."

"How much?" I couldn't think of a single other thing I wanted inside the moment of the dream. "I want it a lot."

"If I help you, everything will change."

"Will Evan still be Evan? Will he be able to go back to being a wolf? Will Willow be able to say what she wants, do what she wants?"

"Yes."

"Will they be free from the Keyes?"

"Yes."

"That's what I want."

We sat silent together with the mud between us.

"To accomplish what you want," said the dark bubble eventually, "you have to act, too. Watching is no longer enough."

"That's okay. I want to act. I can't stand not being able to do anything about this."

"Evan will not change, and Willow will not change, but you will change."

I wasn't sure I wanted to ask anything else about this. I had been prepared to turn into a poodle or a chihuahua for no other reason than the amusement of someone else. This was much more important. "Will it hurt?"

"Yes."

"What do I change into?"

"My son."

I didn't know how to deal with that, and I didn't know what it meant. I had more than enough parents. But then, Father Boulder had always been ... a father to me, in the same way the lake was like a mother. How different could this be? "What do I have to do?"

"Put your head under the mud."

"But—"

"Put your head under the mud."

"But I won't be able to breathe."

"That's the only way I can help you."

I sat in the mud's enveloping warmth and thought about that for a while. If I died by drowning in mud, I'd be letting down Pop and Granddad and Evan and Willow and even Mom. If I didn't duck under the mud I could go home and open the store at nine, and life would go on, only with a wound where my relationships with Evan and Willow were, and acres of worry. Or I could go to Lacey five and plead with the Keyes, but I had a pretty clear idea that that wouldn't do any good, only get me in deeper trouble.

If I did duck under the mud there was a chance that Father Boulder could help me. I couldn't imagine how. But he had never lied to me about anything.

I thought about Evan being marched away under someone else's power, locked up by people he didn't trust so that they could teach him how to behave. I thought about Willow, having to watch this happen to him. I thought about Mom, who had escaped the cage of her first family, and then escaped the cage she had made of her second family, and who was finally learning not to build cages. I thought about Pop, wanting everything to stay the same, maybe finally figuring out that it wouldn't, accepting Evan into our lives one way and then another, capable of more change than I had suspected.

I thought about me. Willow had come, and Evan had come, and everything had changed. I loved it. I wasn't ready to let go of either of them, no matter what the Keyes wanted. I didn't want things to go back to the way they were before.

I took a deep breath, gripped my nose between thumb and forefinger, and ducked my head under the warm, sticky mud. For a little while it felt great being surrounded by solid warmth; I'd never felt it on my face before, kissing against my lips and eyelids, crowding into my hair. I felt like I was floating inside a hug.

It crept into my ears. I shook my head, but that didn't stop it. Finally I stilled myself. I hadn't been able to hear anything, anyway ... until my ears were full of mud; then I could sense that things were going on around me, sending the vibrations of movement to where I could almost hear them. Nothing was happening close to me, though; I knew that through my skin and my ears.

Presently my breath got stale, and I breathed it out. It formed bubbles and rose away from me. I tried to follow it and swim up to the surface to get more air, but I didn't know which direction to swim; I was weightless, no clues from gravity. I thrashed around, the mud embracing my every move, giving way and filling in, inescapably friendly.

Finally I had to open my mouth and nose, and the mud came in, heavy and slow. It tasted a little like chocolate and a little like sulfur. It came down my throat and into my nose instead of air. I swallowed it because I needed to swallow something. I tried to choke, but I couldn't even cough, just felt my chest and throat spasming. I thrashed, trying to drive the mud back out. There was nothing to hold on to. There was no way I could fight. Everything in the world was mud.

I saw whole galaxies of purple and pale green stars on the insides of my eyelids. I felt like my head was about to explode.

Then it did explode. My whole body exploded. Pieces of me went everywhere, and the mud embraced them all.

Hurt like hell at first. Slowly, the pain faded. Ultimately, being dead was very restful.

I opened my eyes and looked up at blue sky with pine tops, and speckled gray sandstone around the edges of the view. I pulled long cool draughts of air into me, wondering how my head could still be on my body, and how I could still have lungs, or for that matter, eyes to see with, since I could remember what it felt like having them pop. With each deep breath I felt my way into my body, hands and feet, arms and legs, head, chest, back, butt, everything. I was alive.

I was alive, and the world smelled and tasted slightly different. Blue looked bluer. Green almost glowed. The gray and white stone of Father Boulder reminded me of something else.

Flesh.

I put my hand against the rock and felt humming life under the surface.

I closed my eyes for a little while, then opened them

and studied myself. I was still wearing whatever I had thrown on last night—turned out to be jeans and a worn flannel shirt of Pop's I had found for Evan in the trunk in the attic—and I was still curled up on top of Father Boulder, only there was something different about my position. Stone pressed against me from more directions than just down.

When I was sure I was all there I sat up. I was sitting in a cup on top of the rock just the right size to hold a curled and sleeping me.

I began to shake.

Father Boulder was a constant. He wasn't supposed to change, no matter what else happened. I closed my hands on the lip of the cup and held on while I shook. I felt hot, and hotter, and then hotter. I wondered why my hands weren't bright red, the way Pop's face got when he was yelling.

After a while the heat faded and so did the shakes. I climbed out of the cup. The tennis shoes I had stomped into the night before were missing; my feet were bare. "What happened?" I said, sitting on the still-smooth slope of the rest of the rock.

Lie on the ground.

The voice came from the rock under me, only it wasn't so much spoken as felt.

He'd never talked to me while I was awake before. Maybe I was imagining it.

On the other hand, what could it hurt?

I climbed down off Father Boulder and lay on the needle- and moss-carpeted ground, pressing my palms to the soil. Time drifted past. I realized I had left my watch in my room. I realized I was hungry. I realized this was probably the end of independent life for me; as soon as I got home Pop was going to take away all my freedom. So I might as well do whatever the hell I wanted to right now. Mostly what I wanted was to find out whether Evan and Willow were all right.

My skin felt prickly all over. I wondered if ants were

walking on me. I resisted the urge to scratch, even though the prickling intensified into the unbearable range, and it was everywhere, even on my face. I closed my eyes and waited.

All right. Pull the cloak around you. Go to the place of strangers.

I sat up. Cloak? Cloak? I looked down at myself and realized I was incredibly dirty. Dirt was packed under my fingernails. My skin was covered with dirt so deep I couldn't see my natural color, and my clothes were filthy. I slapped at a sleeve and dust flew up. My scalp itched. I scratched, and dirt cascaded down. My hair was caked with it.

Jumping in the lake would feel really good. I brushed off the back of one hand.

Stop it. Pull the cloak around you.

Cloak? What cloak? I put my hand down, feeling among the dirt and moss and pine needles to see if there was some sort of cape on the ground. Dirt rose up and coated the back of my hand again.

Spooked, I jumped to my feet. I peeked inside my shirt and saw my chest was covered in a layer of dirt. Drowned in mud, covered in dirt, I thought. I wondered what my face looked like. My feet were deep dirt-brown.

Dirt was the cloak.

Ewww.

Okay.

I knelt, closed my eyes, grabbed dirt and sifted it down over myself. At first I was only conscious of how much I hated the feeling of being filthy. It itched. It felt wrong. All I wanted was water. Even my throat and the inside of my nose felt coated with dirt. I couldn't smell anything, and all I could taste was dirt, but I noticed I wasn't coughing anymore.

I stopped scrabbling in the dirt after a while. I had a feeling of completeness. I couldn't imagine being any dirtier. I opened my eyes and stood up, and suddenly

I didn't itch anywhere anymore. I couldn't even feel the dirt, any more than I felt my own skin from inside.

I walked down the slope toward the place of strangers.

My knock left a streak of dirt on the door. I stooped and grabbed another handful of dirt to restore my hand.

The door took a while to open. Elissa stood there. She was wearing the white see-through dress, and she held a burning stick of incense in one hand. "What is it you want?" she said.

"Evan, and his snow crystal. Willow."

"Go away."

"No."

"There are more restrictions we can place on you than silence without violating salt covenant. Go away now and we will leave you alone."

I came toward her, and she backed away.

"I forbid you to cross this threshold," she said, her voice heavy with vinegar and steel.

"You invite me. Ceaselessly you invite me." The voice was low and muddy. It came from the dirt. The words tingled against my skin. Inside the dirt, I walked right into the house.

"Rory!" Elissa cried, backing toward the living room. The dirt walked me after her, which scared me. It felt like my clothes had come alive and were controlling my body.

The whole family was still sitting around the table in the living room. Smoke rose from the fire in the little brass bowl in the center. The *skilliau* rock lay in front of it, and Granddad's creel was still right behind it. Rory, dressed all in black and looking much less like a nice vacationing tourist, sat between the table and the fireplace, with fire at his back. He had a silver wand in his hand. At his left, Willow cradled a green glass bowl of water on her lap. She looked frightened, trapped, and upset. To Rory's right, Lauren held a bone;

next to her, one boy held a leaf, and beyond him, the other a feather. Bennet sat beside Willow, holding a chunk of quartz, and Evan, still twisted tight somehow, his eyes dull, clutched a handful of dirt.

"You called me and I have come," said the dirt on me.

"Nick?" said Willow.

"Silence!" Rory snapped at her.

"What do you want?" asked the dirt.

"Who are you?" Rory whispered.

"I am what you speak to morning, noon, and night, what you invite, what you summon. Now I am here."

Rory sketched some signs in the air with his thumb. Suddenly everything except Rory looked different. A yellow ghost wolf sat where Evan had sat. Willow had an outline of yellow flame; Lauren's lines were sketched in wavering green; Elissa's were too. Bennet and the older boy looked like red rocks, and the younger boy was pale blue and see-through.

I remembered Evan heating the pot of water and saying, "Sign fire." I remembered him looking at my ring of blue flame and saying it had something to do with air. Maybe yellow was fire and blue was air; red rocks might be earth, and green would be water, I guessed.

As for me, I was standing in the middle of a ghost volcano, red-hot lava spilling down from above my head to pool and puddle on the floor around me. I could almost feel the heat.

In a moment the images faded.

The Keyes stared wide-eyed at me for a while. Dirt held me still. Evan still looked tranced and dull, but Willow was staring at me with her mouth half-open.

After a heavy silence, Rory said something in the other language.

"Yes," said the dirt.

Rory spoke in the other language, a passionate torrent

of questions. The answer from the dirt was always, "No."

He cried one last question. The dirt said, "Did you honor me? In many ways you did. In this most important way you did not." It held out my arms, and my head looked down at myself, then up at Rory again.

"This is yours," he said. His voice sounded tired.

"Yes."

There was another long silence. I thought about that. I belonged to the dirt? I belonged to Father Boulder? I belonged here, at Sauterelle?

And my memory stone was in the lake somewhere.

"How can we honor it?" asked Rory.

"Give it what it wants."

That silence stretched a while, too. At last, Rory said, "What do you want, Nick Verrou?"

"Evan. His snow crystal. Willow. And I want you to leave me alone."

Everyone sat still for a long moment. Only the little fire moved. The face formed above it, looked at me and laughed silently, then stretched back into smoke.

"This isn't just up to me," Rory said. "Evan's and Willow's parents placed them with us, trusting us to care for them."

"Transfer the trust to me," said the dirt. "I will honor it."

"*Skilliau* being a parent? I have never heard of a thing like that."

"You forget," said the dirt, its voice deeper still. It held out my arms to Rory, and then . . .

Then all my edges blurred. Skin and bones, blood and muscle, hair and nail and breath, nerves and brain, everything that made me human melted out from inside me, throwing me back into the night's dream, where the mud came into me and I into it and we mixed and I was a bubble in the mud. "I am *skilliau's* parent. I am the parent of everything," the dirt said. Its knowledge was inside me. I knew what it felt like to be weathered by hail and rain and lightning, flood and frost, and how the small stirrings in it excited it and woke it, and how small stirrings grew to be larger stirrings, how grass bladed up to eat sun and in turn be eaten by other things that had once been earth, how stirrings grew and spread and intensified until so much was stirring, plants, animals, insects, birds, tiny things and giant things, how even dirt's loving grasp on itself was broken as feet lifted loose, only to return, and wings lifted farther; but everything came home to rest eventually; everything was born of dirt and everything came home to dirt, and I was dirt.

"Power," whispered Rory. "I did not know."

The dirt laughed. It lowered my arms that were arms no longer. Stirrings inside me itched and ached and flowed as what I recognized as myself reformed inside the cloak of dirt. "Do you any longer want what you have asked me for?" the dirt asked Rory. "Or do you wish me to withdraw?"

I tried to imagine what it would be like if dirt withdrew from you. Would it take gravity away? Would it keep everything you could eat away from you? Would your body stop working? Or maybe it just meant we would walk out the door. Then what?

My mother had cut me off from her, and then I had told her to stay away. My father and I had so far not connected on a comfortable level. I was inside dirt. I knew it was my ultimate parent, one that I would never leave no matter where I went, one that would never leave me.

Rory blinked. Then he sang a long complicated song in the other language. Elissa and Bennet joined in for some of it. The dirt on me grew warm for part of it, cool for another part of it, and then sizzling hot near the end, but it didn't hurt me. It sang some of the time too, deep, muddy responses to some of the things Rory sang. Rory unbuttoned a pouch at his side and pulled out a sliver of clouded quartz. He held it in his open hand. It lifted from his hand and floated across the room and I reached for it, pulled it out of the air.

Evan relaxed and took some deep breaths. Color returned to his eyes.

They all sang some more. Willow took the bowl of water from her lap and set it on the table. Her shoulders untensed. "Dirt," she said in a low voice.

"Child," said the dirt.

"If I bind to you, do I unbind to my family?"

"Only if you wish to," said the dirt.

"Thank you," she whispered. "Thank you for choice."

Dirt raised my arms and said something in a voice like a mountain talking. Rory, Bennet, and Elissa repeated it in voices like pale echoes. The children cast the objects they were holding, leaf, bone, and feather, into the fire, and spoke farewell words. A shudder went through me. I felt like a sleepwalker waking up in midstride. The weight of power and history and gravity eased off my shoulders.

"Honor the terms," said the dirt. "Now we can talk." Then I was walking toward the front door. Then I was out in the open air.

10

Stones

"**O**h, God," I said. "Oh, God."

A moment later and Evan was behind me, the door slamming shut in his wake, and then his arms were around me, dislodging dirt. He still clutched his handful of dirt. "Iloveyouiloveyou," he said. He released me and danced around me like a delighted dog.

"Willow?" I said.

"She wanted to stay. She wants to talk to them. She'll come if you want."

"If I want?" Skewed déjà vu of our whole relationship: my wanting her not to want me to do things unless we both agreed first. I shook my head. "When she wants. Come on."

Dirt and I walked into the woods, wending the secret ways with Evan behind us until we came to the clearing where Father Boulder stood. Evan stopped at the edge of the trees, staring, as I climbed up on top and sat with my feet dangling in the me-shaped cup in the rock.

"This place," Evan whispered.

"I don't know what just happened," I said. "It sounded like whatever this dirt stuff is adopted you. I don't know what that means. It adopted me too. I said it was okay."

"Oh, Nick!"

"Is it okay with you?"

He stared at me. He blinked. He closed his mouth and nodded, slowly at first, and then vigorously.

I set the sliver of Evan's snow crystal at the bottom of the cup. Sandstone welled up to envelop it, and kept welling up, filling in the cup and pushing my feet up until the rock was smooth again. I patted the rock. "Thank you," I said. "Thank you."

My pleasure.

"May I come in?" Evan asked.

The dirt said, "This is your place. I am your parent now."

Evan walked, with a hesitation between each step, over to Father Boulder, held his hands near the rock, skimming the air around it. "Oh, Nick. This stone. This place! Did you know where it was all along?"

"I come here a lot."

"*Sirella.* Talk about paying attention to all the wrong things. I could have asked you a few questions and known all this. . . ." He shook his head, smiling.

"This is Father Boulder," I said, patting the rock. "Now he has your crystal."

"Mmm." Evan asked a question in the other language, and the dirt said yes to him. He pressed against Father Boulder, embracing rock with his arms as wide as they could go.

"Do you understand what just happened? Is this all right?"

"It's more than all right, little brother. You amaze me. Can I—?" He kissed the rock, stepped out of Pop's overalls, and lay on the ground, and a misty minute later he sprang up as his wolf self. "*Ruh!*" he said. He leapt up onto the rock and sat beside me.

I raised my arm to put it around him, but then thought, no, I'll get him all dirty. He nudged me with his head. I hugged him anyway.

"*Ruf,*" he said. He licked my cheek and sneezed.

I let him go. "Yeah," I said. "I don't know if I ever get to take a shower again."

"How did you—" He cocked his head. I was so happy I could understand him even though I was no longer his fetch that I hugged him again. "How the heck did you ever come up with this plan? How *could* you?"

"Father Boulder gave me a dream."

"Wow."

"I think . . . I died in my dream."

He stared at me with wide yellow eyes. He sniffed me. *"Wuff,"* he said. "Hard to tell. Lift your hand."

I raised my dirt-encrusted hand, and he waved his paw above it. Instead of the gas-blue ring of flame I'd seen there the first two times he and Willow had tried this, there was a glowing red liquid mountain, its base just the size of my palm.

"Oh, Nick," he whispered as the mountain faded. "I'll never be able to thank you enough."

"This means something, huh."

"You've changed alignments. I've never heard of that before."

"I like the way it sounds." I flattened my hands against Father Boulder. "The dirt was great," I said. "Can I take it off now?"

Lick your hand, he said.

"Eww!"

Lick your hand.

I closed my eyes for a second. I had done everything Father Boulder had told me, and he had kept all his promises. Some of what he had told me to do hurt, but he had kept his promises. I sighed. I lifted my hand to my mouth and licked dirt off the back of it, wondering what, in the greater scheme of things, this meant. I was getting tired of everybody else having greater schemes.

The dirt tasted gritty and dusty, with a faint overtone of sweet. It was not about to become my taste treat of choice. Water would have helped. After I had licked a couple inches of skin clean, Father Boulder said, *Enough.*

I swallowed a few more times and almost managed to work up some spit. My stomach felt prickly. "Whoa," I said. I felt like a sparkler was shooting out sparks inside me. It was strange but not unpleasant.

That's all I need for now, said Father Boulder. *You may drop the cloak.*

"Thanks," I said. I knew everything had changed, just as he had said it would, but I couldn't figure out how, or what it might mean to me. There would probably be plenty of time for questions—the rest of my life.

I looked at the sky. The sun was somewhere between ten and eleven. "I have to go home."

"I'll come with you," said Evan.

"Good."

On the way back to the store I took off my clothes and jumped in the lake with them. The water embraced me. I floated for a while, just feeling the water all around me, warm against my skin—that couldn't be true, it was still morning, and the sun hadn't had time to warm the top layer of lake water—but I felt comfortable, much more comfortable than I had felt submerged in mud in my dream. For a while I rested, floating, with my eyes closed.

Then I dived down, still hanging onto my clothes, and scrubbed myself and my clothes as well as I could. I stayed under for a while. I opened my eyes and stared at a dim green world that went on away from me in all directions. I stared up at water-warped sky.

This was a safe place.

I left most of the dirt in the water.

"Any explanation at all?" Pop asked, lowering his *Hitchcock's.* His voice was calm, even friendly.

"I had to save a life," I said.

"I like that one. You fall in the lake?"

"Yep."

"Somebody was drowning, I take it?"

"Pretty much. Did Granddad get his cereal?"

"Of course." He looked at Evan the wolf, who stood beside me. "So where's the other Evan?"

"Uh," I said. I looked down at Evan too. I wondered if he would ever return to human form again. Maybe he would know it was safe now that his uncle didn't have the snow crystal. Maybe he had never wanted anything but to be a wolf. Maybe that was his idea of enough. "It's hard to explain."

"He said he was going to come up to the motel this morning with me. He unreliable too?"

That stung. "Pop ... I've been reliable for years, haven't I? These last few days haven't exactly been typical."

He ran a hand over his head and said, "You're right. I didn't mean to say that. I been expecting a lot from you, and getting it, too. I been sitting here giving it some thought. You know, I might be able to run this place without you after all."

My first feeling was a rush of hurt. For five years I'd been doing a lot of everything around this place, and not even for money. This was the thanks he gave me? The relief didn't even have time to show up before he said, "Maybe for a little while, anyway, sometimes. I guess you probably have a few summer things to do. I'm glad you got your dog back."

"I am too," I said.

"What happened to your friend? Explain it to me even if it is hard."

I looked down at Evan, who stared up at me. "It doesn't make a whole lot of sense, Pop, but Granddad understands it. This Evan and the other Evan—"

"No, Nick."

"They're the same."

"No, Nick. You gotta stop telling these whoppers."

"Pop ..."

He shook his head.

"Should I prove it to him?" Evan asked.

"No," I said. "Maybe later."

"I take it you're having a conversation with him now," Pop said.

I looked at him and bit my lower lip. After a minute I said, "Pop, did you know Mom was weird when you married her?"

"What!"

"You must have figured it out at some point."

"What does your mother have to do with any of this?"

"Well, she was my mother."

He frowned out the door. Presently he said, "Yep, I knew she was weird when I married her."

I sighed and said, "So, I can talk to Evan."

He drummed his fingers on the counter, staring beyond me. "Okay," he said at last. "Give me time. I forgot how to think about this stuff and stay sane. Gotta work my way back up to it."

"Okay."

"You ready to come back to work? I've got people to check out at the motel."

"I need a hot shower and something to eat."

"Customers can find their way in here, I guess. I left them a note."

"I'll be down as soon as I can."

He nodded and lifted his magazine again. I hesitated a moment, then walked past him and into the hallway to our part of the building. I paused just before I lost sight of Pop, and glanced back at him. He was staring at me. We both looked away.

I dug my fingernails into the soap; it was the only way I ever cleaned them, but it wasn't working on this particular type of dirt. I'd have to use one of the manicure tools in the store, I thought. Then I thought, what the hell am I thinking about? Did I or did I not just have the most intense experience of my life? Had I really died in my dream? Had I really faced all those sorcerous people and turned into mud and back, freed the captive prince and princess, and come out of it almost unscathed? Lord Calardane would be proud of me.

The shower still smelled like mildew, and work was still waiting for me. In a weird way I found that comforting.

Even though I washed my hair twice, sandy dirt stuck to the comb after the shower. It didn't seem too visible in my hair in the steam-fogged mirror. I ignored it and got dressed, thinking I would have to do laundry tonight up at the motel.

It occurred to me as I tied the laces on my old tennis shoes that I really, actually could load up a backpack, take Evan, and head for the hills. Everything I knew about camping I had read in books and magazines, but we had a lot of outdoors magazines in the store; I had been mentally practicing camping for years. The Venture Inn store sold most of what a person needed to spend a night or two in the wilderness. If we ran into any trouble, I had the feeling Evan could come up with some unorthodox way to handle it. Or maybe I could. Dirt was everywhere. I looked out the bathroom window at the forest and the sky and thought, yes.

Megan and Kristen were in the store when I had finished my cereal in the kitchen and Evan and I pushed past the curtain. Pop closed his magazine, and headed for the motel without even one scold.

"Oh," Megan said, squatting and holding out a hand to Evan. He went to her and smelled it. "You're okay! I'm so glad. And . . . I'm so sorry," she said. She raised her hand and tentatively stroked his head. He let her. "I feel like such a chicken."

"They're really scary people," I said. "They're the scariest people I ever met."

Evan said, "Tell her you fixed their wagon."

Megan looked up at me, waiting, her hands snagged in Evan's ruff.

"He says I fixed their wagon."

"You *did?* How could you, when that creepy man could just stare at you and make you do stuff?"

I gazed over her head. A line of cobweb hung from the ceiling. I would have to get a broom. "Evan got in worse trouble. I didn't know what to do. I thought about asking Pop to help me." I looked at her. "I even thought about asking you to help me. Finally I thought of this other friend I have, and he helped me."

"Does that mean we can relax?"

I wondered. What more could the Keyes do to me? If I had seen me being dirt, *I* would have been scared of me. "I think so."

"Maybe start over?" she asked Evan. He licked her nose. She hugged him. "This is *sooo weird.*"

"It's a really, really good trick," Kristen said, drifting closer and staring at Evan. She sounded a little lost. "Nick, is this the strangest summer ever? I keep wanting to sleep through it."

"Where's Ian?"

"He's boring." She put a *Cosmo* on the counter and handed me money.

"Stay awake and keep looking around." I gave her change.

She looked at Megan and Evan. She glanced at me, licked her lip, focused on Megan again, and said, "Megan, do you really want a boyfriend who's a dog?"

"I guess I do," said Megan, rising. "Or a wolf, anyway." Evan sat watching her, tail curled around his feet, his mouth hanging open in a panting grin.

Kristen frowned. She stared at me. "Changed my mind. Don't want to sleep through it. Okay?"

"Good," I said.

She rolled her *Cosmo* up and tucked it under her arm, gave me a smile, then shook her head, frowning down at Evan.

"Next time let's swim in the lake," Megan said to Evan, "some place far from Lacey's."

"*Ruh!*"

"Like, today?"

"Tell her to wait," Evan told me. "Ask her to leave her number. I'm not sure you and I are finished with everything."

I got out a piece of scratch paper. "He'll call you," I said, handing Megan a pen. Kristen shook her head again while Megan wrote. She smiled, though.

Willow came by just as I was closing the store. I was running out the register tape for Pop, watching the strings of numbers in their categories, thinking that if I paid attention to this stuff I would figure out how the business was doing and whether it was reasonable for me to ask Pop for enough credit to buy camping gear, when she leaned across the counter and grabbed me and kissed me. She smelled like evergreens and tasted like clover.

"Hey," I said, when I could.

She climbed across the counter, let her legs down behind it, grabbed me, and kissed me again. Then she let me go and rubbed tears out of her eyes.

"What?" I whispered. I lifted my arms and put them around her just to see what it felt like.

"It was so awful. It was just terrible. I have never been so glad to see anyone in my whole life as I was when you came walking in that door like a big old dirt pile. They don't understand Evan at all. They couldn't even see they were killing him. They wouldn't listen to me. I kept trying to make them stop. I used to think I was so hot, but Elissa's a lot stronger than I am. Plus they really know how to act in concert, those Keyes. Rory gathers them all together and they turn on a spigot, and whoosh, power." She leaned against me a moment, then straightened and stroked her hand through my hair. She frowned and studied her palm.

Her eyebrows rose. She showed me what she was looking at. Grit clung to her skin.

"I have the feeling it'll never all wash out," I said.

She smiled, her eyes golden. "It was beautiful."

"It wasn't me."

"It was enough you, and it wouldn't have happened
without you."

I touched the dirt on her hand. "Why do you want
to stay with them when dirt would have let you out
of it?"

She sighed and said, "They're my family. Your family is your family, even when they're acting like idiots.
And who knows, maybe they'll listen to me and I can
tell them what they need to change, once they stop
telling me what I need to change."

Your family is your family. . . .

I thought about Mom's address and phone number,
hidden in my bottom dresser drawer.

Willow frowned. "You know, you could still pretend
to be a fetch, and I could take you home to the Hollow,
and we could figure out about my baby brother. . . ."

"I'll have to ask Pop if I can have some time off."
I had no clue how I could solve a case ten years old,
but it was the first time anybody had asked me to detect anything.

Willow was still kissing me when Pop came to pull
the tape off the register. He walked back through the
curtain, shaking his head.

"What the heck did they want with Granddad's creel,
anyway?" I asked Evan that night when I was getting
ready for bed.

"Why do you keep asking me questions like that?"
he said, rolling around on his back on the rug. He
looked at me from upside down, his mouth open in a
grin, his tongue hanging out the side of his mouth. I
glared at him. He rolled over and sat up. "It's some
complicated thing about the—the spirit of a thing that's

been used for years. They needed something local and human-touched to use in the summoning. Uncle Bennet can find stuff like that; he's a kind of walking dowser. So he decided that thing was what he needed. Are you satisfied now?"

I brushed my teeth and wondered.

The second time I saw Willow disappear, she knew I was watching her. I sat on the edge of the lake as the sky lightened in the east, deep night blue bleaching toward dawn white. My feet were in the cold water, my toes dug into the mud and feeling as if they could root there. I knew the mud should be freezing, but somehow it felt comfortable. Other things had changed since I had changed alignments; Evan had helped me test it. I had lost the super-salesman voice—couldn't remember how to make it come out of my mouth. I had decided not to tell Pop yet.

I could still see through most false or acquired images, though. I asked Evan why he had looked like a wolf to me, when Mom had still looked like Mom even when she thought she was disguised. "Think about it," he had said.

The only reason I came up with was that somewhere deep inside, he really had the soul of a wolf. I remembered the flicker of him I had seen when Rory did the spell that made everyone look different and me look like a volcano. Wolf.

Willow stood a little distance from the bank. She was wearing her orange leotard/swimsuit this time. "I'm a fire sign, but I can do this water prayer anyway," she said. "I'll teach you, if you like."

Then the sun edged up above the ridge and cast light across the lake. Willow lifted handfuls of water and held them toward the sun, singing. Her voice was beautiful—how could I not have noticed last time?—and I could almost understand what she was saying. It was about how water was in everything, and light was in everything, and earth, and sky, and she thanked everything that all things mingled to make a world where so many wonderful things happened. The water slid down her arms in slow motion, catching light against her skin, and then she *was* the song, everything together, sun, water, air, earth, sound, motion, and stillness; and she turned transparent; she became the prayer.

My breath caught inside me. I pressed my hands to the ground. I was conscious of earth under my feet, under my body, sun touching my face, water around my legs, air waiting to enter me. I let air in and repeated the only phrase I could remember from Willow's song, the words foreign and not quite right as they crossed my tongue, but close enough, because everything flickered, and for an instant I felt all of everything flowing into and out of me and through me, as though my heart pumped earth and my lungs breathed fire, my bones carried water and my skin kissed air.

Then I settled back out of it, feeling heavy and cold as clay. The sun was pulling free of the treetops, and so bright I couldn't stare at it anymore. Willow dropped back into sight, too, and turned to smile at me. "Not so hard," she said.

I sat for a while just breathing deep, until I felt alive again.

"You okay, Nick?" She waded over and sat beside me, splashing water up with her feet.

"I'm okay. Evan said it was a woman's mystery."

"That's because he's too lazy to do proper devotions."

I wiggled my toes in the muck. "If you can do that, why do you need to do anything else? It was fantastic."

"You can't stay there all the time," she said, splashing harder. She kicked water at me and giggled. "Unless you're some kind of religious fanatic or something, and just want to dissolve. I'd rather kiss you."

We ended up in the water—under it some of the time. A moment came when we were just floating, our

hands clasped. I stared up at the sky, indelible burning
blue in the center, paler toward the edges; and at the
hills rising from the lake, under cloaks of pointed pines
that caught sun in the pale new green tips that ended
their branches. Above us an eagle soared like a spinning
thought, edging up and away, and my heart rose as
though trying to fly, and then broke. This was as perfect
a place and a moment as I could remember. If I could
be here, why did I ever need to be anywhere else?

How could I ever leave this place?

Then I thought about what Willow had said about
being inside of prayer. The moment moved past it.
Other things happened. Even though I knew how to
dissolve, I didn't want to. There was still a world worth
watching all around us.

AVONOVA PRESENTS
MASTERS OF FANTASY AND ADVENTURE

SNOW WHITE, BLOOD RED 71875-8/ $5.99 US/ $7.99 CAN
edited by Ellen Datlow and Terri Windling

A SUDDEN WILD MAGIC 71851-0/ $4.99 US/ $5.99 CAN
by Diana Wynne Jones

THE WEALDWIFE'S TALE 71880-4/ $4.99 US/ $5.99 CAN
by Paul Hazel

FLYING TO VALHALLA 71881-2/ $4.99 US/ $5.99 CAN
by Charles Pellegrino

THE GATES OF NOON 71781-2/ $4.99 US/ $5.99 CAN
by Michael Scott Rohan

**THE IRON DRAGON'S
DAUGHTER** 72098-1/ $4.99 US/ $5.99 CAN
by Michael Swanwick

GHOSTCOUNTRY'S WRATH 76838-0/ $5.50 US/ $7.50 CAN
by Tom Deitz